P9-DCN-446

A CONTRACT IS A CONTRACT . . .

Max Maxon is an ex-marine who makes his living with a gun. Sasha Casad is a rich teenager trying to catch the next spaceship home. Max's job is to get her there alive. Somebody's trying to stop them—somebody with plenty of money and firepower. That doesn't bother Max. A contract is a contract. Against all odds, he's going to fulfill this one . . . and then he's going to make somebody *pay*.

●　　●　　●

Praise for the work of William C. Dietz, author of the "Drifter" trilogy and the "Sam McCade" series:

"Slam-bang action!" —**David Drake**

"All-out space action!" —*Starlog*

"Good solid space-opera, well told."
　　　　　　　　—*Science Fiction Chronicle*

Ace Books by William C. Dietz

WAR WORLD
IMPERIAL BOUNTY
PRISON PLANET
ALIEN BOUNTY
DRIFTER
DRIFTER'S RUN
DRIFTER'S WAR
LEGION OF THE DAMNED
BODYGUARD

BODYGUARD

WILLIAM C. DIETZ

ACE BOOKS, NEW YORK

If you purchased this book without a cover, you should be aware that this book is stolen property. It was reported as "unsold and destroyed" to the publisher, and neither the author nor the publisher has received any payment for this "stripped book."

This book is an Ace original edition,
and has never been previously published.

BODYGUARD

An Ace Book / published by arrangement with
the author

PRINTING HISTORY
Ace edition / October 1994

All rights reserved.
Copyright © 1994 by William C. Dietz.
Cover art by Bruce Jensen.
This book may not be reproduced in whole or in part,
by mimeograph or any other means, without permission.
For information address: The Berkley Publishing Group,
200 Madison Avenue, New York, NY 10016.

ISBN: 0-441-00105-X

ACE®
Ace Books are published by The Berkley Publishing Group,
200 Madison Avenue, New York, NY 10016.
ACE and the "A" design are trademarks
belonging to Charter Communications, Inc.

PRINTED IN THE UNITED STATES OF AMERICA

10 9 8 7 6 5 4 3 2 1

*This book is dedicated to all
the freaks, misfits, and outcasts
of the world. God bless 'em one
and all.*

1

"Market discipline must be maintained."

Chairperson of the Board
Margaret Hopworth-Smith

We rose from the depths of the Urboplex like a plague of sewer rats, drifting upwards on crowded platforms, riding the humanity-packed escalators, or climbing hundreds of stairs to emerge blinking from seldom-used exits.

We were a hard-eyed lot, younger rather than older, and almost universally desperate. For we were the bottom feeders, the lowest-ranking members of a long, hard food chain, willing to do what it took to survive, and well aware of the fact that whatever value we had was related to brawn rather than brains. Something I've been short of ever since a portion of mine were blown out during the Battle of Three Moons.

You remember, the Battle of Three Moons was the key battle in the Labor War fought between the deep-space tool heads and the corpies. I was a Mishimuto Marine back then, and, according to my service record, one tough hombre. Anyway, the loss of that much gray matter makes me a bit slow at times, which is why I eke out a living as a bodyguard instead of doing something more respectable. Not that I have many clients, which accounts for my willingness to do less desirable tasks as well.

I left the low-rise lift tube, walked the short distance to the high-rise tube, and stepped inside. It was packed with the usual mix of droids and day workers. The robots didn't give a shit, but the humans made room for me. Lots of room. More than I needed. It might have been an especially polite crowd, or it might have been the fact that I stand seven feet two inches tall, weigh two-fifty, and have a triangular-shaped skull plate. It extends across the back of my head and points forward towards my nose. That, plus a lot of short, prematurely white hair, makes me stand out in a crowd. The white eyebrows, bright blue eyes, and squared-off chin help too. But *all* of us tend to stand out, the men and women who live by the gun, and risk their lives for less money than a taco vendor makes in a day.

Not that we are *better* than taco vendors, because it takes real guts to go home to a crummy little cube, kiss the wife, play with the rug rats for an hour, grab some sleep, get up in the wee hours of the morning, make the tortillas, fry the soy, prepare the lettuce, cheese, tomatoes and salsa the customers expect, haul your stuff two miles through scum-infested corridors, and set up shop. Not just once, but day after grueling day. Now that takes guts. *Real* guts. More guts than most shooters have.

The doors whispered closed, the platform moved upwards, and the air was thick with at least thirty kinds of fragrance, cologne, perfume, deodorant, and shampoo. I grinned. No matter what sort of scent my fellow passengers wore, it wouldn't cover their lower-level stink. Fear and poverty works its way in through your pores, penetrates your guts, and pollutes your soul. It makes you do what you're told, say what's safe, and kiss corpie ass.

Which could account for the fact that the lifers keep us around. You can program a droid to kiss your butt, but they *have* to obey, and that takes all the fun out of it. No, there's nothing quite so elevating as to have a real honest-to-god sentient by the short hairs. That's real, that's fun, that's power!

A woman caught my attention. She was on the other side of the platform and looked good in her T-shirt, waist-cut jacket, and matching pants. She might have passed for anything if it hadn't been for the telltale bulge of a cross-draw hip holster and the wary look on her face. Our eyes met and she gave me a slow, deliberate nod. The kind one pro reserves for another. I nodded in return, knowing we understood each other in ways the people around us could never comprehend. We knew what it was like to kill people no worse than ourselves, to sleep with one hand on a gun, and live with our backs against the wall. Yeah, we knew and it didn't make a damned bit of difference. Because knowing doesn't mean jack shit. Life sucks, and that's a fact.

An ad for Duane's Big and Tall Shop was projected into both my ears as the lift tube's computer ran a superficial analysis on my appearance and chose what it deemed to be the most appropriate commercial.

The platform slowed and stopped on Surface Levels 1, 2, and 3 before the woman and I stepped off. We avoided each other but knew we were after the same thing. Money. Five hundred smackers for a single day's work. More moola than I had made during the previous month. It's rare for a real dyed-in-the-wool member of the Big Board to put out a call for *one shooter,* much less two hundred and fifty, so there would be plenty of takers. Especially since there were no requirements beyond "a reasonable degree of mobility and a valid weapons permit." Or so the ads said.

And, thanks to the preference shown to disabled veterans, I had a permit. Brain damage and all. Scary, isn't it? But that's how it is in a world where poppers pop, snatchers snatch, and bodyguards guard.

The day workers scattered for their temporary jobs while I made my way through a labyrinth of corridors, sky bridges, and hallways before arriving at Droidware HQ. I have trouble with directions sometimes, so I had scouted the path twelve hours before and committed it to memory.

As with most corporations, the lifers had taken good care of themselves. The lobby was a huge affair that featured acres of dark red carpet, tons of gray-white marble, and what must have been a thousand board-feet of real mahogany. A golden "D" graced the back wall and shimmered with internal light. The woman at the front desk was real. Real pretty and well aware of it. She stared at the top of my head as she handed me the baton. "To your left."

The baton tugged towards the left and I obeyed. The woman I had seen in the lift tube had arrived ahead of me and disappeared through a pair of double doors. I followed. Outside of some small vid cams that oozed over the walls and ceilings, the hallway was completely bare. The woman passed between another set of double doors. I followed and stepped out into a good-sized auditorium. A bin had been provided for the batons, so I added mine to the rest.

The auditorium was equipped with rows of starkly utilitarian chairs and a small stage. The floor consisted of polished concrete and slanted down towards an industrial-size drain. Not the sort of place to entertain share owners, but just right for an assemblage of greasy, grimy, lower-level scum like ourselves.

Fifty or sixty shooters had already arrived and managed to look studiously bored. I knew a few of them and nodded politely. No one asked me to sit next to them, nor would I have accepted if they had. It's better that way, in case you end up on opposite sides of a fight, and a whole lot safer. Friends can betray you. Strangers can't.

I chose a seat towards the back, found that my legs wouldn't fit, and stuck them out into the aisle. A hard case with a fist-flattened nose nearly tripped on them, opened his mouth to say something, and caught his reflection in my skull plate. I smiled and he moved on.

Shooters of every possible size and description continued to arrive until the place was more than two-thirds full. It was then that the lights dimmed, the forward wall shimmered, and some broadcast-quality 3-D video appeared. The piece ran ten minutes or so, and did a bang-up job of describing Droidware Inc., the high-quality robots that walked, crawled, rolled, hopped, skipped and jumped out of its highly automated factories, and the almost godlike crew of full-time employees who ran the company. All thirty-six of them. The last of these, a grotesque apparition who had what appeared to be a hundred-year-old head on a twenty-five-year-old female body, bid us welcome and introduced a man who appeared as if by magic at the center of the stage.

I say "a man," although he didn't look much like a man, since vat-grown analogues and complicated electromechanical systems had replaced most of his original organs. Just one of the many fringe benefits associated with life-long employment. Machinery whirred as the lifer surveyed the crowd. His voice was distinctly artificial.

"Good morning, ladies and gentlemen, and welcome to Droidware Inc. My name is Jaspers, Ralph Jaspers, and I'm in charge of Competitive Management at the big 'D.'"

Jaspers paused as if to give our pea-sized brains time to absorb this vital piece of information and continued. It appeared as if a well-intentioned PR type had instructed the lifer to gesture with his hands, and he waved them in every possible direction. "You were invited here because we need your help to deal with a competitive threat."

I felt my gut tighten. A competitive threat? Was Droidware Inc. about to declare war on one of its rivals? The big board had been pretty successful at limiting open conflict between the companies, but it happened once in a while, which accounted for some rather large standing armies. Armies I no longer cared to be part of. If I had learned anything in the Mishimuto Marines, it was that war sucks.

It seemed that Jaspers could read minds, at least simple ones like mine, and extended a synthiflesh-lined palm. "No, this is *not* the beginning of a corporate war. The competitive threat I referred to stems not from one of the many fine corporations that offer products similar to ours, but from the nasty criminal element that preys upon our droids."

The audience shifted uneasily, since many of them were part of the "nasty criminal element" that Jaspers referred to, and wondered where this was headed. I thought I understood, although my brain is notoriously unreliable, and prone to the occasional error. Still, I knew that Droidware Inc. manufactured some of the best robots on the market: a fact that attracted thieves and discouraged potential customers. After all, why buy a Droidware model if others were almost as good, and a lot less likely to be stolen?

It was a common sight in the lower levels to see a team of

scrappers blindside a droid, drag it into a passageway, and strip it for parts. Parts that quickly made their way into the illegal black-market robotics shops, where they were used as components for low-end bots that eroded Droidware's market share. Yeah, some companies had armed their robots, but scrappers still found ways to steal them, and their weapons too. And nobody cared either, since the droids had put millions of flesh-and-blood people out of work, and were owned by the same companies that refused to employ us.

"So," Jaspers continued, "we decided it was time to do some housecleaning. We spent months preparing for this day. Our agents have identified the most successful scrappers, know where they live, and how they operate. We have grid coordinates for the illegal factories that purchase black-market parts, profiles on how they operate, and detailed information about their security systems. Your job is to take that information and put it to good use. Similar efforts are underway around the world. Questions?"

The most obvious question was "Why should we help you make robots that take jobs away from human beings?" But the answer was obvious. Robots were more efficient than people were, amortized themselves in two years, and never asked for a day off.

The second most obvious question was "Why not order the Zeebs to do it?" Especially since they were indirectly controlled by the corporations, but the audience knew the answer to that one as well. The Zeebs kept order on the streets but lacked the training and incentive to do anything more. Sure, the corpies liked to complain, but since anything that resembled *real* law enforcement might get in the way of profits, they left things as they were. We were silent. Jasper liked it that way and nodded his approval. "Good . . . let's get down to business. Plans have been laid and are ready to be executed. Before we move to that step, however, there are some minor housekeeping matters to deal with. Corporate security informs me that twenty-seven members of the audience lack the weapons permits necessary for this kind of operation and will not be allowed to participate."

I don't think anyone was surprised to learn that Jaspers was in radio contact with his goons. I remembered the baton and the vid cams. The corpies had taken our mug shots, fingerprints, and lord knows what else. More than the minimum amount of information necessary to run us through the so-called "Citizen's Registry," and come up with twenty-seven unlicensed shooters. Shooters who had lost their permits or never had one to begin with.

Doors popped open around the perimeter of the room, and uniformed soldiers stepped in. They wore the burgundy-and-gray uniforms of the Droidware Dragoons and held riot guns cradled in their arms. Their was a universal hiss of indrawn breath followed by the loud whisper of fabric as hands went to weapons. Some people stood while I remained perfectly still.

There are sizeable gaps in my memories, but my dreams are quite vivid. One involves a group of soldiers firing into a crowd. I don't know if the massacre really took place, or if I was there, but I'm afraid that it did and I was. So I had seen what double-ought buck does to a crowd and knew what the industrial-strength drains were for. Jaspers held up his hand.

"Please be calm. There's no reason for alarm. Those individuals who do *not* have valid permits will be detained for a period of six hours and compensated for their time. Their weapons will be confiscated but they will be released unharmed."

"Why?" a man off to my right demanded suspiciously. "Why detain us?" He stood in a half-crouch, hand on gun, eyeing the Dragoons with open dislike.

"Because those who *do* have valid permits would like to arrive down-level unannounced," Jaspers replied calmly, "and because you are *not* authorized to carry a weapon."

The rest of us, those with valid permits, nodded sagely, and said things like, "Right on," "You can say that again," and "Tell 'em how it is, J-man!"

There was little doubt that the non-permitted shooters would sell us out if they had the chance. We looked at the man who had asked the question, and he wilted under the weight of our stares. He and twenty-six other people were led from the room. I wished I was one of them. The concept of getting paid for *not* working appealed to me. I should be so lucky.

The last of the rejects was no more than out the door when the rest of us were divided into what Jasper called "Sanction Teams" and placed under the command of steely-eyed ex-military types. And, being a steely-eyed ex-military type myself, I approved.

Judging from the way they carried out their briefings, the team leaders had done their homework. There were twelve people on my team, and our leader was a hard-eyed, tight-assed woman named Norris. She was pretty in a pinch-faced "don't mess with me" sort of way, and I liked her style. We had gathered towards the rear of the auditorium, and she was talking about the equipment piled at our feet. She stood at parade rest.

"Forget the hardware you brought with you. According to data provided by the scanners built into the entry hall, you people are armed with everything from double-barreled Derringers to Hicap Machine Pistols. Rather than mess around with such a wide variety of ammo, and take the time to assess the reliability of your hardware, we decided to issue Glock Disposables." Her arm blurred, and an ugly-looking block of metal and plastic appeared in her hand. I recognized it as the weapon in question. She sounded like a drill instructor.

"The Glock .9mm semi-automatic disposable hand gun was designed for police use but will meet our needs rather nicely. You will notice the protruding twenty-five-round magazine here, the over-sized safety here, and the thumb-activated laser sight there. Each weapon is capable of firing up to three magazines prior to deactivating itself." Norris smiled. It appeared and disappeared so fast I couldn't be sure that I'd seen it at all.

"So, if we lose a team member," Norris continued, "and the scrappers grab their weapon, there's a limit to how much damage they can inflict with it."

The guy next to me cleared his throat nervously. He had the soft, pot-bellied look of an off-duty security guard. "What if we need *more* than three magazines?"

Norris raised a quizzical eyebrow. "Then we are in deep shit. Seventy-five rounds should be more than adequate for this particular mission, but if it isn't, then use your own piece as a backup. Satisfied?"

He wasn't, but the man swallowed and nodded his head anyway. I made a mental note to stay as far away from him as I possibly could. They guy had "casualty" written all over him, and I had no desire to die.

After that we were issued one-size-fits-damned-near-everybody body armor, feather-light headsets, and a call sign. Norris invented them on the spot, and mine was "Lurch." It could have been worse, so I didn't complain.

Then, exactly one hour and fifteen minutes after Jaspers had started his presentation, we were ready to go. And not through the public walkways as I had assumed, but down through the nearly empty lift tubes, stairways, and corridors normally reserved for Zeebs and other officials. It had taken me the better part of an hour to reach the surface from Sub-Level 38 of the Sea-Tac Residential-Industrial Urboplex. It took less than fifteen minutes to make the trip back down. Not to Sub-Level 38, but to Sub-Level 35, which is almost the same thing. A fact which I found to be rather interesting, since it meant the entire transportation system was *intentionally* rather than accidentally screwed up. I had just started to ask myself why when my call sign surfaced in the middle of the mumbo-jumbo that had passed through my ears but missed my mind. "Is that okay with you, Lurch?"

I had absolutely no idea what Norris was talking about and decided to take a chance. "Umblepop. I mean, yeah, sure."

"Good," Norris said smoothly, "then come up here with me so you'll be handy when the time comes."

I groaned internally, worked my way forward, and joined Norris at the head of the column. "Never volunteer for anything." That's the second or third maxim of every military organization I ever heard of, and I had somehow managed to violate it.

A pair of Zeebs approached. The Zeebs take their name from the skin-tight suits they wear. Suits that are white with diagonal black stripes. They look great on Olympic athletes and terrible on everyone else. Including this pair.

Norris motioned us against the wall. The first cop, a nasty piece of work with meaty thighs, started to say something but bit the words off when Norris flashed some interactive I.D. It recognized the Zeeb, read out some code, and the police continued on their way. I don't know about the others, but I was impressed.

I waited for the order to move out, but Norris stared into space, listened to a voice via her earplugs, and subvocalized a response. She nodded, said something else, and turned to us. "Okay, boys and girls, take five but stay off the air. We're waiting for teams three, eight, and sixteen to reach their launch points."

I leaned against the wall. You had to give the corpies credit.

They might be assholes, but they were competent assholes, and knew how to get things done. Like launching all the teams at once so it would be impossible for one set of scrappers to warn the rest. Yeah, the plan was well conceived. But even the best laid plans have a tendency to come apart when the shooting starts. Norris interrupted my thoughts.

"Okay, people, time to rock and roll . . . Now remember, don't fire unless fired at, and watch out for noncombatants."

The truth was that it was damned hard to find any noncombatants below Sub-Level 15 or so, but we understood what she meant, and nodded obediently. I had no desire to grease the pathetic slobs that worked in the scrappers' sweat shops, and the others didn't either.

Still, it didn't hurt to check our weapons and the backup mags slotted into pockets on the front of our chest armor. I didn't like the Glock's teeny-weeny grips, but the laser sight was nice, as was the heavy-duty magazine capacity. I was scared and felt an almost overwhelming need to go to the bathroom.

Norris pushed an access card into the slot by the door and waited for it to slide open. She stepped out and I followed. The corridor was packed with people. They took one look at us and ran, or tried to, since the bodies behind them blocked the way. Someone screamed, neon shimmered, and the usual flow of down-level water splashed out from under our boots as the crowd parted and Norris led us to the right.

I saw a sign. It was shaped like an arrow. Angry red letters jerked down towards a pair of graffiti-covered metal doors. When Norris spoke, her voice sounded a full register higher than it had before. "Those are the doors, Lurch! Break 'em down!"

I suddenly knew what I had unintentionally volunteered for and damned near shit my pants. But there didn't seem to be a whole lot of choice, so I picked up speed, aimed my shoulder at the doors, and hit them as hard as I could. They gave, thank god, a lot more easily than I was ready for, and I fell forward. Somebody stepped on my back in their eagerness to follow Norris wherever she was going, and I gave them a silent blessing. They were welcome to my share of whatever bullets happened to be waiting.

The whole team had splashed past by the time I did a push-up, wiped the water from my chin, and staggered to my feet. I heard a confused babble of voices through my earplugs and stumbled forward, not so much out of loyalty to the team as from a sense of self-preservation. The hallway was long and dark, punctuated here and there by rectangles of light with a lot of deep, dark shadows in between. I knew that any one of them could conceal a gun-toting, fire-breathing, homicidally inclined free-market capitalist. The team represented safety in numbers, and I had a strong desire to be safe.

I glanced into the doorways as I ran by and was treated to the sight of dismal rooms packed with ragged-looking pieceworkers. Most were adults, but a third or more were children, their eyes dull as they clipped one component to the next. Some of the brighter workers had seen the team, the guns, and the body armor and jumped to the correct conclusion. They were on their feet and headed for the nearest exits.

The rest sat where they were, parts clutched in grimy hands, waiting for instructions that would never come. I wanted to tell them it was a bad idea, that it was quitting time, but doubted they would listen. Jobs were hard to come by, even crappy ones, and they weren't about to split without one helluva good reason.

A sledgehammer hit me between the shoulder blades. I heard the boom of a handgun and hit the floor facedown. I'd been doing a lot of that lately, and I hoped it wouldn't ruin my good looks. The combination of inertia and the slime-covered floor carried me down the corridor. I rolled, thumbed the laser sight, and watched the ruby-red dot dance across the ceiling. I forced it down, found the scrapper, and squeezed the trigger.

The Droidware body armor had saved my life. The scrapper wasn't so lucky. Either he wasn't wearing any, or what he had was too thin. The outcome was the same. My slugs picked the man up, threw him backwards, and bounced him off a wall. He was still in the process of falling when Norris blasted my ears. "Hey, Lurch! Where the hell are you, anyway? We could use some help up here."

I felt like telling her to kiss my ass, but old military habits kicked in, and I did what I was told. I lumbered up the hall, aiming my weapon at every shadow I encountered, half expecting to catch one between the eyes. Any hint of radio discipline had disappeared, and my plugs were filled with garbage.

"Watch it . . . watch it . . . the little one has a gun." "Cover my back, damn it . . ." "Come to poppa, little robot . . . daddy has a present for you." ". . . Not a god-damned scrapper in sight . . ." "Whoa, momma! Check those buns!"

It was about then that I caught up with the rear guard, a scrawny little weasel with the rather appropriate call sign of "Snotface." He motioned me forward, and I had just pulled up alongside him when the fecal matter hit the fan.

The scrappers seemed to come from nowhere and everywhere at once. They poured out of the shadows, dropped from overhead accessways, and popped out of doorways like so many jack-in-the-boxes. And every friggin' one of them had a little kid strapped across their chests, leaving their hands free to do other things. Like blow our heads off.

The kids screamed, the scrappers opened fire, and Snotface took one through his open mouth. I sensed more people fall and heard Norris give the only order she could. "Ignore the kids! Shoot the bastards!"

She was right, I knew that, but couldn't bring myself to do it. The rest of the shooters opened fire while I stood there with a gun in my hand, unable to pull the trigger. The children came apart like so many cheap dolls as a hail of bullets hit them and were stopped by the body armor between them and the scrappers.

That's when I saw her. A little girl with straight black hair, doll-fine features, and a thumb in her mouth. She didn't scream, struggle against the straps that held her in place, or do any of the other things you would have expected. She just hung there, watching the destruction, waiting to die.

Something primal worked its way up through my throat and came screaming out my mouth. I felt the slugs hit my body armor as I made my way forward. A smaller man might have stumbled, might have fallen, but my size worked in my favor. The bullets hit and I kept coming.

I saw the scrapper had long greasy locks, bad teeth, and a two-day growth of beard. He grinned, knowing that I couldn't shoot without hitting the girl, tilted his gun up towards my highly reflective head, and started to squeeze the trigger.

I guess I'll never know why the little girl took her thumb out of her mouth and grabbed his hand, but I'm real glad that she did, because it gave me sufficient time to cross the intervening space, grab the bastard's head and spin it halfway around.

The move was all strength and no science, but it worked anyway. Bones crunched, the scrapper's eyes rolled back in his head, and he slumped towards the deck. I grabbed and held him long enough to free the girl. She looked into my eyes, smiled approvingly, and pointed towards my skull plate. "Shiny!"

I smiled in return. "Very shiny. Do you like it?"

The little girl nodded, slipped her thumb back into her mouth, and waited for whatever life would bring next. The firefight was over by then. It took the better part of an hour to find the girl's terrified mother and hand her over.

Norris was super-pissed by the time I got back, and threatened me with all sorts of dire consequences, but so what? It wasn't like she was my boss or anything, so I kissed up enough to get paid, double-checked to make sure the right amount of money had been dumped into my account, and headed for home. I was tired, and a shower seemed like the best idea I'd ever had.

2

"Death to Droids!"

*Graffiti found in the main
corridor of Sub-Level 31,
Sea-Tac Residential-
Industrial Urboplex*

I live on Sub-Level 38 of the Sea-Tac Residential-Industrial
Urboplex. Not a very pleasant place to hang your hat, but a lot less
expensive than Level 37.

The door buzzed, and, having just sent out for a pizza, I made
the reasonable assumption. But reasonable assumptions are almost
always wrong, and this was no exception.

I opened the door and found myself face-to-tentacle with two of
the ugliest-looking androids you ever saw. One looked like a
recently buried corpse, and the other resembled Hollywood's idea
of what aliens *should* look like, but probably don't. A grotesque
thing with lots of facial tentacles, pointy teeth, and a bad case of
artificial halitosis.

Well, form has a tendency to follow function, and androids look the way they do for a reason. But I missed that. Just like I miss a lot of other things. I was polite. "Yes? May I help you?"

A micro-robotic maggot crawled out of the corpse's nose, took a look around, and disappeared under his coat collar.

"Are you Max Maxon?" The words came along with the almost overwhelming stench of rotting carrion.

I held my breath and considered the possibilities. A bill collector? No, I had debts alright, plenty of them, but none large enough to rate one droid, much less two.

Old enemies? Possibly, but given how low I'd sunk, why kill me? A real enemy would let me live.

That left clients, a rare and exotic breed that almost never, repeat never, samples life thirty-eight levels underground. Still, there's a first time for everything. I hadn't worked for androids before, but what the hell, I'm a liberal kinda guy, so I took the chance.

"Yeah, I'm Maxon. What can I do for you?"

"We work for Seculor Inc.," tentacle-face said politely.

I swallowed hard. Damn my screwed-up cerebral cortex anyway! Competitors. A category of visitor I hadn't thought of. And it made sense too, 'cause Seculor was *big*, real big, and had a fondness for weird-looking robots. You know, intimidate the opposition first, and if that doesn't work, blow their brains out. But why waste billable staff time killing something as insignificant as me?

I smiled and allowed my right hand to drift back towards the .38 Super. It's a custom job with an over-sized safety, polished magazine well, squared-off trigger guard, and a triple-port compensator. There's nothing like a few rounds through the ol' CPU to show a droid who's boss.

"Don't do it," corpse-breath said conversationally. "You'll be dead before you can drag that cannon out of your waistband."

I should've known. Androids, especially those designed for security work, are loaded with fancy detection gear. I let my hand drop.

"So what do you want?"

"Thumb this," the alien thing said flatly, and handed me the latest in comp cubes. I almost asked why, saw their expressions, and let it slide. Hey, if the droids wanted my signature they could have it. The cube gave slightly under my thumb, chirped its satisfaction, and gave birth to a tiny disk.

"Your copy," the alien droid said matter-of-factly. He grabbed the cube, popped it into his mouth, and swallowed. God only knows where it went from there.

That was the point at which both droids stepped back, shoved a teenage girl in my direction, and headed down-corridor. People scattered. A zonie looked, dropped his injector, and ran. The girl gave me the look most people do, amazed and somewhat alarmed. There was something else in her expression too. Something that didn't make sense. Compassion? Pity? Awe? I wasn't sure.

So the kid scoped me and I scoped her. She stood about five feet tall, had a pretty face, huge brown eyes, and long, well-shaped limbs. She wore a beret, a black body stocking, a vest, a pouch-belt, a leather miniskirt, and high-heeled boots. Her voice was calm and a little sarcastic. She reminded me of someone, but I couldn't remember who.

"So, are you going to ask me in? Or leave me standing here in the hall?"

Surprised, and a bit taken aback, I gestured for her to enter. She did, gave the room a slow once-over, and wrinkled her nose in disgust. "Have you considered cleaning this dump?"

I looked around. My clothes were where they belonged, tossed in a corner, and the day bed was rumpled, but so what? Most of the empties had made it into the garbage can, and the dishes could wait for a while. I frowned. "And who the hell are you? My mother?"

The kid shook her head sadly, as if she was dealing with a head case, which she definitely was. She pointed at my right hand. "Take a look at the disk."

I brought my hand up and opened my fist. Light winked off the surface of the disk. I had forgotten it was there.

My all-in-one home computer, communications console, and entertainment complex consists of a secondhand Artel 3000. Its basic claim to fame is low-cost, high-quality 3-D imagery. The basic technology was hijacked from the now defunct Ibo Corporation, which copied it from Toshiba.

How can I remember things like that? And forget the disk in

my hand? Beats the hell out of me. Ask the pill pushers. Maybe they know. I inserted the disk and pushed the power button.

Video swirled, locked up, and revealed a middle-aged woman. She looked the way lifers always look. Too old for their bodies and slightly smug. That's what the guarantee of life-long employment does for you, I guess; it frees you from mundane problems like feeding your face, and lifts you above the common herd. People like me and, judging from the way the girl looked, people like her.

When the woman spoke, her eyelids rose and fell like old-fashioned windowshades, and her words came in bursts, like bullets from a machine gun. "I am Administrator Tella. Seculor Inc. has a temporary personnel shortage. We would appreciate your assistance. Keep Ms. Casad alive, get her to Europa Station, and we will pay you fifty thousand credits. Ms. Casad has some expense money. Use it wisely. Do not request help from our company or staff. Your contract follows."

Legal jargon flooded the screen and I hit the power switch. The screen snapped to black. Looking back, I realize I should've questioned how an outfit like Seculor Inc. could possibly run short of staff, trained or otherwise, and if they did, why they'd hire a scumbag like me, but I was brain-damaged and, more than that, blinded by the prospect of fifty big ones.

Fifty grand was nothing prior to the war, when inflation ran two hundred percent per month, and a can of beer cost a hundred credits. But the Consortium won, the executives collectively known as "The Board" got the lid on, and fifty K means something now.

Like the opportunity to be solvent, or better yet to buy my own hole-in-the-wall restaurant. Yeah, that would be great, leaning on the counter and watching the world go by. Pathetic, you say? Well, you have your ambitions, and I have mine.

So, rather than ask the kind of questions I should have, I turned to the girl and said, "Pleased to meet you, Casad. Is there a first name to go with the last?"

She crossed her arms in front of a nearly nonexistent chest. "Sasha."

"Sasha Casad. I like it. All right, Sasha, who's after you, and why?"

"Nobody's after me."

And they call *me* stupid. I heaved a sigh. "Look, Sasha, somebody's willing to insure your health to the tune of fifty big ones. That means snatchers or poppers. Which is the more likely? I need to know."

She shrugged. "Snatchers, I guess. My mother works for the Protech Corporation."

"The new one? That grew up after the war?"

Sasha nodded.

It made a weird kind of sense. The original Protech Corporation had been the victim of an employee takeover, had allied itself with the unionists, and paid the ultimate price when the Consortium won.

But another incarnation of the same company had risen from the ashes and was doing rather well. Or so the flaks claimed. Just the kind of situation the snatchers love. Grab the kid, demand proprietary information, and sell it to Protech's competitors. It's a great scam, and that's where bodyguards come in, though most companies have their own.

Still, Protech was on the rise, and overhead would be a problem. It's hard enough to launch a start-up without funding a top-notch security force at the same time. That would explain why the kid's mother had hired a company like Seculor. What it *didn't* explain was why Seculor had turned to me, but hey, that slipped what was left of my mind. A mind that could remember all sorts of stuff about Protech and forget how to do long division.

"Okay, Sasha. Snatchers it is. Now, why are you here?"

"So you can protect me."

The kid wanted to piss me off, and it was working. I tried to be patient. "No, Sasha. What brings you to Earth?"

I noticed that her eyes were focused on a spot over my head.

"I go to school here."

"And?"

"And I got kicked out."

"Why?"

She shrugged evasively. "Stuff, that's all. Stuff."

I let it drop. She didn't want to tell and it didn't make a helluva lot of difference anyway. Or so I assumed.

The buzzer buzzed.

I gestured her away from the door, pulled the .38, and looked out through the peephole. A long-haired, zit-faced, scraggly-assed kid was standing there clutching a grease-stained box to his chest. My pizza had arrived.

I opened the door, accepted the box, and gave him some cash. He was so busy staring at my skull that he didn't bother to count it. I skimmed a buck off the deal just to teach him a lesson.

I closed the door, locked it, and gestured towards the kitchenette. "You hungry? Want some pizza?"

She nodded, stepped over to the sink, and ran some hot water. The dishes made plopping sounds as they went in. Women. Who can figure 'em?

After the dishes had been washed, dried, and dirtied again, we ate. Sasha occupied my single chair while I leaned against the kitchen counter. I noticed she took small bites, chewed with her mouth closed, and took care of her nails. Her mom would approve. I spoke through a mouthful of pizza. "So, how long have you been dirtside?"

"Eight months or so."

"You like it?"

She gave me a look most people reserve for newly deposited dog squeeze.

"You've gotta be kidding. Earth is an overpopulated, poorly run pus ball."

I shrugged and started on my second piece of pizza. The kid was right. The human race had run out of room. No amount of space habitats, moon cities, or Mars colonies was going to fill the gap. We needed to break free of the solar system, make our way to distant stars, and pollute them for a change. The only problem was that we lacked the means to do so. Conventional drives like the ones that powered existing space ships were too damned slow. No, what we needed was a faster-than-light drive, and there was no sign of one coming along soon. I changed the topic. "So, what's your favorite subject in school?"

This look was even worse than the last one.

"Look, Mr. Maxon . . ."

"Max."

"Alright. Look, Max, I'm not a little girl, so save the 'what's your favorite subject' crap for someone who is."

"Just trying to be friendly."

"Well, don't."

"Gaberscam."

She raised her eyebrow. "Gaberscam? What the hell does that mean?"

I winced. Nonsensical words, numbers, and other stuff has a tendency to leak out of my mouth when I least expect it.

"Right. I meant to say 'right.'"

The kid nodded. "Good."

I used the dishtowel to wipe my mouth and tossed it towards the corner of the room. The prospect of spending the next couple of months with Sasha seemed a lot less appealing than it had before. I was preparing to tell her that when the cookie cutter blew a hole in my ceiling.

Cookie cutters are shaped like an old-fashioned hoop and filled with powerful explosives. They were designed for room-to-room fighting in modern urboplexes and are capable of cutting a circular hole through two feet of steel-reinforced concrete in less than a second. And, due to the shoddy construction found in most of today's buildings, this cookie cutter had only twelve inches of material to deal with.

I was turning, and reaching for the .38, when a two-hundred-and-fifty-pound chunk of concrete hit my bed and bounced a couple of times. Dust billowed away from the concrete, electricity crackled as power lines shorted, and a pair of combat boots dropped through the hole.

The gun bucked in my hand as I put two slugs through the space where a body should be. I heard a grunt instead of a scream. The bastard was wearing body armor! Light flashed as a concussion grenade went off, followed by clouds of thick acrid smoke.

I heard a thumping noise, and a man swore.

"Sasha?"

"Head for the door!"

Head for the door? What the hell was she talking about? And who was she to give *me* orders?

An arm snaked around my neck. I brought the gun up next to my right ear and fired backwards. The assailant fell away. I spun, searched for another target, but couldn't find one. Dust and smoke drifted around me. Light flashed, the second cookie cutter made a thumping sound, and the smoke swirled downwards like water in a toilet.

A getaway! The bastards had Sasha and were getting away! I wanted to follow, jump through after them, but knew I shouldn't. The snatchers would have anticipated such a move and made arrangements to counter it. No, Sasha would be better served if I lived to track her down.

The smoke started to clear. The place was a mess. My ceiling and floor boasted a pair of rather large holes. A body lay draped across the chair where Sasha had been sitting. The top part of his head was missing, but the smile was intact. Or was that a grimace? It was hard to tell.

I looked down through the hole in the floor. There was nothing to see outside of some rubble and Sasha's beret. The snatchers were gone.

I felt stupid. Very, very stupid. The opposition had snatched my client less than an hour after she'd come under my protection, had pulled the job within my own cube, and left me looking like a total jerk. Not the sort of thing to put on your résumé.

There was a loud ringing in my right ear, but the left still worked. The siren made a bleating sound. The Zeebs were on their way. They'd ask questions, lots of questions, while time ticked away. Time I could ill afford to lose if I hoped to find my client and get her to Europa.

I opened a wall locker, grabbed my gym bag, and turned it upside down. A pair of blue shorts and a gray sweatshirt tumbled to the floor. I grabbed a change of clothes, and some spare magazines for the .38, and stuffed them inside.

It was a simple matter to throw the gym bag up through the hole in the ceiling, chin myself on a piece of jagged concrete, and crawl out onto the floor.

I stood to see that a middle-aged woman had been tied to her chair. Rope ran around her like in the cartoons. Adhesive tape covered her mouth, and her eyes bulged with pent-up emotion.

I smiled pleasantly, nodded, and grabbed the gym bag. The door opened smoothly, I stepped out into the foot traffic, and headed up-corridor. A contract is a contract. I'd find Sasha or die trying.

3

"We pay cash for used body parts."

From the sign in front of Arturo's
Pawn Shop, Sub-Level 26, Sea-Tac
Residential-Industrial Urboplex

It took the Zeebs about thirty minutes to summon the meat wagon, ask my neighbors stupid questions, and toss my apartment. Then, having assured themselves that I had nothing worth taking, they left a microbot to keep an eye out for me and headed for the nearest doughnut shop.

Had I been one of the wealthier freelancers, or an honest-to-god lifer, things would have been different. That's because the Zebras work for a company called Pubcor, which makes most of its money providing security to other corporations. I mean, who would you worry about? The people who pay you millions each year? Or the great unwashed horde who ante up six bucks a month? Right. Me too.

22

So, having left the lady's door open so someone would discover her predicament, I joined the crowd on Level 37. It isn't easy for me to blend into a crowd, but I did the best I could. Membership in the great unwashed horde is based on more than appearance. It's a matter of attitude. And to have the right attitude, you need to live the kind of hand-to-mouth existence freelancers do.

It wasn't always that way, I hear. There was a time when companies offered their workers what amounted to lifetime employment. But that ended back around the turn of the century when the last of the communist governments collapsed and capitalism reigned supreme.

After all, why pay employees during periods when you don't need them, especially when the population continues to increase? And automation drives the total number of jobs downwards? So that's how nearly everyone wound up as "freelancers," working when companies wanted them, and waiting when they didn't.

Knowing that, I imitated the slump-shouldered shuffle of a work-starved freelancer, avoided eye contact with oncoming traffic, and moved at the same pace as the rest of the crowd. Sameness. That's the key. People who act differently stand out from the crowd and are easy to remember.

The further underground you go, the worse the conditions get. My particular complex includes fifty sub-levels altogether so 37 is pretty bad. God only knows what 45 or 50 is like. I've never been there. The corpies who run the place save money by leaving every other lighting fixture empty. The substandard plumbing that the original contractor installed bursts on a regular basis, causing unexpected waterfalls that slide down walls or pour through broken ceiling tiles. Additional cable, not included in the original bid, hangs suspended beneath the overhead. Trash, including used condoms, drug injectors, stripped droids, food cartons, soiled clothing, and other stuff too gross to mention piles up fast. The robo-cleaners come through every night, but by noon the next day everything is just the same.

And the human debris is almost as bad. Addicts of every description laying unconscious in the filth, beggars who sold arms, legs, eyes, and god knows what else for a few credits, and street children, wise beyond their years, selling, stealing, and scamming their way through another day. I hate to say it, but Earth is a toilet world, ready to flush.

My first stop was a hallway hotel where I could rent a seven-by-four-foot sleeping compartment. It cost five bucks for twenty-four hours. I slid inside, checked to make sure that it was reasonably clean, and closed the door behind me. Like most sleep slots, this one boasted graffiti-covered walls, a mattress with a patched cover, and a beat-up vid set.

It took ten minutes to disassemble the .38, wipe it down, install a new barrel, and change the firing pin. Something I could do blindfolded if I had to. The change-out isn't foolproof, but it does serve to slow the Zeebs down and weakens their case. Assuming they made a case, which was damned unlikely. Snatchers are far from popular, and without a lifer goading them on, the Zebras could give a shit. Still, you need a license to carry heat, and the Zeebs would like nothing more than to jerk my ticket. So why tempt the bastards?

Yeah, I might have turned myself in and claimed self-defense, but that would have consumed one, maybe two days, and lessened my chances of finding Sasha.

I left the bag in the sleeping compartment, dumped the incriminating parts down a recycling chute, and headed for the escalators. People swirled around me, and an interactive wall ad tried to engage me in conversation. It had a high-resolution flat screen with pinpoint sound. The electronic pitchman had black hair combed straight back, a biosculpted face, and fervor-filled eyes. They followed me as I moved.

"Hey, mister! You look like a guy that has jock itch. Let me show you the Elexar 9000 Groin Grooming System and I'll . . ."

I never found out what he'd do, because the foot traffic narrowed as we approached the escalator and sucked me along with it. The crowd was typical, low-end day workers mostly, wearing beepers that rarely beeped, hoping for the five or six days' worth of work necessary to pay that month's rent. And there were predators too, scammers, zonies, and bangers, all looking for easy prey. And why not? They were self-employed, worked when they felt like it, and didn't kiss ass.

A banger, big in leather and lace, shifted his hockey stick from one shoulder to the other and moved my way. A buddy followed.

I made eye contact, grinned invitingly, and blew him a kiss. I *like* to shoot bangers, and it must have showed. He said something to his companion and they turned away.

The crowd poured off the escalator and headed down-corridor. I followed. Tracking someone through a major urboplex isn't as hard as you might think. Yeah, the halls are packed with people, but the trick is to see *through* them. Look for the things that stand still. Like the expresso stand that occupies the same spot every day, the kids who throw pennies against the wall, and the blind man who isn't so blind.

I don't know why Marvin runs the scam he does, but he's been at it a long time, and knows Level 39 like the back of his hand. I bought an Americano at the expresso stand and drifted his way. Marvin has black skin, wraparound electro-shades, and hair that looks as if it's exploding off his head.

"Shoeshine? Shoeshine to help the po' blind man?"

I stepped onto his stand, sat on the red vinyl seat, and put my boots on a well-worn foot rest. "Poor, my ass. What do you rake in from this racket, anyway? Twenty? Thirty a year?"

Had I been a corpie, just passing through, Marvin would've asked me what color my boots were. But I wasn't, so he let it slide. Carefully manicured hands, stained dark by constant exposure to the polish, slid over my boots. The movement had started as part of the act and evolved into a habit.

"More money than some dumb-assed white-bread shield, that's for damned sure," Marvin replied. "Shit, Maxon, they took the bitch right out from under your god-damned nose and left you looking like a chump. My mother could've done a better job."

Mysterious are the ways of a Marvin, so I didn't bother to ask how he knew about the girl or the fact that I had lost her. "Yes," I agreed sagely, "your mother could have done a better job, as any mirror will attest."

Marvin smeared brown polish on my boots and gave a snort of disgust. "Chrome-headed motherfucker."

"Not so," I replied solemnly. "It's true that I have a chrome-plated head . . . but my relationship with Mom was strictly platonic. Or so I assume."

Marvin laughed. "So what's up? You goin' after her? Or gettin' ready for a date?"

I sipped my coffee, watched an androgynous hall ho strut by, and looked down at the top of his head. A number of tiny silver bells had been woven into his hair. They tinkled as he moved.

"I'm going after her. Got any idea who they were? Or where they went?"

Marvin grabbed a pair of brushes and buffed my boots. "Shit. If you know *who* they are . . . then you know where they went. Everybody knows that."

Marvin likes to piss me off and knows how to do it. I forced a smile. "Thanks for the insight. Nifwamp iggledo reeko. So who the hell were they?"

Marvin looked up and grinned. "Snatchers."

I took a deep breath. "I know that. Who did they work for?"

Marvin produced a rag and snapped it across the top surface of my left boot. "Shit. Ain't my fault if you don't ask the right questions. They work for a company called Trans-Solar."

"And how do you know that XXX672TTT?"

"'Cause they wore matching holo-jackets with the name 'Trans-Solar' written across the backs. And my name ain't triple X whatever, turdface."

"Sorry. They passed your stand?"

"They sure as hell did."

"And the girl? She was okay?"

Marvin shrugged. "A bit mussed but otherwise fine."

"Trans-Solar, huh?"

"That's what I said."

"Deederwomp."

Marvin shook his head sadly. The bells tinkled cheerfully. "Deederwomp to you too, asshole."

I racked my brain trying to remember if the deader had been wearing a jacket, and if so, whether it said "Trans-Solar" on it. As with so many other things, the information was missing.

Marvin gave the rag one last snap and straightened up. My boots looked better than they had for years. He stuck his hand out. "That'll be twenty-five bucks. Twenty for the information and five for the shine."

I stood, slid a greasy twenty-five-dollar bill out of my wallet, and slapped it on his hand. "Thanks for nothing."

"Screw you."

We grinned and parted company, Marvin to work his scam and me to find my client. The crowd closed around me like a river around a raindrop. No matter how poor they might be, most of the people around me meant something to somebody. You know, friends, family, people who cared. After all, what good are accomplishments without someone to share them with? And a background to compare them to? But, according to the disk the corpies had given me along with my medical discharge, I had no family, no friends, and, outside of a talent for mayhem, no marketable skills.

So that, plus my tendency to make mistakes in social situations, had relegated me to the status of the eternal outsider. And, while some might envy my so-called freedom, they didn't sleep alone every night.

But that sounds like whining. Something I detest. Work, that was the answer. The fifty K Seculor had promised me was enough for a down payment on a hole-in-the-wall-café. And, surrounded by my regulars, I'd have someone to shoot the shit with. Pathetic, huh? Well, who said I was anything else?

So, back to business. If Marvin was right, Trans-Solar had put the snatch on Sasha. Now, some other person might have wondered *why* the snatchers revealed their identities when they didn't have to, but I didn't. No, it seemed like an accidental slip-up to me, and I proceeded accordingly.

The first step was to make some travel arrangements and find out where Trans-Solar was located: a task made relatively easy by sliding my single credit card into a slot, waiting for the door to slide open, and stepping into a com booth. The door hissed closed behind me and I damned near gagged on the smell. Someone, or a number of someones, had urinated in the enclosure rather than take their chances in a public rest room along with everyone else. Assholes.

The lights dimmed, and a rather seductive female voice intoned the words that everyone has heard a thousand times. "Welcome to the Pubcom Gateway 4000. Lean forward until your forehead touches the padding, take hold of both grips, and wait for the main menu to appear. You may choose between tactile or voice control. Please indicate your preference now."

"Voice."

"You chose voice. Thank you."

"Bite my ass."

"I'm sorry, but the service you requested is not among those I am programed to provide. Please choose from the following menus."

Characters appeared as the voice read them off. They were pink and floated over a black background. There was everything from a com directory, to on-line games, to travel services, to a gazillion different databases.

When the voice said "travel," I pulled the trigger on my right hand grip. An arrow appeared. I pulled the trigger on the left side and was sucked into the network. This particular sense-surround had been designed by the famous cyber-architect Moshi Chow. It was designed to seem like a futuristic race course, complete with bullet cars, and a pipe-shaped track. A track on which you could drive right side up or upside down.

I gave the grip another squeeze, felt my car pick up speed, and used the arrow to steer. Other cars were all around me. They came in every color of the rainbow and wove in and out with what seemed like death-defying courage.

I gloried in the feel of it and understood how people came to be addicted. After all, virtual reality was everything that reality wasn't: exciting, fulfilling, and forever fun. It was, the critics complained, a carefully orchestrated opiate for the people, subsidized by The Board to keep the workers under control. I tried to think my way through the problem, but my head started to hurt and I gave up.

I felt-sensed my destination ahead, took the proper exit, and was downloaded into a custom-made reality. There was no such place, of course, but it *looked* real, *sounded* real, and, thanks to kinesthetic feedback, *felt* real as well.

My not-real vehicle slowed as it entered a glass-and-steel high-tech building and coasted to a stop. I got out. The car pulled away and accelerated out of sight. The room was huge, or seemed to be anyway, and was rather pleasant.

A network of paths led here and there, passing countless kiosks, each designed to look like the sort of destination you had in mind. I saw tropical gardens, a night club, an English pub, a beach motif, and many more.

Navigating by means of the arrow, I made my way over to what looked like a high-tech control console. A woman, crisp in her ship-type suit, looked up and smiled. Her teeth were slightly uneven. A nice little touch by a programmer somewhere.

"Yes? How may I help you?"

"1111000111000110000100100100100000."

"What was that?"

"I want to visit Europa Station."

The woman nodded agreeably and gestured towards a command chair. "Have a seat."

It felt strange to sit in a chair knowing that I was standing in a com booth.

"How would you like to travel?"

"A space ship would be nice."

The woman smiled patiently.

"No, *how* would you like to travel? First class? Business? Or coach?"

"Well, I normally travel first class, but the rich food plays hell with my waistline, so coach is better."

She nodded as if my response was perfectly believable and consulted a free-floating computer screen. "The fair is $23, 879.12 one way."

I shifted in my chair. "I don't suppose you have anything less expensive? Dowand imbu odlepork."

She shook her head. "No sir, I'm afraid we don't."

"Hmmm. Well, that being the case, perhaps a shorter trip would be best."

She raised a carefully programmed eyebrow. "How short? Mars? The moon, perhaps?"

Like most freelancers, I knew exactly what I had in the bank. There was three hundred credits plus my pay from Droidware Inc. "How far could two people go on $800.00?"

The woman consulted her screen again. "Staros-3."

"Excuse me?"

"Staros-3 is an Earth-orbit habitat. That's how far the two of you could go on $800.00. Assuming you're willing to travel aboard a cargo shuttle with no amenities."

"I see."

Staros-3 fell way short of our destination, but it was a step in the right direction, and a reasonably good hiding place. Something we would need when Sasha was free. And if that seems a tad optimistic, remember that I'm half a lobe short of a full brain, and given to occasional oversimplification.

"Okay, Staros-3 it is."

"Name?"

I gave it some thought.

"Roger Doud."

"The name of your companion?"

"Imbelzweetnorkab."

"Spell it please."

"I meant to say 'Mary Cooper.'"

The woman nodded, and her electronic hands went through the motions of typing while a computer did the real work. "Method of payment?"

"Electronic transfer."

"Account number?"

I quoted the number from memory.

"Authorization code?"

"Privacy, please."

The world went temporarily dark. I gave the code. "Lima beans taste like hammered owl shit."

The computer heard, transferred the funds, and the surround reappeared. The woman smiled.

"Thank you, Mr. Doud. When would you like to lift?"

"Tomorrow evening."

She checked the screen. "That will be fine. FENA Air Flight 124 will board from Gate 426, Surface Port 12, at 3:35 P.M. Each passenger is limited to ten pounds of baggage. Questions?"

"Nope."

"Thank you, and have a nice day."

I liked the sentiment but didn't think it would come true. I decided to forgo the subjective ride and jump to the com booth instead. The voice returned along with the main menu. I asked for the business directory, ignored the characters that floated in front of me, and requested a listing of all Trans-Solar facilities located in the northwest section of the North American continent.

Looking back, I realize it would have been a good idea to learn more about the company in hopes of understanding *why* they had put the snatch on Sasha, but at the time the idea never crossed my mind.

The voice read them off. Trans-Solar had two northwest locations: a downtown business office, and a hangar complex out at the spaceport. It was an easy choice.

The days of enormous high-rise buildings crammed to over-flowing with staff were long gone. A regional business office would house five to ten lifers, some overworked freelancers to make coffee, and some security types to protect them. The real day-to-day administrative work would be done by computers and freelancers telecommuting from home. No, all things considered, the office didn't seem like a place to stash prisoners. Not with a hangar complex to work with.

The entire com booth shook as someone kicked the door. "You been in there long enough. Come the hell out or pay the price!"

I ignored the voice and summoned a map of the spaceport. There was a maze of yellow lines, lots of little red words, and a pulsating orange dot to mark the hangar's location. Maps give me headaches, so I gritted my teeth, squinted my eyes, and forced the information into my unwilling brain.

A boot hit the door and it bulged inwards.

"You better come outta there, asshole! Or I'm comin' in!"

My eyes found the main terminal, made obvious by its size and location, and followed a sequence of yellow lines to an orange dot. North, left at the first intersection, then north again. Right at the third intersection, let four grids pass, and watch for it on the right. I closed my eyes, visualized the pattern, and repeated the directions three times.

The door was ripped aside. A gang banger filled the opening. He was young enough to have peach fuzz and old enough to support fifty pounds worth of chromed chain. He wore leather pants, a matching jacket, and a light blue tutu. He held a piece of rebar, painted to match the tutu, and tapped it against his right shoulder. He grinned. "Hi there. My name's Alice. Wanta dance?"

I showed him the .38. His eyes grew bigger. "Sorry, Alice . . . but my dance card's full. 789123789456123."

I watched him figure the odds, trying to calculate whether he could hit me with the rebar before I pulled the trigger. Caution won out. He bowed and made a sweeping gesture with one arm. "Until next time, then."

I stayed where I was. "Is that a threat? Because if it is, I might as well kill you right now and have done with it."

His face grew paler and he backed away. I nodded agreeably and left the booth. Kids these days. What're you gonna do?

4

"Zombies have eternal peace of mind.
Think about it."

*Ad copy from Mindwipe Inc.,
a wholly owned subsidiary of
the Datastor Corporation*

It took the better part of two hours and three different subways to reach the spaceport. In spite of the name "subways," there was a time when wheeled vehicles, the direct ancestors of today's hover trains, followed the same routes under the open sky. But that was before the urboplex grew up around them, raising "ground level" to coincide with the penthouses where the lifers lived, and leaving the trains to thread their way through the depths below. The trains and the people like me who had little choice but to ride them. Strip lights, alternating smears of white and blue, whipped by.

As with walking the halls, there's some danger to riding the trains. The stops are two or three minutes apart, and a lot can happen in that amount of time. Sure, each car comes equipped with a Zeeb, but they tend to be too young or too old to do much good. The rest have other more important assignments.

My car was a good example. Our Zebra was a woman, pretty once, but gone to fat. Lard rolled back and forth as she moved, and her hips were so big that the regulation sidearm stuck straight out from her waist.

Still, some presence is better than none, and we arrived in one whole piece. Not counting the messenger droid who was ambushed, slammed, and scrapped, all during the sixty seconds or so that the Zeeb spent picking her nose.

A recording announced the airport, the doors whooshed open, and most of the people aboard headed outside. Stepping onto the platform was like stepping onto a whale's tongue. Steel ribs curved up to a high, vaulted ceiling and a PA system gabbled words I couldn't understand.

I followed the crowd onto one of a dozen gleaming escalators, moved to one side as a droid pushed his way past, and listened while a somewhat patronizing voice told me all the things I wasn't supposed to do inside the terminal area.

The faint odor of brine drifted up from the heavily polluted waters below. Not even multiple layers of concrete and steel could keep it out. By the time space travel had become so routine that every city needed its own spaceport, there was very little land available to put them on. That's when the corpies looked around, noticed that Puget Sound took up a lot of space, and decided to pave it over. And why not? It had been a long time since anyone had caught an unmutated fish from Elliott Bay or gone swimming without a dry suit.

Still, it was weird to think there was water under the spaceport, not to mention old shipwrecks, and the ruins of low-lying communities overcome by the constantly rising sea level. The Board was working on global warming, or so they claimed, but the oceans got deeper every year.

The escalators dumped us on the main level. It was huge. The furniture crouched low as if defying people to move it. Each spaceline had its own kiosk, and they dotted the open floor like islands in a nylon ocean. The building shuddered and engines rumbled as a shuttle lifted off somewhere outside. I knew where I was headed, but had every intention of getting there slowly. There would be security, lots of security, and I would have to find a way around or through it.

Now, someone else might have come up with a plan, a clever stratagem to get them where they wanted to go, but not me. Being, as they say, "mentally challenged," I tend to head in the obvious direction and hope for the best. You'd be surprised how often it works.

I drifted towards an expresso stand and bought an Americano. The waitress was fascinated by my chromed dome, knew she shouldn't look, but couldn't help herself. I smiled reassuringly, accepted the coffee, and ambled in the direction of a huge column. It was black with gold bands at the top and bottom.

I used the drink to warm my hands and to justify my lack of movement. People swarmed around me. Judging from the luggage, or the lack of it, the crowd was about evenly split between actual travelers and those who had come to meet someone, wave good-bye, or pick pockets.

I can't remember if I liked to travel, but I think I did. Why else would I join the Mishimuto Marines? Or head out into what spacers call the "Big Black"?

And second only to travel itself I like the *feeling* of travel, the hustle and bustle of spaceports, and the people that ebb and flow like a fleshy tide. Some running, some walking, some trudging heads down, eyes on the floor. Who are they? Where are they headed? And what are they thinking? There are times when I go to the spaceport to commune with them, to share the energy created by their movement, and wonder what they're all about. Strange? Maybe. But it's better than being alone.

But watching is a one-way game, or it's supposed to be anyway. So why was the little guy looking at me? Sure, the head attracts some attention, but the way this character stared at me suggested something else. Trans-Solar security? Possibly, but it seemed unlikely. They had no reason to expect me at the spaceport, or so I assumed. A scammer, then, or an undercover Zeeb, looking for who knows what. My heart jumped. The deader. Had they issued a warrant? Nah, if the Zebras wanted me they'd walk up and take me. I made a note to keep an eye on the man. It wouldn't be hard. He was the only guy around dressed in a bright green sports coat.

A zombie walked between us, eyes blank, a tiny bit of drool

dribbling from the corner of his mouth. He wore immaculate gray livery, high-gloss boots, and a matching dog collar. It was set with diamonds and connected to a six-foot leash. The woman who held the other end was a sight for sore eyes. She was black, about six-six, and dressed in a gray tunic, black miniskirt, and skin-tight leggings. She wore high heels, and they clicked as she walked. A cloud of perfume drifted behind her. It marked the air she breathed as hers and caused every heterosexual male within a hundred yards to salivate. I was no exception.

I felt sorry for the zombie, and slightly superior at the same time, because even *I* can find my way around without a leash. Zombies came into being as the result of some well-intended medical research by a company called E-Mem. Scientists there were searching for ways to enhance human memory when they accidentally came up with a way to *replace* it. And not just memory, but the thing that makes us get up in the morning, and drink that first cup of coffee.

And, as is so often the case with pure research, the real-world applications were an afterthought. As the corpies had grown more and more reliant on computers, and the data stored within them had become increasingly valuable, hackers, and the data pirates they gave birth to, profited accordingly. So when it became possible to electronically record information onto human brain tissue, and to psychologically encrypt it so that not even the most sophisticated data pirate could touch it, the market for zombies was created. Some were brain-damaged from birth, but many weren't.

Why this particular man had been willing to sacrifice most of his identity for a large up-front payment was known only to him. Assuming that he had the ability to remember, that is.

The crowd surged like fish fleeing a shark. I looked and was immediately interested. The bullet-catchers came first, easily identified by the pullover ponchos they wore, each embossed with the Trans-Solar logo. Their function was to literally "catch bullets" should a team of poppers attack their client. It was a high-risk way to make lots of money in a short period of time: a fact well understood by the catchers themselves and the reason behind their frightened eyes and strained expressions.

Four tough-looking bodyguards backed the bullet-catchers and stood ready to respond should someone attack. They looked quite competent. A fact that brought me little comfort and made my mission seem silly.

The lifer they protected was as handsome as the biosculptors could make him and walked with the heads-up confidence of someone who has all the answers. The lifer and his entourage left a vacuum, and I helped fill it. I checked on the guy in the green jacket and found he was following behind me. It was quite a procession.

A comparison of our route to the one that I had so painfully memorized produced a perfect match. I decided to continue. We made good time thanks to the fact that the bullet-catchers forced everyone out of the way. So good that I was worried that we'd hit a corporate checkpoint where the lifer would be allowed to pass and I wouldn't. But the world is a complicated place, and nobody rides for free, not even corpies.

The supposedly "spontaneous" demonstration came out of nowhere along with robo-cams to tape it. People who had seemed like raggedy-assed freelancers moments before rose from their seats, deployed hand-lettered signs and blocked the corridor.

They yelled slogans like "Down with Trans-Solar!" "People before profits!" and "Earth first!"

Greenies. I should've known. Some called them the lunatic fringe, and others regarded them as would-be saviors, men and women, and yes, a dysfunctional android or two, willing to attack the corpies regardless of cost. And the cost was high, as their gaunt faces and ragged clothes could attest. Because to be a greenie was to take an involuntary oath of poverty.

Blacklists were illegal, but everyone knew they existed, and why not? After all, why would a corporation use a freelancer who opposed them? And not in regard to one particular issue but on *everything*. Because that's where the greenies were coming from. They advocated the complete demechanization of society and a return to the land. Land owned by—you guessed it—the corporations.

The two groups came together and exploded. A greenie hit a bullet-catcher, the latter hit back, and the brawl was on. I stepped forward into the thick of the battle.

A woman with hollow cheeks, bad teeth, and fire-filled eyes

swung at me. I hit her harder than I should have. Her eyes rolled back in her head, and she fell. It was only as she went down that I realized she was a bullet-catcher. Somebody hit me from behind. It was a glancing blow and didn't hurt, but I fell anyway. Once on the floor, and hidden by the tightly packed bodies above, it was easy to undo the velcro fasteners and pull the Trans-Solar poncho over the woman's head. I had it half on by the time I stood.

One of the lifer's bodyguards, a Hispanic woman with muscles on her muscles, pistol-whipped a boy and attempted to rally the troops.

"Come on! A fifty-credit bonus to everyone who makes it to the Trans-Solar checkpoint!"

Most of us would have murdered our mothers for fifty credits. We staggered, then surged forward, pushing our way through the greenies. The protesters fell away, hopeful their demo had changed some minds, knowing it hadn't. The status quo was the status quo, and a lot better than some vague "return to the soil" movement. Especially when most of the soil is covered with concrete, contaminated with chemicals, and completely worn out.

Though unable to stop us, the greenies gave chase. We moved down the corridor at a pretty good clip, took a right into a hallway marked "PRIVATE TRANS-SOLAR PERSONNEL ONLY," and headed for a rather elaborate checkpoint. It consisted of a partition made of steel bars, a "kill zone," and another partition of steel bars. It was personed by rent-a-cops, and they were armed with everything short of antitank weapons.

A bodyguard shouted, "Open the gate!" and waved an I.D. card in the air. Laser beams scanned it, a computer approved it, and the gate slid open. We rushed through and it closed behind us. Those towards the rear tried to stop, shoved those in front, and pushed them against a second gate.

I turned to find that the greenies had pushed the man in the green sports coat up against the bars. Our eyes met, and he yelled something, but the crowd noise drowned him out.

A beacon flashed, a buzzer buzzed, and I turned in time to see a female rent-a-cop point towards me from the far side of gate two. "He has a gun! Grab him!"

The .38! Like the idiot I am, I had entered the checkpoint

packing a gun. The autoscanners had found it and were busy spreading the word.

I shoved a middle-aged man with long scraggly hair towards the Hispanic woman. He tripped and fell against her chest. They went down in a tangle of arms and legs. Her gun went off. A bullet hit the ceiling and screamed away.

I took two blows to the chest and heard the gunshots that went with them. I staggered backwards and knew I'd been shot. I looked down, expecting to see a big mess, and realized that the Trans-Solar poncho was bulletproof. Of course! The longer the bullet-catchers stayed alive during an ambush, the longer the lifer would be protected.

The second bodyguard, a white dude with tattoos all over his face, fired as I stepped behind a fat guy. Having raised his hands in protest, the bullet-catcher took a round through the palm of his left hand before it hit the center of his poncho and bowled him over.

I dodged the falling body and felt the gun fill my hand. I brought the weapon up, put a round through the white dude's left thigh, and flinched as a bullet whipped by my ear. The third bodyguard, a twin to the second, corrected his aim. I shot him in the shoulder, realized that his bulletproof underwear had blocked it, and put a round through his gun arm. His pistol clattered as it hit the floor. I was still alive but couldn't understand why. The fourth bodyguard should have nailed me by now but hadn't. I turned, saw the crumpled body, and figured her for a ricochet.

The rent-a-cops, still penned behind gate two, tried for a clear shot but couldn't find one. Bullet-catchers scattered every which way. The lifer did his best to get behind them, but it didn't work. A pair of women pushed him forward. "Here . . . shoot the bastard and leave us alone!"

I grabbed the sonofabitch, put the gun to his head, and marched him towards the second gate. The rent-a-cops shuffled their feet and wondered what to do. The smell of expensive cologne filled my nostrils. I spoke into his right ear. "Open the gate and do it now."

Sweat trickled down his temple and his hands fluttered helplessly. "Don't hurt me! I'll double what they're paying you!"

"Sounds good," I said. "Lepforg gortnoy. Open the gate!"

A well-manicured hand came up, hesitated for a moment, and stabbed the keypad. The gate started to move, and the rent-a-cops surged forward. I took the gun away from the lifer's head long enough to bounce a round off the floor in front of them. They backpedaled in a hurry.

"Place your weapons on the floor and do it now!"

The ranking rent-a-cop, a woman with a blue Mohawk, looked doubtful. The rest waited for orders. I shoved the .38 into the lifer's ear. He got the hint. His voice quavered. "Do what the man says."

Blue-hair frowned unhappily, did a squat, and placed her handgun on the floor. Her troops did likewise. I figured most of them for backup weapons, but didn't plan to push my luck. I edged the lifer around until the rent-a-cops were between me and the cage. I waved the .38.

"All right . . . into the cage."

The rent-a-cops backed into the cage palms out. A snarl hurried them along. I kicked the door closed, hoped it would take them a few minutes to get it open, and motioned towards the far end of the corridor. "Come on, pretty boy . . . let's run."

He did as ordered, huffing and puffing after the first hundred feet or so, expelling the words one at a time. The floor was cleaner than most of the plates in my apartment, and our shoes made squeaking sounds as we ran. The corridor turned to the right, and we followed.

"What"—pant, pant, pant—"are"—pant, pant—"you"—pant, pant—"going"—pant, pant—"to"—pant, pant—"do"—pant, pant—"with"—pant, pant—"me?"

"Well," I replied, glancing over my shoulder, "cross-country competition is out, and that being the case, I'll trade you for a girl named Sasha."

He looked at me sideways. His eyes grew bigger. "Sasha"—pant—"Casad?"

"That's the one. Where the hell is she?"

"And your name"—pant—"is?"

I started to get annoyed. The tables had turned somehow, and he was interrogating me. I reached out, grabbed his collar, and skidded to a halt. The .38 wouldn't fit inside his left nostril, but I did what I could to shove it there anyhow. "My name is 'tell me where the girl is or I'll blow your sinuses out through the top of your head.' "

His eyes grew even bigger. "I know who you are! Please, forget the girl, and listen to what . . ."

I turned the gun to the right and squeezed the trigger. The bullet went out through the side of his nose instead of up through his brain. Blood sprayed all over the place and the lifer screamed. He covered his nose with his hands and I rammed the .38 into his gut. "Now listen, asshole, I'm done playing patty-cake with you. Take me to the girl, or I'll drop you right here."

I wouldn't have dropped him right there, but he didn't know that, and did as he was told. His voice was muffled. "All right, all right, just leave me alone."

There was a shout from the other end of the corridor. It was the Hispanic bodyguard. She was pissed, and so were the rent-a-cops.

I sent two rounds in their general direction and gave pretty boy a shove. He staggered, caught his balance, and began to run. I followed. The steel door was fifty feet ahead. The lifer slowed, used the wall as a brake, and fumbled with the keypad. His blood-covered index finger skidded from one key to another. He started over. I turned, aimed low, and sent three rounds down-hall. Eight, nine, and ten. That left me with four rounds and a spare magazine.

A rent-a-cop threw up his arms, tumbled head over heels, and grabbed his right knee. The Hispanic woman shouted something obscene, raised her gun to return fire, and stopped when she realized that even a slight miscalculation could result in her client's death. I grinned.

The door opened. Pretty boy dived through in hopes of leaving me stranded outside. It didn't work. Bullets clanged off the door as it closed behind me. I looked for and found the inevitable keypad. I clicked the "emergency lock" button five or six times and heard the heavy-duty bolts shoot home. The door shook as the rent-a-dorks discovered what I'd done and expressed their displeasure.

I looked for pretty boy, found him plucking Kleenex from a blood-spattered box, and whacked him over the head. He collapsed in a heap.

I checked for people, didn't see any, and took a moment to look around. Art hung on the walls, plants sat just so, and the furniture invited me to sit down and relax. I didn't.

"Welcome to Trans-Solar, Mr. Maxon."

The voice came from behind me. I turned to find myself looking down the barrel of a hand-held cannon. My .38 hung straight down, so far out of position that it might as well have been home, sitting in a drawer. I wondered if I could bring it up before he was able to squeeze the trigger. The man smiled and shook his head. I let the .38 drop. It made a soft thump as it hit the carpet. The man nodded approvingly. "Wise. Very wise."

The man was bald, or nearly so. What hair he had left was pulled back into a ponytail. He was handsome without being pretty and wore his clothes with negligent ease. His eyes were blue and very intelligent. "We've been expecting you."

"Really?" I said stupidly. "How's that?"

"Come now, Mr. Maxon," the man replied. "Even you are smarter than that. My men wore their jackets logo-out so you'd know where to look."

Blood rushed to my face as I realized how stupid I'd been. It was so obvious, so god-damned obvious, and I'd missed it. But why? They had Sasha, and that was the objective, wasn't it? I tried to sound nonchalant. "Yeah, that was pretty transparent, alright."

"Exactly," the man agreed. "But it worked, and you were a good deal more resourceful than my staff gave you credit for." He gestured towards pretty boy's crumpled body. "Curt will remember you for a long time."

"Ibelsnork mopocky," I said nonsensically, doing my best to maintain eye contact, while Sasha emerged from a side door and held a finger to her lips. She tiptoed in our direction, selected a piece of stone statuary off a side table, and closed the distance. She wore a bra, panties, and nothing else.

I was afraid she'd blow the whole thing by giving herself away, or by hitting the man so lightly that it did little more than piss him off. Little did I know. Sasha brought the statue back like a baseball bat, gave him a good thump to the side of the head, and stood ready to follow up if the occasion demanded. It didn't. The lifer's eyes went blank, and he hit the floor in an untidy heap. Good. Smug bastards piss me off.

I kicked the .44 out of reach, checked his pulse, and found it was steady. Sasha seemed somewhat casual for a teenaged girl. "Is he dead?" She retrieved the .44 and held it barrel down.

I frowned. "No, but you hit him awfully hard. I'm surprised his head didn't fly off."

Sasha hit the cylinder release, checked to make sure that all five of the .44's chambers were loaded, and flipped the weapon closed. The whole thing was done with a degree of expertise that should have bothered me but didn't. Her voice was casual but tight. "He tried to rape me."

The bra and panties suddenly made sense. As did the swellings around the sides of her face. "I'm sorry."

She shrugged and smiled crookedly. "It wasn't your fault."

Well it *was* my fault, or so I assumed at the time, but there seemed little point in dwelling on it. The door shook as something heavy hit it. "Get your clothes on. It's time to leave."

Sasha nodded, strode towards the side door, and disappeared inside. I drifted that way and caught a glimpse of a rumpled bed and the leather straps that had connected her hands to the headboard. She grabbed her tights and pulled them up around her waist. They were ripped. She nodded towards the straps. "They were long enough to use my teeth on."

I nodded my understanding. The girl was more than I'd thought at first. She had guts, and I admired that. I gestured to our surroundings. "Any way out of here? Other than the front door?"

Sasha settled the miniskirt into place and turned her attention to the high-heeled boots. I tried to imagine someone running in them and couldn't.

"Yeah, I think there is. I didn't exactly have the run of the place, but there's something towards the back."

I nodded, hit the .38's magazine release, and slipped the near-empty magazine into my pocket. The backup slid home with a satisfying click. I pumped a round into the chamber, checked to make sure the safety was off, and slipped through the door. Rats always have more than one way out of their nest. All I had to do was find it.

There was a dull thump, a wave of air hit my back, and the door crashed inwards. I turned, waited for the inevitable rush, and punched three rounds through the smoke and dust. Sasha appeared by my side, held the .44 with both hands, and loosed a round through the doorway. The recoil pulled the gun up overhead. She brought it back down. Someone screamed and she grinned.

"Come on!" I grabbed her hand and jerked her towards the rear of the office. There were cubicles, storage rooms, and yes, a door with the words "Emergency Exit" lit up above it. Bullets whipped past us as we pushed it open, spied the circular staircase, and started downwards. The corpies were only seconds behind us. I had my client back. The question was, for how long?

5

"We're not proposing to pump
it dry, for god's sake . . . just
pave it over."

*Land Commissioner Donald
Siranni on plans to "cap"
Puget Sound*

A massive concrete pillar ran down through the center of the spiral
staircase. One of Sasha's spiked heels caught in the open mesh.
She managed to pull it out and continued on tiptoes. A door
slammed and the stairs shook as the rent-a-cops started down. We
had a two- or three-minute lead. Not enough at the speed we were
traveling. "Sasha! Lose the boots! We won't make it otherwise!"

The kid grabbed the rail and stopped. I squeezed past, turned,
and gestured for a boot. She shoved one in my face. I grabbed,
pulled, and felt it come loose. The second boot was easier. I threw
both aside.

I heard a shout, sent a slug up the stairwell, and headed down.
Sasha followed. We took the stairs two, sometimes three at a time,

always conscious of the fact that the corpies were close behind. There were lots of landings, and doors off each, but all of them were locked. I kept going, knowing the stairs had to end sometime, and hoping that maybe, just maybe, there would be a way out.

The landings were numbered and the numbers got larger. Finally we were on "Level 50," and nothing but a door stood between us and whatever lay beyond. I pushed and nothing happened. We were trapped.

"Stand aside." Sasha held the .44 in both hands. She was already in the process of squeezing the trigger when I yelled "No!" The word was lost in the boom that followed.

The bullet bounced off the steel plate that protected the lock mechanism, hit the wall next to my shoulder, and whined up the stairwell. I hoped it would hit a corpie and knew that kind of luck had been reserved for someone else. My ears rang as Sasha brought the gun down for another try. I told her what to do.

"Ebertok asu nabledock!"

Sasha frowned and her finger tightened on the trigger.

I tried again. "Aim for the keypad instead!"

She nodded and corrected her aim.

I turned and was watching the stairs when she fired the next shot. It was as loud as the first. A few more of those and I'd be deaf.

"Maxon! Look!"

I looked. The slug had transformed the keypad into a mass of shattered plastic and tangled wires. Sparks sputtered and a tendril of smoke drifted away. I kicked the door and it swung inwards. We entered together. I saw a corridor and a second door. There was no sign of a lock. Good. Sasha gestured to the corner next to the door. "Stay here and slow 'em down. I'll scout ahead."

Who the hell had died and left her in charge? I started to ask, but she was gone before I could organize the necessary words. So I stayed where I was, watched the stairs, and fired when I saw legs. They retreated upwards in a hurry. The corpies yelled something, tried to draw me out, and I ignored them. I heard the now-familiar boom of the .44.

"Maxon! Come on!"

I wished there was some way to lock the door, couldn't think of one, and backed away. Sasha held a second door open and gestured with the .44. The bore looked big enough to drive a truck through. I made a note to teach her something about gun safety. Assuming we lived long enough to make the effort worthwhile, that is.

I moved through the door and out onto a concrete jetty. Dark water lapped all around. There was a variety of equipment, including a pair of light-duty cranes, fuel pumps, cargo modules, and a high-speed launch that sat on a cradle. The line of bullet holes just above the heavily stained waterline gave mute testimony to what had happened. That, plus the fact that the security station resembled a small-scale fortress, hinted at unseen dangers.

The apparent dangers, both naked from the waist down, stood with their hands behind their heads. The woman had nice legs and an attitude to go with them. Her nudity didn't bother her in the least. She looked at me and smiled. The man kept his eyes on the deck. Sasha was pleased with herself. "They were busy playing hide the submarine when I surprised them."

I frowned to demonstrate my disapproval of her unladylike analogy and gave thanks for the human sex drive. Assuming that our pursuers had called ahead, this pair had been too busy to notice. "I heard a shot."

"Oh, that," Sasha said nonchalantly. "I fired a round to get their attention."

Sasha seemed to be of the opinion that ammo grew on trees. I scowled at the guards and gestured towards a cargo module. "Climb to the top and sit on your hands."

The man hurried to obey. The woman followed, and so did my eyes. My lust was rather short-lived, however, since the corpies chose that particular moment to arrive, firing as they came. The fact that they were shooting at Sasha, and not at me, should have set some thoughts in motion but didn't.

Sasha brought her cannon up and squeezed the trigger. A rent-a-cop was plucked off his feet and thrown backwards into the crowd. I grabbed the girl's wrist with my left hand and towed her towards the far end of the jetty. The .38 bucked and corpies dove for cover.

A man, hidden until now, appeared from our right. He wore mechanic's overalls and held a wrench in his hand. Sasha swung the .44 in his direction and pulled the trigger. The hammer fell on an empty casing. I shot the man through the thigh and lectured Sasha as he fell. "This ain't no movie, kid . . . you gotta count your rounds."

She looked ashamed, and it was then that I noticed the bloody footprints. Sasha had come down who knows how many stairs in her bare feet and cut them to shreds. All without a whimper. I felt like the biggest sonofabitch in the world and wished I could take the comment back. Her attention was elsewhere. "Maxon, look!"

I looked in the direction of her pointing finger. The boat appeared to be about twenty-five feet long, had lots of lights, and, judging from the shape of its hull, had been designed for speed rather than cargo capacity. Just the thing for harried executives or fugitives like ourselves. I shoved Sasha in that direction. "Jump! I'll cast off."

"You know how to drive one of these things?"

"Of course," I lied. "Now jump." She jumped. The boat bobbed slightly as she landed.

I ran to the point where the forward line had been wrapped around a bollard, found that someone had used a double-reverse-something-or-other-knot to secure it, and swore as my fingers strained to undo it. A rent-a-cop opened up with a submachine gun, and Sasha's words were nearly inaudible. "I dumped the other line! Come on!"

Bullets whipped past Sasha's head as I ran towards the boat, jumped the ever-widening gap, and tumbled into the cockpit. I was still sorting myself out when the starter whined, the engine caught, and the boat surged forward. The bow hit the jetty a glancing blow, bounced off, and roared away. Corpies ran the length of the jetty. Fire flickered from the muzzles of their guns as empty casings arced through the air. A piece of side glass shattered, tiny bits of fiberglass peppered my face, and an invisible hand tugged at my sleeve.

I fought my way forward, shouldered Sasha out of the way, and assumed control in time to avoid a head-on collision with a support column. She seemed happy to relinquish command.

Someone fired a scope-mounted rifle. The windscreen shattered, and miniature geysers erupted all around us as he or she emptied a clip.

I didn't think of it then, but would eventually realize that the

sniper *could have* hit me had he or she really wanted to, and had
missed on purpose. Then we were gone, beyond the range of the
rifle, and hidden by almost total darkness. My heart beat a mile a
minute as I remembered the columns that held everything up,
searched for the right pictograph, and flicked the appropriate
switch.

The spotlights were mounted on a bar over the flying bridge.
Some had been shot out, but a dozen or so remained. They
illuminated a row of concrete pillars that marched off into the
distance and disturbed hundreds of bats. The miserable little
bastards swooped down, sailed through the lights, and flapped
away. An unexpected waterfall poured from above, spattered
across the bow, and ran the length of the boat. Drainage from the
spaceport? A broken pipe? There was no way to know.

I looked back to where our wake broke white against concrete
columns and the lights from the jetty seemed to wink off and on.
I glanced at Sasha as I turned towards the bow. Her hair blew
straight back, and she reminded me of someone else, though I
didn't know who. Had that thought passed through my mind
before? I strained but couldn't remember. "Did you see another
boat?"

She shook her head. "Just the one that had been hauled out for
repairs."

I nodded. "Do us both a favor. Go below and look for holes."

Sasha frowned, as if disappointed that she hadn't thought of
that, and backed down a short ladder. I basked in my moment of
brilliance, edged towards the exact center of the channel, and
wondered where the hell we were going. Well, we'd get there
pretty damned fast, that was for sure. The wind pressed against my
face, and the pillars whipped by like pylons in a race. Sasha
reappeared at my elbow. "You were right, Maxon."

"The name's Max."

She looked impatient. "Max, schmax. We're taking water. Lots
of it."

"How fast is it coming in? Could we plug the holes?"

Sasha looked doubtful. "I don't think so. It's half a foot deep
and rising fast."

I swore under my breath. It would be just my luck to escape a hail of gunfire only to drown a few minutes later. "Can you swim?"

Sasha shook her head. "Swimming pools are in short supply on Europa Station. How 'bout you?"

"Not a lick. Not that I can remember, anyway."

Her eyes left mine and darted away. "Shit."

"Yeah."

We were silent for a moment. A pillar flashed by. She looked my way. "Did you see that?"

"What?"

"The column had words on it."

"So?"

"So, slow down. If that column had words on it, the next one might have them too."

It made sense, although the practical value of reading the words escaped me. I eased the throttle back and took a look at the speedometer or the nautical equivalent thereof. The needle dropped as our speed fell off. The boat bobbed up and down as its wake caught up with it. Sasha pointed at the next pillar. "Look!"

I looked. The column bore the likeness of a skull and crossbones with words underneath. The boat had drifted close. I slipped the engine into reverse and goosed the throttle. "What does it say? Your eyes are younger than mine."

"It says, 'Death to corpies. Proceed at your own risk.' "

I nodded agreeably. "A noble sentiment indeed. It's time to haul ass."

Sasha nodded. I moved the transmission lever into the "forward" position, brought the throttle up, and felt the boat surge forward. It took longer than before, and the wheel felt sluggish. A hand darted in to flip one of the many switches that lined the control panel. There was a humming sound, and water gushed from the boat's side.

"Jeez, Maxon. It says 'Bilge Pump.' What hell were you waiting for?"

I felt blood rush to my face. "Sorry . . ."

She looked angry. "Sorry isn't good enough! A mistake like that could get us killed."

I kept my eyes straight ahead. What could I say? The girl was right. I *did* make mistakes, and one *could* get us killed. A hand touched my arm. I looked in her face and saw the anger had disappeared. Something else had taken its place. Something I couldn't quite name.

"I'm sorry, Max. That was a stupid thing to say. You came after me, and that took guts. I won't forget it."

I couldn't remember anyone saying something that nice to me. A whole host of emotions bubbled up from deep inside. I wanted to say something suave but knew I'd cry instead. So I settled for a nod and tried to look impassive. I couldn't tell if she bought it or not.

We continued that way for another forty-five minutes or so, water gushing out of the boat's side while it sank lower and lower in the water. That's when the floaters roared out of the darkness. Their small, sledlike boats wove in and out of the pillars like shuttles on a loom. There were ten or fifteen of the speedy little craft, and each boasted a two-person crew. The drivers hunched behind their control panels while their gunners stood within cagelike structures and aimed their pintle-mounted weapons in our general direction. They wore black scuba suits and enough armament to embarrass a marine. I hit the throttle and the boat surged forward, but it was too late.

Four or five of the sleds turned inwards, pulled alongside, and bumped our hull. Four of their neoprene-clad gunners were aboard a half-second later and aimed some rather ugly-looking machine pistols in our direction. I considered the .38 but rejected it as a bad idea. A member of the assault team gestured with his weapon. "Throttle back. Keep your hands where I can see them."

I looked at Sasha. She gave a tiny, almost imperceptible shrug. I pulled the throttle back. The boat nose-dived, regained its equilibrium, and wallowed in the waves the sleds had made.

The man spoke again. "Good. Place your hands behind your head and step away from the controls." He pointed the machine pistol towards Sasha. "You too."

We did as instructed. Another member of the assault team, a woman this time, patted me down. She found the .38 and held it beneath a light. "Nice, very nice, but not the sort of heat that corpies carry."

My voice came as a croak. "We aren't corpies."

She grinned. Rubber framed an average face. Her skin was

unnaturally white. "No shit. That would explain why you look like hell and the boat's full of holes. What happened to your head, anyway?"

"A guy blew my brains out and the medics stuffed them back in. They couldn't find the top of my skull, so they installed a metal plate instead."

The woman thought I was joking and laughed appreciatively. "I like your sense of humor. Now, explain how you got the boat and what you're doing in our territory."

That's when Sasha jumped in. She was concerned that I'd screw things up, and I couldn't really blame her.

"We found a hole in Trans-Solar's security, tried to hijack some proprietary information, and were caught in the act. We headed downwards, wound up on a jetty, and stole this boat. Finding you was chance and nothing more. End of story."

The woman nodded slowly. There was a smile on her face. "And quite a story it is. Parts of it could even be true! Well, never mind. You really pissed 'em off, that's obvious from the condition of the boat, and that makes you okay with us. Here, take your cannon back."

I accepted the .38 and stuck it down the back of my pants. Sasha's .44 had been confiscated as well. A man handed it back. The woman offered her hand. It was strong but cold. "My name's Murphy. What's yours?"

There wasn't enough time to think of a good lie, not for me anyway, so I told the truth. "I'm Max Maxon . . . and this is Sasha Casad."

"Max . . . Sasha . . . glad to meet you. Now stand by while we bring some pumps aboard."

Sleds bumped the hull, pumps were handed up, and two of the floaters headed below. Within minutes the hoses were connected, the pumps were started, and water gushed over the side. It was all done with a minimum of motion and conversation, as though they'd done similar things many times before.

Murphy looked over the side and nodded her satisfaction. "That should do it. I'll take the wheel if you have no objection."

Neither of us had been all that excited about steering to begin with. We shook our heads in unison. Murphy smiled, waved the sleds off, and inched the throttle forward. The bow came up in one smooth motion, steadied, and hung there as if suspended from above. The sleds roared along to either side, dashing back and forth across our wake, narrowly avoiding the pillars. It looked like fun. Murphy yelled over the sound of the engine, "What will you do now?"

Sasha was unaware of our travel arrangements, so I took over. "We need to get topside as soon as possible."

Murphy nodded thoughtfully. "You owe my family for the cost of our fuel, and the use of our pumps, but the boat is yours. By *our* laws, anyway. What will you do with it?"

I was about to give it to her gratis when Sasha took over. "We plan to sell it, pay our debts, and keep the balance. Would you like to make an offer?"

Murphy flicked the wheel to the right, skidded the boat around some floating debris, and straightened it out again. "Boats like this are hard to come by. We use them to run contraband in from the ocean. The corpies try to stop us, but we usually outrun them. My father will give you a good price."

Sasha looked skeptical. "No offense, but others might offer us a good price as well, and we owe it to ourselves to listen."

Murphy nodded, as if Sasha's comment was not only appropriate but expected. "True, but that would take time, and Max says you're in a hurry."

I wanted to say something agreeable, but Sasha sent a scowl in my direction. "We'll listen to any reasonable offer."

These people had saved our bacon, but when it came to business the girl didn't have a sentimental bone in her body. A little gift from her corpie-type parents, perhaps? But it didn't bother Murphy. She nodded and pointed towards the bow. "That's Floater Town. We'll be there in five minutes or so."

I looked and saw a collection of lights that seemed to hover just off the water. Reflections zigzagged across the surface and shattered as the water undulated up and down. The engine noise dropped to a rumble as Murphy eased the throttle back and allowed the boat to settle in the water.

There was a single approach to Floater Town, and it carried us through a maze of mines. Some were submerged while others bobbed near the surface. How Murphy was able to pilot our boat through the maze was a mystery. Perhaps she had memorized the route, or maybe the small earplug she wore had something to do with it. Whatever the method, she proceeded slowly, as did the sleds, which formed a single line behind us.

Floater Town boasted other defenses as well, including a number of heavily armored barges, attack sleds, and automated weapons blisters that clung to the ceiling like concrete limpets. And later, as we cleared the mines, I saw four sixty- or seventy-foot submarines, all moored side by side and painted to resemble sea monsters.

Murphy maneuvered the boat alongside the dock with nary a bump. A burst of reverse power was sufficient to neutralize our forward motion. A gang of cheerful-looking children, as sleek as seals in their rubber suits, ran to handle our lines. Murphy slipped the gearshift to neutral, switched the bilge pump to shore power, and killed the engine. Water continued to spill from the hoses. "The pumps will hold her for now."

Sasha nodded impassively and followed Murphy over the side. She winced as her feet hit the surface of the dock. Murphy saw that and frowned. She gestured towards a gear locker. "Sit on the box. Hold your feet up one at a time."

Sasha shrugged but did as she was told. The bleeding had stopped, but the lacerations were easy to see. They were red towards the center and edged with blue. Shame swept over me like a wave. I had meant to remember her feet, I really had, but my memory, fickle as always, had betrayed me once more.

Murphy called for help. A pair of muscular young men appeared, swept Sasha off the locker, and carried her down the dock. Standards had been placed every twenty feet or so and cast interlocking circles of light. A wave rolled in out of the darkness and the dock shifted beneath our feet. The rest of Floater Town did likewise, undulating up and down before settling down.

None of the buildings were more than two stories tall, and all rested on some sort of flotation system. Some were built on barges, some squatted on rafts made from fifty-gallon oil drums, and others rode homemade pontoons. Most were rather dilapidated, having the appearance of well-maintained shacks rather than formal dwellings. Still, there was lots of elbow room, and that was attractive, in spite of the unending darkness and the press of a barely seen concrete sky.

The men carried Sasha into one of the more prosperous-looking structures, and we followed. I barely had time to see the hand-lettered sign that said "Murphy Enterprises," and the metal booster tanks that held the place up, before I was ushered into a combination living room and warehouse.

Coils of nylon line hung next to all manner of floats, fishing gear, spear guns, nets and other less identifiable items. And there was furniture too, shabby-looking stuff for the most part, but solid and comfortable. Everything was in shades of gray, as if the external darkness had managed to reach in and leach the color out of the walls, furniture, and fittings.

Sasha was receiving better care than I could provide. People ran hither and yon and yelled insults at each other as they gathered medical supplies and worked on her feet. I used the time to examine what seemed like an anomaly. A large, rather splashy painting, blue the way the ocean is supposed to be, and full of tropical fish.

"Do you like it?"

I turned to find Murphy at my side. The rubber hood hung between her shoulders. Her hair was so short that it was little more than brown fuzz. She wore gold studs in both earlobes.

"Yes, I do. Is it yours?"

She smiled. "If you like it, then yes, it is. Come. My father wants to see you."

I turned and saw Sasha trying on a pair of black, high-topped sneakers. They were more practical than the high heels had been, and would be good for shipboard use. Or so I assumed, because in spite of the fact that I had spent several years in space, I couldn't remember a thing about it.

It was then that I noticed that the two young men still hovered in the background, and realized that Sasha was more than a girl; she was an attractive young woman. An urge to separate her from her male admirers bubbled to the surface. "Sasha . . . Murphy's father wants to see us."

Sasha said, "Be right there," turned to her fan club, and said something I couldn't hear. They laughed and headed for the door. I wondered what she'd said but didn't dare ask.

Murphy led us in the direction I least expected to go, down-wards. A short flight of stairs carried us down into an underwater room. It hung between the massive booster tanks that provided the building with buoyancy. Armored glass enclosed three of the four walls, and underwater floods illuminated the surrounding area. I watched in open-mouthed amazement as a big ugly fish swam through the brightly lit water, flicked its tail, and disappeared into the surrounding gloom.

"Beautiful, isn't it?"

The voice came from the man who sat with his back to the single solid wall, separated from me by a semicircular desk, which, judging by the cables that squirmed out the back of it, housed some rather sophisticated electronics. He had thinning hair, a high forehead, and bright blue eyes. They seemed lit from within and capable of seeing straight through whatever they looked at. He stood and held out his hand. He wore khakis and was very fit.

"Mr. Maxon . . . . Ms. Casad . . . welcome to my home."

"Thank you," I replied. "We appreciate your help."

I heard a thumping sound and turned to see what had caused it. Two rubber-suited children hung outside the window waving and making faces through their masks.

"It's the twins," Mr. Murphy said apologetically. "They love to show off."

Sasha said, "You have a wonderful family," and seemed to mean it.

"Thank you. We have six boys and five girls, which is ten more than the corpies would allow us to have topside, and about eight more than we planned. But the Murphys are a passionate lot and not always given to practicality. Please, be seated. Would you like something to eat? To drink?"

My stomach rumbled, and I realized that it had been a long time since the pizza. Sasha looked interested as well. "Something to eat would be nice, if it isn't too much trouble."

Mr. Murphy settled back in his chair. "No trouble at all. Maureen? Would you be so kind?"

The woman who had introduced herself as "Murphy" nodded and headed upstairs.

"So," Mr. Murphy said comfortably. "Maureen tells me that you have a boat for sale."

I nodded, but Sasha answered. "Yes, we do. And a rather nice one at that."

Mr. Murphy grinned and countered with a position of his own. "Boats are supposed to float. Yours would sink if the pumps failed."

Sasha shrugged. "Holes can be plugged, and besides, it's the engine you're after anyway."

Now this was a revelation to me, but it made a weird sort of sense, since hulls are a lot easier to fabricate than high-tech engines. Sasha had known that from the start, while I had taken the situation at face value.

Negotiations went on for some time, with points being scored on both sides, as the dollar spread gradually narrowed. I ignored the conversation for the most part, content to devote most of my attention to the soy-steak sandwiches Maureen had delivered, and the pot of scalding hot coffee. I knew a deal had been struck when both parties stood and shook hands. Mr. Murphy spoke first. "You're a tough negotiator, Ms. Casad. Who taught you to slice a deal that thin?"

Sasha grinned. "Dear old Mom. I had to write a business case in order to get seconds at dinner."

Mr. Murphy nodded approvingly. "Start 'em early, that's what I say. How do you want your money?"

The words seemed to pop out of my mouth. I was as surprised as they were. "Cash mostly, but we could use some clothes, and a pair of space-certified weapons."

If Mr. Murphy thought my request unusual, he gave no sign of it. He nodded understandingly. "You'd never make it past security with regular firearms, and you'd be crazy to use them even if you could. Some of those habitats are surprisingly thin-skinned. Maureen . . . take a look in the armory. A pair of Browning .9mm flechette guns might meet their needs."

We made small talk until Maureen returned with two plastic cases. She handed one to each of us. I thumbed mine open, pried the weapon from its nest, and looked it over. It had all the latest enhancements, including some carefully placed weights to add heft in normal gravity situations, an over-sized safety to accommodate gloved hands, a thirty-round magazine, a ninety-round gas reservoir, and a flat black nonreflective finish. The box included thirty rounds of ammo, fifteen standard or "killer" rounds, and fifteen injector or "drug" rounds. I tried to remember when and where I'd learned those names, but couldn't.

"So what do you think?"

I looked Mr. Murphy in the eye. "We'll take 'em. We'll need shoulder holsters, four spare magazines, and a thousand rounds of ammo. Half killer and half drug. And some clothes. Two outfits apiece and a bag to tote them in."

Yeah, I had some clothes stashed in the sleeping compartment on Level 37 of the Sea-Tac Urboplex, but I wasn't likely to see them again.

The other man raised an eyebrow. He looked at Sasha. "That'll drop your cash down to $4,000.00."

Four thousand dollars? The girl was amazing!

Sasha looked at me and nodded. "If Max says we need that stuff, then we need it."

I felt warm all over, like a puppy that had been patted on its head, and grinned like an idiot.

The rest went quickly. We changed into one set of new clothes, stowed our weapons in their holsters, loaded the spare magazines, and stashed them in the pouches provided for that purpose. My shirt, jacket, and pants were black, as were my shoes. We were just about to leave when Sasha pointed at my head. "That skull plate is visible from miles away. You should cover it with something."

She had a point. The Murphys had agreed to escort us as far as the surface, but that was the extent of their protection. We'd be on our own after that, with who knows how many poppers and rent-a-cops hot on our trail. So a ball cap, with the word "Captain" spelled out in gold letters, and scrambled eggs across the bill, served to complete my outfit. I didn't see the money, but Sasha assured me that it was secured around her waist in a money belt.

And so it was that we took leave of Floater Town, headed up towards the stars, and a future that neither one of us could be sure of.

6

"Why pay for frills when FENA flies for less?"

The tag line from FENA Air's
Urban Graffiti campaign

We were on Level 45 when Maureen handed us over to a runaway android named Rita and waved good-bye. I hated to part company with her, but understood why she couldn't accompany us. There was a rather large bounty on her head and plenty of poppers looking to collect it.

Rita, for reasons known only to her manufacturer, had been equipped with four arms. She used them to good effect, pulling herself up the access ladder with monkeylike agility and babbling all the way. ". . . And that's why they built the siphon, to provide the spaceport with water, which it needs for a multiplicity of purposes . . ."

I tuned her out, stopped for a moment, and looked down. I've never had trouble with heights, which is a good thing, because it was quite a drop to Level 50. Yeah, there were platforms at each level, but you could see through the steel mesh all the way to the bottom.

Sasha was fifteen or twenty rungs below me, moving with the quick, easy confidence of someone raised with the void all around, our knapsack bouncing on her back. I had offered to carry it, but she had refused.

"Hey!" Rita called. "I haven't got all day . . . let's get a move on down there."

I forced myself up again. We had managed a three-hour nap, but my body ached for a full night's sleep. The siphon consisted of a vertical pipe that was five or six feet across and painted the lime-green color that bureaucrats always choose. The structure vibrated next to my shoulder as vast quantities of sea water were pumped to the surface, desalinized, and purified. Or so they claimed, but, as anyone whoever drank the stuff can attest, it tastes like shit.

Beads of water condensed on the pipe's surface, coalesced into puddles, and streaked down towards the sea. I wondered if they had individual identities, and if so, whether I had swallowed them years before.

The climb went on and on, until my legs ached, and my back was sticky with sweat. I wanted to stop, wanted to rest, but Rita was tireless. Having explained the siphon, and the desalinization plant up above, she had transitioned into the story of her life.

". . . exactly why, but it might have been a faulty component, or some sort of power surge. But whatever the reason, I went bonkers, left the job, and never returned. Sure, the android hunters came looking for me, but I made my way to Floater Town and went to work for Murphy Enterprises . . ."

A low-grade utility bot was doing some routine maintenance work on Level 2, but we crowded past and continued the journey upwards. The top landing was more spacious than all the rest. I heaved myself onto it, gave a sigh of relief, and looked around. I saw a hoist, some over-sized valves, and a maze of pipes. Sasha appeared over the edge, pulled herself inwards, and stood panting on the platform. It did my heart good to see she was tired as well.

Rita gestured us into motion and led us towards a steel fire door.

She hadn't stopped talking. ". . . which is why I can't go with you. But there's no need . . . since you'll be inside Surface Port 12 and quite close to your gate. Well, here we are."

She turned. Unlike robots designed for frequent interaction with human beings, Rita had been given a frozen manikin-type face. It was locked in a perpetual smile. Her voice came from a speaker located on the front surface of her plastic throat. "It's been nice to spend some time with you. Some people say that I talk too much. I hope it didn't bother you."

I suppose it's stupid to worry about a machine's feelings, especially when everyone agrees that they don't have any, but I wanted Rita to know that we appreciated her help. I held out my hand. She took it. "No, Rita. It didn't bother us at all. Thanks for getting us here safely. Take care of yourself."

"I will, Mr. Maxon. Good-bye, Ms. Casad. Have a safe journey."

Sasha sent one of her "you are a hopeless idiot" looks in my direction and said, "Thanks."

Rita, her face wooden as always, nodded.

We opened the door and stepped outside. There was a loud click as it closed behind us. So much for that line of retreat.

A moon flight had landed, and passengers were streaming towards the baggage area. They were contract workers for the most part, miners with dilated eyes, technicians who ate too much, and pilots who had pushed one load too many. They walked like ancient helmet divers, forcing themselves forward under the weight of Earth-normal gravity, sweat beading their foreheads.

I nodded to Sasha and we stepped out into the flow. We, like the other passengers headed for Gate 426, struggled against the current like fish swimming upstream. Assuming there was a river in which fish still swam, that is. I stopped below a bank of monitors. "We're looking for FENA Air Flight 124."

"There it is," Sasha replied, pointing upwards. "Flight 124, Gate 426."

"Good."

I caught a flash of green from the corner of my eye, turned, and saw a man back into the crowd: the same man who had followed me to the checkpoint and tried to speak with me through the mesh. Who the hell was he, anyway? What did he want? And how had he found us with such ease? I took Sasha's elbow. "Come on. We've got company."

"Who? Where?"

"Over towards the right. The little guy. In the green sports coat."

"What about him?"

"He's a greenie, or I think he is. He was part of the crowd that chased pretty boy into the Trans-Solar checkpoint."

"A greenie in a green sports coat?"

The connection had escaped me. I pretended it hadn't.

"Yeah. Weird, huh?"

"It sure is. Let's shoot him and stash the body."

I frowned. "Getting a little bloodthirsty, aren't we?"

She shook her head impatiently. "I didn't say *kill* him, I said *shoot* him, as in trank him."

"Oh," I said stupidly. "That's different. Let's do it."

We looked, but the man was gone. Sasha frowned. "Assuming it *was* the same man, and assuming he's interested, how did he know when and where to look?"

I shrugged. "Beats me. I made the reservations under phony names."

Her eyes locked with mine. "I had the expense money. Until the corpies took it, that is. How did you pay?"

"I transferred some funds from my bank account."

"Smart," she said sarcastically. "Real god-damned smart. Phony names don't mean shit when you give them an account number. The greenies have sympathizers everywhere. One of them pulled a record of your transactions, gave the information to the guy in the green sports coat, and bingo, he was waiting for us to show."

Sasha didn't point out that Trans-Solar could have done the same thing and probably had. She didn't need to. Even I could figure that out. The shame was familiar by now. Like a relative you don't like but can't get rid of because they're part of you. But something good came of it as well, a rare moment of blue sky when my brain actually functioned.

"This is more than a standard snatch, isn't it? Why are the greenies after you, anyway? And what's the deal with Trans-Solar?"

Sasha's eyes clouded over and her head turned away. Her voice was flat and unconvincing. "You know as much about it as I do. My mother might be able to tell us, but we'll have to reach her first."

I tried to see through the words to the truth beyond, but the patch of blue sky had disappeared. My hands made fists at my sides. "Have it your way, Sasha, but remember, you're the one they're after. 0011100100111."

Her eyes came back to mine. They were softer now, like those of a mother with her child. "You did the best you could. What's done is done. We'll lose them on the habitat. Come on."

We made our way down the corridor. The line in front of Gate 426 was relatively short and consisted of down-and-outers like ourselves. There were some spacers, a tech type or two, and a couple of beat-up androids. One had a faulty servo and whined as it moved.

We shuffled forward and stopped in front of the counter. I identified myself as Roger Doud and proved it by providing the account number I never should have given them in the first place.

The ticket agent was an android whose torso ended at the countertop. He had the solemn manner of an undertaker and an electronic speech impediment. "Your ffflight is on time. Please ssstep through the detector and wait to be called. Thanks fffor flying FENA Air."

The detector looked like an over-sized free-standing door frame. Sasha stepped through and I followed. Buzzers buzzed, lights flashed, and a pair of lunchy-looking rent-a-cops lurched to attention. Neither was exactly athletic, but the woman was the more obese of the two. She used her nightstick as a pointer. "Stand over there. Spread your legs. Put your hands behind your head."

I didn't like her tone, but there was no point in making a scene. I obeyed. The man stepped up, blew garlic in my face, and passed a wand over my body. My first thought was the .38. But it was stashed in Floater Town, where Maureen had promised to clean it occasionally. And the Browning .9mm was not only legal, but made entirely of plastic, and therefore undetectable. No, the problem was my skull plate. The man stood on tiptoes to pass the wand over my head and grunted when it made a whining sound. "Take the hat off."

I did as I was told.

The man looked at my head and nodded. "Put it back on." He turned toward his partner. "No problem, Gert. This guy's got enough metal in his head to build a Class A shuttle. Let him pass."

The woman nodded, stared at my head as if it was the first one she'd ever seen, and allowed us to join the passengers in the holding area. It had been furnished with the same low, crouching furniture that graced the rest of the spaceport. The androids huddled together as if for mutual protection, and everyone else spread out. Sasha sighed. "So much for the disguise."

I said, "Sorry about that," but didn't really mean it. That's the great thing about being stupid. You worry less.

I took a look around and wondered how I felt the first time I headed into the Big Black. I'd been a good deal younger back then, nineteen according to the records, so it stood to reason that I'd been scared. Scared of zero-G boot camp, scared of the unknown, scared of dying. And I was still scared of dying, though I wasn't sure why, since living was a major pain in the ass. Sasha's voice brought me back. "Max?"

"Yeah?"

"They called our names."

"Oh. Sorry."

We followed the others through a door, down some stairs, and onto a loading dock. A man looked up from his portacomp as we approached. He was dressed in a dark blue jumpsuit with "FENA" stitched over the left breast pocket, a pair of ear protectors worn around the neck, a pair of black combat boots with pink laces. He gestured towards a cargo module and the autoloader that supported it. Both were snuggled up to the edge of the dock. "Your carriage awaits. I will call your names. Please enter your assigned tubes. Aarons, tube one. Axel, tube two. Benning, tube three. Cooper, tube four . . ."

Sasha shook her head in amazement. "I've spent a lot of time in space but never seen anything like this."

I felt defensive. "Sorry, but you had the expense money, and this is what $800.00 will buy."

Sasha smiled apologetically, stood on tiptoes, and kissed my cheek. "Don't worry, Max. Tube four is fine."

I touched the place where she had kissed me. Was it my imagination, or was that particular spot warmer than the surrounding skin? I wanted to say something, wanted to thank her, but she had lowered herself into a tube by the time I was ready. My alias was called shortly thereafter. I looked, but the man in the green sports coat was nowhere to be seen.

I trudged over to the cargo module, peered down into tube twenty-four, and inhaled the powerful odor of disinfectants. I kneeled, placed a hand on the cold concrete, and jumped. There was padding in the bottom and all around the sides. I bounced slightly and looked around. There was nothing much to see except for a tiny, almost miniscule vid screen, a headset with mic, and some waist-high tubing. I was still trying to understand what the tubing was for when a voice said, "Have a nice trip," and a lid slammed closed over my head. There was a moment of complete darkness followed by a yellow glow as the light came on over my head.

The vid screen came on about the same time that the cargo module jerked, swayed, and went horizontal. The screen swirled and coalesced into a picture of a pleasant-looking, middle-aged freelancer. I fumbled the headset onto my head in time to hear most of her spiel. ". . . join us aboard FENA Air. Now, settle back in padded comfort while your high-tech passenger module is loaded aboard one of our first-class ships, and lifted into orbit.

"The trip to *Staros-3* will take approximately two hours. If you wish to catheterize yourself, please do so now, as the safety restraint system will make movement difficult during the journey itself."

Now that I knew what the tube was for, I was determined not to use it. The woman continued to talk. ". . . medical emergency, then please notify the ship's crew via your headset, and they will make sure that medical personnel are waiting when we dock with *Staros-3*.

"So, settle back into the padded privacy of your personal transportation enclosure, and enjoy the trip."

Personal transportation enclosure? Who the hell did they think they were kidding? My enclosure was little more than a padded mailing tube, completely inaccessible during flight, and vulnerable to all sorts of potential dangers. Not to mention the fact that my accommodations would push the average claustrophobe over the edge in a matter of minutes.

The universe jerked as the autoloader came to a halt, then started into motion again as the cargo module was pushed up and into the shuttle's belly, where it was hooked to the ship's life support systems. Oxygen hissed in through a nozzle located next to my head, caressed my cheek with an ice-cold hand, and slid down my neck.

Maybe the oxygen stirred it up, or maybe it would have made itself known anyway, but the thick odor of sweat, vomit, and god knows what else oozed out of the tube's nooks and crannies, overwhelmed the disinfectants, and filled my nostrils with a sort of funky perfume. It made me gag.

The restraint system was activated without warning. The first thing I noticed was a snug feeling as the padding pushed in around me. Then it had me in a soft but insistent embrace that allowed for almost no movement at all. But the laws of physics prevailed, and I felt the additional half-gee as the shuttle accelerated down the runway and blasted off. Though unable to see outside, I had seen countless takeoffs on television, and knew how it was supposed to work. Or thought I did, anyway.

Unlike the space shuttles used back in the 1990's, the current equivalents used standard runways for takeoff. Once airborne they used air-turbo-ram-jets to reach Mach 25, or more than 17,000 mph. The trick was to compress the air through the use of turbines at lower speeds and use the force of the incoming supersonic air stream to compress the air at higher speeds. Or was it the other way around? In any case, rockets kicked in at Mach 16 or so, boosted the shuttle to Mach 25, and thus into orbit.

There were other factors too, such as the high-strength, temperature-tolerant materials that went into the hull, and the complicated technologies that cooled the aircraft's skin. Taken together, they made the trip into orbit as routine as a flight from Los Angeles to New York had been a hundred years before. Unless you were making the trip in a glorified mailing tube, that is . . . which I don't recommend to anyone. How do I remember this stuff? And forget less complicated junk? It's like I said before . . . Beats the heck out of me.

Unable to move, and with nothing to do but watch the unending commercials that FENA Air pumped onto the vid screen, it was easy to fall asleep—something I did rather quickly. When I awoke, it was to mild nausea induced by zero gravity and a gentle bump as the shuttle docked with *Staros-3*. The inevitable announcement followed. Video swirled and the woman reappeared. She seemed happy with the way things were going.

"Welcome to *Staros-3*. There will be a short wait while your module is unloaded and steered into one of the habitat's locks. Once the lock has been pressurized, and it's safe to leave your enclosure, the door will open and you may exit. On behalf of FENA Air, and your flight crew, it has been a pleasure having you aboard."

The woman disappeared and was replaced by live pictures of the docking process. It felt good to see what was actually going on. My stomach lurched as the module was freed from the shuttle's cargo bay and pushed towards the habitat's lock. The push was supplied by a one-person tug, no more than a sled with steering rockets, but sufficient for the job. The task was trickier than it looked, since the habitat had some spin on it, and the operator had to take that into account.

Once we were inside the lock, automatic cargo-grappling equipment grabbed hold of our module and clamped it in place. That's when the process came apart. There was a forty-minute delay while modules filled with more important materials—like food, water, and toilet paper—were nudged into the lock, followed by a thirty-minute pause as the technicians made repairs to a faulty hatch mechanism, and a fifteen-minute wait as the doors closed and the bay was pressurized.

So, by the time the restraint system had released us from its mushy grasp, and we were allowed to climb out of the tubes, everyone had to pee in the worst possible way. Everyone except for the androids, that is, and a woman who had either catheterized herself prior to takeoff, or discovered a way to pee while standing up without wetting her pants in the process.

Gravity was about half Earth-normal, which caused most of us to move with extreme care, the exceptions being the androids, who had been programed for this sort of thing, and experienced spacers like Sasha, who made it look easy.

And so it was that a small group of grim-faced passengers shuffled, pranced, and groped their way towards the habitat's center, encountered more gravity the further they went, and barged into a unisex rest room. There were a sufficient number of booths, but the fixtures were strange, and it took me five minutes to decipher the pictograph-style instructions and make mine do what it was supposed to. Sasha was waiting when I emerged. She seemed amused. "It's nice to have you back. I wondered if I'd see you again."

"Funny. Very funny. It's not my fault that you need an engineering degree to operate the toilet."

She looked quizzical. "What about all those years in space?"

I tapped the skull plate. The hat got in the way, but she understood. "Brain damage, remember? I can't recall anything prior to my discharge from the Mishimuto Marines. Well, most of the time, anyway, although I have flashes once in a while, and dreams that seem real."

Sasha shrugged. "Yeah, it seems funny, that's all. Well, let's get busy and find our cabins."

I felt my face go blank. "Cabins?"

Her expression said it all. But there was no comment this time, and no recriminations, as she'd had time to think the matter through and made a conscious decision to tolerate my lapses. I didn't know which was worse, being yelled at for being stupid, or escaping criticism for the same reason.

We headed for the habitat's Administrative Control Section, waited through a line, and asked a graffiti-covered android for separate cabins. None were available, so we agreed to share a double, dropped one thousand four hundred and fifty dollars of the money Sasha had collected from Murphy Enterprises, and retreated to the cafeteria. It boasted a 360-degree view, and, thanks to the fact that we were a full hour ahead of the next shift change, there were plenty of tables. They had padded edges, were welded to the floor, and came with four stools apiece.

So there we were, sitting at our table and gazing at what was left of Mother Earth, when the man in the green sports coat appeared. I should have been surprised, but wasn't somehow. He had carefully combed hair, narrow-set eyes, and heavily creased frown lines. A sack dangled from his right hand. The contents were round and about the size of a bowling ball. He gestured towards the table. "Mr. Doud . . . Ms. Cooper . . . may I join you?"

I looked at Sasha and she shrugged. "Sure, why not?"

" 'Why not,' indeed," the man said as he took his seat. "It's so much more pleasant when people talk rather than fight. Although," he said, placing the sack on the table, "violence *does* have its place. Isn't that so, Mr. Doud? Or should I say Mr. Maxon?" His eyes were pale, pale blue, like denim that's been washed too many times.

I shifted my weight from one side of the stool to the other. "I guess so."

The man shook his head in mock wonderment. "Tsk, tsk. You're far too modest." He turned to Sasha. "You should have seen him, my dear, charging through the Trans-Solar checkpoint like an avenging angel, shooting anyone who got in the way. But I did my part, yes I did, and saved his life."

I thought back to the fight and remembered the bodyguard with the bullet between her eyes. "You did that? You killed the bodyguard?"

The man nodded calmly. "Yes, I did, and you're quite welcome." He stuck a hand across the table, and I took it. "The name's Nigel Trask. Glad to meet you."

He shook hands with Sasha while I tried to figure things out. "But why? Why did you help me?"

Trask shrugged. "Anyone who attacks Trans-Solar is a friend till proven otherwise."

"Why? Did Trans-Solar do something to make you angry with them?"

Trask looked surprised, as if the answer was so obvious that only an idiot would miss it, which was probably true. "Trans-Solar, along with the other spacelines, oppresses humanity through the drug called technology."

Sasha entered the conversation sideways, sliding in between the two of us so smoothly that Trask didn't notice, and I wasn't offended. "So you're a greenie?" It was more statement than question.

Trask stiffened. "Labels are somewhat tedious, but yes, I favor a return to the agrarian past."

Sasha nodded. "So that explains your opposition to Trans-Solar. But where do *we* fit in?"

"An excellent question," Trask replied solemnly. "And one I was sent to get an answer to. Where *do* you fit in?"

Sasha spread her hands over the table. "Nowhere. Mr. Maxon and I are neutrals in the war between the corporations and you."

"There are *no* neutrals in our war. Trans-Solar snatched you for a reason. What was it?"

Sasha shrugged. "I have no idea why Trans-Solar had me snatched. Ransom, perhaps?"

"No," Trask replied, "I don't think so. Not the normal kind, anyway. Trans-Solar is too big, too important, to waste its resources on a two-bit snatch, so it's safe to assume they didn't. What about Murphy Enterprises? What's your connection with them?"

Sasha looked puzzled. "Murphy who? Never heard of them."

Trask allowed an eyebrow to drift towards his hairline. "Really? That's not what Rita says." He grabbed the top of the sack and gave a powerful jerk. The cloth came away and Rita's head rocked from side to side. A power saw had been used to remove it from her body. An auxiliary power pack had been hard-wired into her circuitry and was taped to her plastiflesh neck. Her eyes popped open and looked around. "Hello, Mr. Maxon. Ms. Casad."

A lump formed in the back of my throat. Poor Rita. She had fallen out of the frying pan and into the fire. "Hi, Rita."

Her face was wooden as always. "I'm sorry, but they forced me to tell them everything I knew."

Trask nodded agreeably. "The android is correct. She *did* tell us everything she knew. And a boring lot of garbage it was. Her kind are an abomination, an expression of The Board's contempt for humanity, and must be destroyed."

So saying, he produced a pair of insulated side cutters, selected one of the wires that ran from the power supply into Rita's throat, and cut it in two. Sparks crackled, the smell of burnt insulation filled the air, and Rita's eyes rolled back in her head. She was dead. I was angry, but Sasha seemed entirely unmoved. "That was unnecessary."

Trask returned the side cutters to a pocket. "Perhaps, but enjoyable nonetheless, and it *did* get your attention. Now, tell me about your connection with Murphy Enterprises."

Sasha shrugged. "We took one of Trans-Solar's boats, used it to escape from their thugs, and sold it to Murphy Enterprises. End of story."

Trask stared at her as if able to see through her skull and into her brain. "Alright, that compares favorably with what Rita told us, but there could be more. Things she didn't know. Things she didn't hear. So we'll wait and see what happens. But mark my words, if your mother's company is working to unleash some sort of new technological hell on the human race, then we'll learn of it, and do everything in our power to stop you."

Sasha looked him right in the eye. "I have no knowledge of what my mother's company might or might not be working on."

Trask nodded, but it was clear that he didn't believe her, and you know what? Neither did I.

7

"Management is not responsible for radiation-induced genetic mutations that may be experienced by guests, visitors, or crew of *Staros-3* during or after their time aboard."

Fine print found on the back of each
Staros-3 boarding pass

There were lots of things to do, like losing Trask, and getting off *Staros-3*, but we were tired and went to bed instead.

In spite of the exorbitant amount of money we had paid for the cabin, it was little more than a shoebox. The beds folded down from the bulkhead and occupied most of what little bit of deck-space there was. That put the mattresses side by side, but I don't mess with clients, especially when they're almost twenty years younger than I am. The sheets had seen better days, but most of the holes had been patched, and they were reasonably clean.

Sasha started to remove her clothes, frowned, and gestured for me to turn my back. Hookers, the only women with whom I had recent experience, didn't care if you looked or not. I turned my back and made a note to be more careful in the future.

I brushed my teeth in the tiny sink, took my turn in the fresher, and was careful to wear a towel when I emerged. There was no need, however, since Sasha had turned the lights down and was already asleep. I dried myself off, slipped into my spare underwear, and got into bed. It felt wonderful. I don't know if the ensuing dream stemmed from the cafeteria's heavy-duty spaghetti sauce, my return to space, or something entirely different, but it was a real lulu.

● ● ● ● ● ●

Sweat beaded the pilot's forehead. She was very young and wore little more than shorts, a tank top, and her lieutenant's bar. She had great nipples and I had watched them as she conned the boat through ten thousand miles of asteroid-strewn blackness. She bit her lower lip and whispered a mantra of her own making: "Holy mother full of grace, help me make it through this place, Holy mother full of grace . . ."

I grew tired of it after the first thousand times or so, but pilots are a weird bunch, and it's best to let their idiosyncrasies go. There were three ships in all. I had the point position, Lieutenant Daw was number two, and our CO Major Charles Wamba rode drag.

It was a bad mission, the kind recon always gets, full of floating variables, insurmountable obstacles, and ugly ways to die. But that's what the Mishimuto Corporation paid us to do, to kill as many of these nasty-assed tool heads as possible, and make it back if we could. But this was different, a little something thought up by the oxymorons in military intelligence, and intended to bag information instead of bodies.

My briefing had been provided by a man who turned into a woman with no face. She explained that Mishimuto owned stock in a small start-up company, that the employees of said company had gone over to the strikers, and might have taken proprietary information with them. And that's where we came in. Our team was supposed to sneak up on the miscreants, surprise them, and recover the missing data. The only problem was that they had taken refuge in a research station called T-12, right smack dab in the middle of the asteroid belt, and defended by a rather sophisticated automatic weapons system. Not a walk in the park.

My thoughts were interrupted when the pilot screamed, "Shit! Shit! Shit!" and pointed at the screen. Her eyes grew wide with horror and exploded as we hit the asteroid.

• • • • • • •

I sat up. My body was drenched with sweat, my heart was trying to beat its way out of my chest, and my breath came in short gasping sobs. I have at least one nightmare a night, so I'm fairly used to them. But this dream had a coherency the others lacked, as if memories were trying to put themselves back together and couldn't quite make it. It took an hour or more to fall asleep. It seemed as if a few minutes had passed when Sasha opened the fresher, used both hands to towel her hair, and kicked my bed. "Up and at 'em, Max. We need to get off this tub."

I yawned, pulled my clothes on, and followed her to the cafeteria. Breakfast cost a hundred and fifty-two dollars. Each. And it wasn't all that good. Nor was the company, since Trask sat about fifty feet away. Earth hung behind him like a backdrop, a not so subtle reminder of what he was all about, and an indictment of generations past. He was engaged in earnest conversation with a serious-looking black man, but took a moment to bow sardonically, to which Sasha lifted her coffee cup in reply. Her words belied the smile. "I don't trust that man. Let's find some work."

We had no other choice. Our bankroll was dwindling fast, and Sasha refused to ask her mother for help because to do so would reveal our location to anyone who monitored Earth-Jupiter radio traffic, and that was practically everybody. The fact that I'd have to earn my passage while simultaneously guarding Sasha from the forces of evil didn't exactly appeal to me, but it was either that or give up any hope of a fifty-thousand-dollar payday.

But *wanting* work and *getting* work were two different things. Almost every shipping line large and small had a cubicle-sized business office aboard *Staros-3,* and none of them were interested in us. What jobs there were went to specialized droids, experienced spacers, or people with the right connections. So we trudged from cubicle to cubicle, waited through what seemed like endless lines, and were refused by men, women, and androids alike.

Oh, we came close once, when the Regis Line offered Sasha a job as a hostess, but there was no slot for me. I actually *felt* the fifty thousand slip through my fingers, but Sasha shook her head and led me into the hall. Yes, it was strange that she didn't leave me behind, but I had no reason to question a decision that put money in my pocket, and wasn't smart enough to think it through.

I did notice one thing, though, and that was the fact that Sasha looked more and more discouraged, as if the weight of the whole world rested directly on her shoulders. With the exception of the kiss, she had never been exactly friendly, but there was an air of desperation about her that I'd never seen before. Not even when we were running from the snatchers and poppers. I tried to talk to her, tried to cheer her up, but it didn't seem to help. She seldom spoke and became increasingly depressed.

We were exhausted by mid-afternoon. We skipped lunch in an effort to conserve our funds, returned to the cabin, and settled in for a nap. I awoke four hours later to find Sasha gone and a note on her bed. "Max, gone for a walk, back soon, Sasha."

"Gone for a walk"? Was the girl out of her mind? Yes, of course she was, though the whys and wherefores were a mystery. And I had failed to think of that, just as I had failed to think of so many other things. Visions of Trask and the Trans-Solar goons danced in my head as I splashed water on my face, slipped my arms through the gun harness, and headed for the door. I paused for a moment, performed one of the small rituals that keep me alive, and stepped out into the corridor. Everything looked dark and ominous.

The bulkheads were thick with multi-layered graffiti. They closed in around me and pushed a thousand day-glo images through my eyes. The crowd swirled, became annoyed with my relatively slow pace, and pushed on by. Robo-hawkers, disabled spacers, whores, and itinerant lawyers begged for alms. The smells of sweat, incense, food, smoke, and ozone filled my nostrils and forced me to breathe through my mouth. It was, I decided, even worse than the Sea-Tac Urboplex, and the closest thing to hell I'd ever seen. I watched for Sasha, and did my best to think like a teenaged girl, going where she'd go, doing what she'd do, but it didn't seem to work. I checked the cafeteria, the retail shops, and the business section, but she was nowhere to be found.

Finally, in an act of what can only be described as desperation,

I did what I should have done early on, and stopped at one of the
habitat's public terminals. There, for the absurd fee of twenty
dollars, I was allowed to ask about Sasha's whereabouts. I even
remembered to use her alias. The answer came back almost
instantly. The voice was synthesized: "Mary Cooper is located in
cubicle fourteen of the *Staros-3* medical facility. Mary Cooper
is . . ."

I ducked out of the booth, shouldered a dweeb out of the way,
and followed the red-cross-shaped pictographs towards medical.
Had she been mugged? Raped? Shot? The possibilities were
endless, and all of them filled me with fear. Fear, and a sense of
shame, since I was her bodyguard and had failed to protect her.
Never mind the fact that she should have woken me, should have
told me where she was going, it was still my fault. I was a
grown-up, and she was a kid, and it was my responsibility to
prevent such things.

The shoe was on the other foot now, with the crowd moving
more slowly than I liked, which was too bad for them. I'm big,
strong, and perfectly capable of taking advantage of that when I
want to. Most people scattered, and those who didn't got shoved.
I kind of hoped that some asshole would take offense, would give
me an excuse to work off my anger, but no one did. Maybe it was
the chrome-plated skull, my size, or the nasty grin. Whatever it
was worked and allowed me to reach the medical center in record
time.

The receptionist had long orange hair. It had been teased up into
a point and allowed to droop like a halfhearted question mark. His
smirk told me what he thought about big men with chromed heads.

"Mary Cooper. Where is she?"

"She's in cube fourteen, and who may I say . . ."

The route was obvious and I took it. The cubicles were tiny affairs
screened with curtains. The numbers got larger. Twelve . . .
thirteen . . . fourteen. I whipped the curtain aside.

Everything was white including the paint, the bed, and the gown
Sasha wore. She stood with her back to me looking in a mirror.
The sudden commotion caused her to turn. One hand clutched the
front of her gown while the other started towards her gun. The
second hand topped, fluttered for a moment, and fell to her side.
A bandage covered her left eye. Gauze ran around her head. Tears

rolled down her cheeks. My heart jumped to my mouth. "Sasha . . . what happened? What did they do to you?"

Her mouth moved but nothing came out. It seemed natural to move in, put my arms around her, and let her sob into my chest. She felt small and very, very fragile. Finally, after what seemed like a long time, the sobs died away. She pushed me away and wiped a hand across her mouth. "Sorry about that . . . it was stupid . . . and very weak."

"Stupid? Weak? What the hell are you talking about?"

Her voice grew stronger as she turned and shook out her pants. "No big deal. I sold an eye, that's all."

The words rolled around the inside of my head like twenty-ton ball bearings. Images flashed through my mind. I imagined Sasha lying on an operating table as a doctor pried her eye out of its socket and dropped it into a basin. It made me queasy. "You did what?"

She was defensive. "We need money. I sold an eye. People sell organs all the time. It's no big deal."

I may be stupid, but even I tweak eventually. This was more than a schoolgirl on her way home, more than a skirmish in some corporate war, this was *big*. So big that teenaged girls were willing to sell their eyes to move from one place to another. I grabbed her shoulder and pulled her around. *"Why,* Sasha, *why*? Why would a girl sell an eye? And don't give me that bullshit about taking you home. Are you running drugs? What?"

Tears welled in her remaining eye, brimmed over, and trickled down her cheek. She shook her head. "No, I'm on a mission for my mother. An important mission. That's all I can tell you."

I heard my voice get louder. "For your *mother*? What kind of mother would want her daughter to sell an eye?"

Sasha stood tall. She wiped the tears away. Her face grew hard and defiant. I saw hatred in the eye that remained. As if I were responsible somehow. "Who the hell are *you* to judge? My mother does what she *has* to do. And so do I. So shut the hell up and step aside. I'm getting dressed."

We walked through the corridors in silence, she with her thoughts, I with mine. What she'd done was monstrous. What sort of parent, what sort of mission, could justify a thing like that? There was no way to tell, but one thing was for sure. Anyone who was willing to sacrifice herself to that extent would do the same with me. I would have to be very, very careful. Our cabin was just ahead. We slowed down.

Habits are interesting things. They can hurt you or help you, and I need all the help I can get. That's why I make a fetish out of small things, like checking the load on my handgun every morning, and plastering a tiny piece of transparent tape across my door when I leave. These things were a struggle at first, but they're second nature now, and I do them without conscious thought. Except when something unusual happens, that is. "Don't touch the door. Someone's been in our cabin."

Sasha frowned. "How do you know?"

"I left a piece of tape across the door. It's broken."

"So what do we do?"

I thought about it for a moment. The wheels turned slowly but turned just the same. "You hungry?"

People came and went in both directions. Sasha watched them. "Yeah, but what does that have to do with the door?"

"Let's order some room service."

I placed the call from a com booth down the hall. It took fifteen minutes for the autocart to arrive, use its electronic pass key, and roll inside. I waited for a bomb to go off, for assassins to peer outside, for a thief to run down the corridor. Nothing.

Minutes passed, the autocart emerged, and the door closed. We waited for the robot to trundle away, keyed the proper code, and stepped inside. Our dinner sat steaming on a carefully set fold-down table. The rest of the place was a mess. What few belongings we had were scattered about like toys in a child's room.

I stated the obvious. "It's been searched."

"Yeah," Sasha agreed. "But by whom?"

I shrugged. "Trask is a distinct possibility, but why wait till now? My money's on Trans-Solar. It took some time . . . but they caught up with us."

Sasha didn't agree, but she didn't disagree either, which was almost the same. We balanced trays on our knees. Sasha took some pills as an appetizer. I envisioned her big brown eye, a strand of nerve still attached, rolling around the bottom of a kidney-shaped basin. Or worse yet, being installed in a lifer's head. My appetite vanished and I felt an almost overwhelming need to cry. But bodyguards don't cry, not in front of clients anyway, so I poked at the food and pretended to eat it. Not so Sasha, who had the appetite of a stevedore, and cleaned her plate with a piece of bread.

It was a simple matter to throw our dirty clothes into the knapsack, slip out the door, and meld with the crowd. The room charges would continue to mount, but that was better than checking out, which would signal our departure. Sasha set a brisk pace. I struggled to stay abreast of her and watch for tails at the same time.

"Dorlop impog asup 95601."

"What did you say?"

"I asked where we're headed."

"A ship called the *Red Trader* leaves in two hours. She's headed for Mars, which is not the most efficient way to get where we want to go, but some progress is better than none."

"She's a passenger ship?"

Sasha laughed then stopped as if something hurt. "I wish. No, she's little more than a clapped-out freighter, and we're members of the so-called crew."

I frowned. "Then why sell your eye?"

Sasha spoke patiently as if to a child. "Because the jobs *cost* five thousand dollars apiece."

There was nothing to say so I didn't.

Staros-3 was shaped like the letter H, with living accommodations clustered around the center bar, and docking facilities, solar arrays, and other facilities located along the four extremities. They were variously identified as Leg One, Two, Three, and Four. The *Red Trader* was docked on Leg Three so we headed in that direction. I checked our tail for any sign of Trans-Solar's goons, or Nigel Trask's greenies, and damned near missed the black man. The same man I'd seen with Trask. He caught my eye and waved. Sasha made a grab for my arm, but it was too late. I waved back.

He was there within seconds, his eyes darting from one to the other, summing us up. He had intelligent eyes, a rather aquiline nose, and thin, expressive lips. His suit was white, or had been once, before the accumulated grime stained it gray. We stepped into an alcove to escape the traffic. "Mr. Maxon . . . Ms.

Casad . . . this will only take a moment. I know you're in a hurry. Mr. Maxon . . . may we speak privately?"

I looked at Sasha. She didn't like the situation one bit. "Speak your piece . . . but I'm staying here."

The man bowed in acknowledgment. "As you wish." He turned, blocking Sasha with his body. "My name is Philip Bey. I have a message for you. Mr. Trask wants you to know that our associates have performed some research, and the Mishimuto Corporation discharged two marines who suffered brain damage identical to yours. They experienced the same reduction in cognitive function, the same loss of memory, and had skull plates similar to your own."

"They did?" I asked stupidly. "Where are they? What happened to them?"

Bey looked me in the eye. He was so direct, so sincere, that I felt sure he was telling the truth. "The first committed suicide within months of discharge. The second has been in and out of mental institutions ever since her release from the Marine Corps. A man who claimed to be a relative took her on a day-trip. She hasn't been seen since."

Thoughts plodded their way through my mind. They were like elephants linked trunk to tail. Slow, ponderous things that barely moved. I looked to Sasha for guidance. She refused to meet my gaze. I turned to Bey. "What does this mean? What are you saying?"

Bey shrugged. "Mr. Trask believes that you are in danger. He's aware of your upcoming journey and suggests that you remain here with us. We will pay your expenses plus five thousand dollars."

I frowned, moving the thoughts by force to will, determined to make my own decision. Five thousand dollars would have been a fortune only days before, but I had my sights set on *fifty thousand,* and there was Sasha to consider. A contract is a contract, and I had agreed to escort her home. Besides, the greenies were as bad as the corpies, so why stay with them? I shook my head. "I'm sorry about those other guys, but there's no reason to think they're connected to me, and I'm under contract."

I looked at Sasha, and where I had expected to see approval, I saw something like sorrow instead. It seemed I couldn't do anything right.

Mr. Bey bowed slightly. "As you wish. I shall inform Mr. Trask."

The old Sasha seemed to reassert herself. "Do that . . . we have a ship to catch."

Bey looked at Sasha's bandages. "Yes. I hope the accommodations are worth the price. The god called 'technology' demands many sacrifices. Your eye was little more than a down payment."

Sasha turned white and headed up-corridor. I followed. So much for getting off *Staros-3* unobserved. The greenies might be strange but they didn't miss much. I hurried to catch up. The *Red Trader* was connected to Lock 3-C. We stopped outside the lock, called the ship via vid screen, and identified ourselves to a woman so fat I could barely see her eyes. If she had virtues, charm wasn't one of them. "Well, it's about damned time. You got the money?"

Sasha held a certified check in front of the scanner. The woman nodded. "Good. Get your asses aboard. We got a schedule to keep."

The screen snapped to black. The lock yawned and swallowed us whole. The hatch made a hissing sound as it closed. The umbilical that connected the *Red Trader* with *Staros-3* was already pressurized. The second hatch opened quickly. The umbilical was pleated to accommodate slight movements of the ship or the habitat it was moored to.

Six or seven steps were sufficient to carry us into a rather spacious lock. Sections of paint had been worn away, leaving islands of magenta. A rubber mat gave slightly beneath my feet and air jets cooled my face. I was still inspecting the space suits racked to either side of the compartment when the inner hatch irised open and a man entered. A funny smell followed him in, like when you visit another person's apartment, or skirt the edge of an enthnoplex.

He had thinning black hair, feral eyes, and a hatchet-shaped nose. He wore a filthy tank top, baggy shorts, and bright orange high-tops. His eyes went from my skull plate to Sasha and stuck like glue. "And what have we here? Some nice-lookin' poontang, that's what. Hi, honey, my name's Lester, what's yours?"

Sasha gave him a look that would have killed most men. "Screw you."

Lester licked his lips and rubbed his crotch. "What a coincidence. That's exactly what I had in mind."

I stepped forward, gathered some of the tank top in my right hand, and lifted Lester clear of the deck. His feet kicked and his fists beat against my arms. "Put me down!"

"Apologize to the lady."

"All right! I apologize. Now put me down."

I put him down. He pulled his tank top straight and looked daggers in my direction. "Come on. The captain wants to see you."

We followed Lester out of the lock, down a passageway wide enough to accommodate standard cargo modules, and right through an access corridor. The ship was surprisingly roomy. And why not? It had been constructed in space, where shape made no difference and size was limited by little more than the cost of materials and the energy it would take to push them around. So, given a desire to move large quantities of cargo all at once, and the need to retain a competent crew, the corporations were inclined to build large rather than small. It was one of those thoughts that offered themselves when it made little difference and were impossible to find when I really needed them.

Lester took a left and led us past a number of cabins to a brass plaque that read "Captain." It had been polished to a high gloss, and the hatch to which it was affixed stood slightly ajar. Lester rapped three times. His knuckles made very little sound, but a voice yelled "In!" nevertheless.

Lester turned in our direction. I could see that he wanted to say something, to take a parting shot, so I raised an eyebrow. "Yes?"

He scowled, did an about-face, and marched down the corridor.

The voice was annoyed. "I said 'In,' damn it!"

We entered. The combination office-cabin, for that's what it seemed to be, was spacious. The decor could only be described as eclectic, since it incorporated everything from ultra-modern fiber chairs to an overstuffed sofa with a paisley print. The common element was food—cartons, plates, and remnants of which were scattered everywhere.

The captain was even more monstrous than she had appeared on video and was supported by a specially modified forklift. Yards and yards of shiny black cloth had been used to make pajamas for her over-sized body, and the slightest movement sent light rippling in every direction. She had piggy eyes, and they were filled with malevolence. "What you staring at, chrome-dome? You ain't so pretty yourself. Give me the money."

Sasha handed her the check. A small, well-kept hand reached out to accept it. Light flashed off a multiplicity of rings. The captain held it up to the light, saw that the electro-threads were intact, and gave a grunt of satisfaction. She poked it down into the crevasse between her massive breasts and gave us the look most people reserve for dog turds.

"Good. Consider yourselves duly sworn in and all that other crap. Now here's the deal. I run a tight ship, I don't take shit from know-nothing ground-pounders, and I expect a full shift's work. Clear?"

We nodded.

"Good." She looked at Sasha. "So, sweet stuff. What happened to your eye?"

Sasha met her gaze without flinching. "I sold it."

The captain nodded, as if selling an eye was the most natural thing in the world, and nothing to be concerned about. "Right. Find an idiot named Kreshenko. Tell him you're the help he's been asking for, and keep an eye on Lester, he'd screw a droid if he found one equipped with a hole."

The forklift whirred and carried her to a combination desk and console. She searched through the junk, found a disk, and flipped it in my direction. I caught it and she nodded approvingly. "You're in charge of the farm. Your predecessor drank himself to death. Don't make the same mistake. Read the disk, memorize the contents, and don't mess up."

I nodded stupidly, hoped I could comply, and knew I couldn't.

The captain reached for a bag of Oreo cookies, spilled some into the palm of her hand, and shoved one into her mouth. The words were muffled. "Good. You can have cabins G and H. Now get to work."

We were halfway out the door when she stopped us. Crumbs dribbled down her chin. "One more thing . . . the dart guns are legal . . . but keep 'em holstered."

We shrugged, nodded, and hit the hall. It seemed as if secrets were damned hard to keep. The ship broke free of *Staros-3* about an hour later, accelerated away, and started the long, slow journey to Mars.

8

"Although technically competent, Lester Hollings demonstrates certain behaviors consistent with a psychopathic personality. I recommend close supervision by qualified mental health professionals."

A notation from Lester Hollings's personnel file that had been scrubbed from memory but was later found on a backup matrix

I spent the first forty or fifty hours sleeping, exploring the ship's cavernous interior, and becoming acquainted with the rest of the crew. And a jolly bunch they were too.

In addition to the porcine captain and the hormonal Lester, the *Red Trader* boasted an over-the-hill pilot, a cook nicknamed Killer, and a detail-obsessed load master named Kreshenko. There were fifteen or twenty androids too, some of whom had names, and some of whom relied on numbers for identification. The most notable of these was known as "the phantom," after the character in "Phantom of the Opera," and was said to be in desperate need of a full-scale electronic tune-up. I decided to keep an eye peeled for him.

All of which was interesting but didn't help me learn my job. A job that was connected with the hydroponics section, or "farm." It seemed that production had fallen off, and, given the captain's preoccupation with food, I was in deep trouble. Especially since the captain kept the pressure on Killer and he kept the pressure on me.

Finally, after another close encounter with a cleaver-waving cook, I retired to my cabin and sat in front of my computer screen. The cursor winked at me like an electronic pervert, well aware of my weakness, and happy to exploit it. The problem stemmed from the fact that a penny-pinching corpie had equipped the *Red Trader* with manual PC's, denying me the voice recognition systems that I had learned to rely on, and plunging me into despair.

I inserted the disk, hit the key that made things go, and watched characters flood the screen. I stared at them, forced the images into my mind, and waited for knowledge to flood my brain. It didn't. The characters remained as meaningless as ever, cutting me off from the information that I needed, and filling me with rage.

My fist came down so hard that the keyboard jumped. It wasn't fair, damn it! I *must* have been able to read, *must* have been able to understand those squiggles, or the Mishimuto Corporation would never have recruited me. Hell, I'd been an officer, for god's sake, and surely *they* knew how to read.

But the chunk of metal that had taken my memories had taken my capacity to read as well, leaving me unable to do anything more complicated than killing people.

The rage died away and tears of self-pity trickled down my cheeks. I thought of the others, the ones Bey had mentioned, and wondered if they felt as I did. Was that why one of them had committed suicide? Why the other had been confined to a mental institution? And what about the skull plates? Were they a coincidence? Similar injuries treated in a similar way? Or something more?

The questions crowded around me and made my head hurt. I pushed them away and turned my attention to the problem at hand. I didn't understand the characters, so I'd get some help from someone who did. There were a variety of techniques available, and one of them would work. True, this situation called for a more complicated scam than usual, but there was no reason to believe I couldn't come up with one.

I withdrew the disk, glanced at the time, and stood up. The cabin was small compared with those assigned to the regular crew, but comfortable nonetheless. I had a bunk with overhead entertainment console, a locker ten times larger than my wardrobe, and a desk-computer combo. The only trace of the previous occupant was the half-empty bottle of hooch stashed under the mattress and a black sock in one of the drawers.

I stepped into the corridor and knocked on Sasha's door. There was plenty of time, since her shift didn't start for another hour so. Her voice was muffled by the steel hatch. "Yes?"

"It's Max."

"Are you alone?"

I looked around. Lester was nowhere in sight. The corridor was empty. "Yup."

The hatch slid open. The bandage had been replaced with a black eyepatch that gave Sasha a piratical air. And that, plus the bra and panties, was reminiscent of the more exotic strip shows I'd seen. It was nice to be trusted yet somewhat disturbing at the same time. I felt like Uncle Max, eccentric, but essentially harmless. Sasha had no idea that she'd offended my delicate male ego and motioned me inside. I slipped into scam mode.

"Hi, how's it going?"

"Lester's a pain in the ass, but otherwise fine. How 'bout you?"

"Oh, nothing much," I said casually. "The captain's on my case . . . but what else is new?"

Sasha nodded understandingly. "Yeah, I know what you mean. I'm so tired of working on Kreshenko's inventories I could puke. I'll bet the guy dreams about decimal points. What's your job like, anyway?"

I shrugged. "That's the problem. I haven't started yet . . . and the captain's pissed. Not to mention Killer."

Sasha stepped into her pants and pulled them up around her waist. I tried to ignore the fact that she had nice legs and failed. She looked surprised. "You haven't started? Why not?"

I produced the disk. Light glinted from its surface. "1001100101111000011110. This stuff is complicated. I wouldn't want to screw up."

Sasha nodded understandingly, as if my tendency to screw up was an ongoing problem, which it definitely was. "You want some drill? No problem. Let's take a look."

I felt the thrill of victory as she slipped the disk into her console and hit the appropriate key. "Where shall we start?"

"From the top," I answered quickly. "And read it aloud. I learn better that way."

Sasha nodded and started to read. "The Nutralife 4000 food maintenance and production system is intended for use on Class IV ships carrying no more than twenty crew and passengers. It is essential that this system be provided with sufficient oxygen, water, and nutrients. Failure to provide these materials in sufficient quantities will reduce the system's capabilities to provide dependents with a balanced diet and nullify the Nutralife 4000's warranty."

Then she paused, frowned for a moment, and pointed at the screen. "What's that word?"

I shook my head slowly. "Beats the heck out of me."

Sasha raised an eyebrow. "Really? You don't know the word 'and'?"

Blood rushed to my face. I tried a bluff. "Of course I know it . . ."

She held up her hand and looked as concerned as a person with a black eyepatch can. "Admit it, Max . . . you don't know how to read. It goes with the brain damage."

The way she said it was sort of sad, as if accepting the truth of something she'd suspected all along, and managed to ignore. "People think you're stupid when you can't read."

I felt her fingers on my hand and looked up into her face. It was the nice Sasha, the same one who had kissed my cheek, and was occasionally sympathetic. "You're far from stupid, Max. Disadvantaged, yes, and strange at times, but far from stupid."

The compliment was rather heavily qualified but I decided to accept it anyway. Doing so made me feel warm, loved, and damned near human.

Sasha looked at her watch. "I have about forty-five minutes. Let's get to work."

She read, and I listened, and the information began to accumulate. Other sessions followed, and two cycles later, on the eve of the very shift when Killer had promised to eject me from the main lock, I was ready to go. Or semi-ready, since there were vast tracts of highly technical information that had gone in one ear and out the other.

But Sasha had instructed me to take heart from the fact that no less than three of the ship's androids were assigned to the farm and would handle the real as well as the intellectual heavy lifting. No, my role was to supervise and provide something the instruction disk called "psycho-reinforcement," but sounded a lot like petting. So, armed with my newfound knowledge and the very best of intentions, I headed for the farm. It was located about two-thirds of the way down the length of the ship's hull and consisted of two sections.

The first was reminiscent of the way a revolver works. Nine cylinders rotated around a central axis, but rather than bullets, each chamber contained a thirty-foot-long hydroponics tank. Rather than using soil, which was heavy and therefore expensive, the tanks contained trays full of water mixed with nutrients. Each tank was shielded against radiation, received sunlight via external solar collectors, and had its own internal irrigation system.

Rotating as they did around a central axis, the tanks paused in each of the nine possible positions for two hours at a time. Retractable decking slid into place and allowed my robotic assistants to open the chamber and take care of the more mundane chores like seeding, trimming, and harvesting. And what a harvest it was!

I arrived on the maintenance deck just in time to see the androids remove the last of some basketball-sized tomatoes. One of the robots, a rather functional-looking unit with four legs and three arms, spotted me and minced over. Multi-colored paint drippings covered him from sensors to foot pads. They were the residue of a maintenance assignment, and the source of the nickname: Picasso. Like most higher-order androids, Picasso had the ability to supplement his original programming through on-the-job experience, and his speech reflected that fact. "Hey, dude . . . what's happening?"

"I've been assigned to run the farm."

"All right! 'Bout time the captain sent a bio bod down here. The veggies are fine but the aniforms are antsy as hell. We shoot the breeze with 'em, and shovel their shit, but it ain't the same. Come on . . . I'll take you into section two."

I followed the robot past the still-open module. Though smaller than Picasso, and built more like spiders, the other androids stood waist-high and were equipped with all sorts of highly specialized sensors, cutters, and grabbers. Picasso handled the introductions. "The one with the stickers all over his torso is known as Decal, and the other one prefers the official designator of Agrobot Model XII."

Decal was the more friendly of the two and trundled right up. "Could I have the privilege of knowing your name, sir?"

"You can call me Max."

"Thank you, Mr. Max. Your predecessor programmed me to generate large quantities of alcohol. A surplus has accumulated since his death. Should I make more, or wait for you to consume existing supplies first?"

I couldn't help but smile. "I won't need as much as my predecessor did. Save what you have but don't make any more."

To the extent that a machine can look relieved, this one did, and rolled away. Picasso explained as we walked towards section two. "You made his day. Operating the still ran counter to his main mission and made him less efficient than specs called for. The result was an internal dissonance that had to be resolved. Yeah, nothing bothers a droid more than countervailing objectives, and we get 'em all the time. No offense intended."

"And none taken," I assured him. "Humans provide each other with countervailing objectives every day."

Picasso turned a paint-splotched sensor in my direction. "Really? How strange. Well, it's like I tell the others: 'They were smart enough to invent us, so they must know what they're doing.'"

I wasn't so sure, but it didn't seem appropriate to say so. The hatch slid open and we entered section two. The rich, almost sweet smell of animal feces filled the air. I decided to breathe through my mouth. Even though I knew what to expect, the reality of it surprised me. The aniforms saw us and started to moo, bleat, grunt, and cackle. Cubicles lined both sides of the corridor, and each one contained one or more biologically engineered life forms. The cows came first.

Like their distant ancestors many times removed, the cows had heads with ears, eyes, and mouths, but that's where the resemblance ended. Necks that had been long were shorter now and connected to rectangular bodies that rested within identical stainless-steel boxes. Legs had been deemed unnecessary and eliminated, along with tails and carefully selected bones. They all looked alike, which wasn't surprising, since they were clones. The aniforms had been designed for one thing and one thing only: meat. The mooing had grown to almost frantic intensity as nineteen pairs of big brown eyes stared into my face and begged me to make contact. It seemed as though something unexpected had occurred during the long process that created them.

Not only had each successive generation of cows become a little bit smarter, they had become more emotionally dependent as well, until ongoing social interaction had evolved from something they tolerated to something they couldn't do without. And the same was true of the sheep, pigs, and chickens.

And that was my function, to visit them on a regular basis, and keep them happy. Failure to do so resulted in steady weight loss and tougher meat. Which explained why the captain and the cook were so concerned. "Go ahead," Picasso shouted over the din, "pet them."

Having never touched a farm animal before, I was scared. I reached out to the nearest cow and its head met my hand. The aniform's hair felt short and wiry. I ran my hand up towards the top of its head and saw its eyes close in ecstasy. A shiver ran through its black-and-white-spotted body and reminded me of the moment when Sasha had kissed my cheek.

Was the cow feeling the same warmth I had? If so, I could understand the importance of the contact. But there was no way to tell, and I continued to stroke the cow's head. The thought of killing, much less eating, the aniform made me sick.

Droids aren't supposed to feel emotions, but I would have sworn that Picasso sounded wistful. "An android can pet them all day long without the slightest sign of pleasure. A human comes along and they go crazy. Why?"

I gave the first cow a final pat and moved to the next one. "Beats me. Some kind of evolutionary linkage or something?"

"Maybe," Picasso said doubtfully, "but it still seems strange."

Time passed, and Picasso turned his attention to shoveling shit. I was halfway through the cows and well on my way to the sheep when the captain called. Her voice came from a speaker mounted over my head. There was a vid cam as well but duct tape covered the lens. "Hey, Maxon, you there?"

"Yes, ma'am."

"Well, I'll be damned. He's actually doing some work for a change."

"Yes, ma'am."

"Well, get your ass to the bridge. We got trouble."

There was a cacophony of disappointed moos, baas, grunts, and cackles as I turned towards the hatch and made my way forward. "What kind of trouble?"

"Bad trouble. It seems that Lester made a move on your skinny-assed friend and she put a dart through what was left of his brain."

"He deserved it."

The captain's voice followed me through the hatch. "Probably . . . but that's beside the point. Lester was our engineer and we needed him."

"Give me a break. This ship has backups for its backups. I assume Lester was no exception."

There was a long silence followed by the sound of the captain clearing her throat. "Well, Lester *was* supposed to have a fully qualified assistant, but I couldn't find anyone to fill the position."

I remembered the long lines outside every business office on *Staros-3* and knew the captain was lying. The miserable bitch was using a phony identity to line her own pockets. I knew better than to say anything, however. "How unfortunate."

"Exactly," the captain agreed. "Now get your butt up here."

I entered the "holy of holies" four minutes later. It was roomy and almost entirely automated. Banks of seldom-used manual controls glowed softly, air whispered through duct work, and the star field hung almost motionless on a curvilinear screen. The entire crew had gathered around the captain's thronelike command chair. There was Wilson, the round-shouldered, gaunt-faced pilot; Killer, his whites stained with what looked like blood; Kreshenko, his carefully shaved face devoid of all expression, and the captain, who looked as she always did: fat.

I saw Sasha and hurried over. She had an angry-looking bump on her left temple and her clothes were ripped. The question sounded lame even as I asked it. "Are you alright?"

She gave me one of those "how could anyone be so stupid?" looks and shook her head. "Never felt better."

But the size of her remaining pupil, the tightness around her mouth, and the quick, shallow breathing told a different story. It felt awkward to put an arm around her shoulders, but I did it anyway, and felt pleased when she made no attempt to escape.

The captain raised an imperious hand. Light glinted from her rings. "Now that chrome-dome has been kind enough to join us, we can begin."

She pulled a pocket comp from her pajamas and read aloud. "Consistent with Comreg 6789.2 paragraph three, it is the captain's duty to hold a formal inquest upon the death of a crew member, and take whatever steps he or she may deem necessary up to and including summary execution. Reports of the captain's findings, plus physical evidence if any, shall be filed at the next port of call."

The captain closed the pocket comp and put it away. A pair of piggy little eyes swung towards Sasha. "So, sweet buns, what happened? And remember, the bridge recorders are running, so this is for keeps."

I felt Sasha shrug and allowed my arm to fall away. "Lester made sexual advances towards me from the moment I came aboard. I rejected them over and over again. So many times that I feared for my safety and carried a weapon."

"Which I told you not to use," the captain said sternly.

"True," Sasha admitted calmly, "remembering that *you* warned me about Lester, and did so in front of a witness."

The captain had forgotten about that, and she scowled accordingly. "Go on."

Sasha nodded slowly. "I got up at the time I usually do, took a shower, dressed, and stepped out into the passageway. I was halfway to the galley when Lester stepped out of a hatch and punched me in the side of the head. I fell. He slapped my face, threatened to kill me, and ripped at my clothes. I reached for my gun . . ."

"Where was it?"

"In a shoulder holster under my left arm."

"So he couldn't see it?"

"Correct."

"Go on."

"I reached for my gun, pulled it out, and shot him in the face."

"And?"

"And he fell over dead."

The captain nodded grimly. She looked around the compartment. "Questions?"

Silence.

"All right, given the fact that Sasha Casad's testimony is consistent with the physical evidence, and is partially confirmed by a security camera located in the vicinity of the attack, I find that Lester Hollings's death was a justifiable homicide, committed in self-defense. Inquest closed."

The captain nodded to Wilson, and he touched a button. She smiled and looked around the bridge. "Okay, everybody, the recorders are off."

Sasha and I turned to go but stopped when the captain said, "Not so fast, chrome-dome. We still have a problem, and you're going to help."

"She means the phantom," Killer said helpfully as he examined a set of absolutely filthy fingernails. "We've got to find him."

I looked at the captain. "Why?"

She scowled. "Because the phantom was programmed to assist the engineering officers, that's why. Barring a major drive failure, or something equally catastrophic, the phantom has enough shit to see us through."

I nodded slowly. "Oh."

Sasha was more inquiring. "Why search for him? Get on the horn and order him to come."

The captain rubbed her chins. They jiggled. "It ain't that simple, honey buns . . . the phantom doesn't like humans."

Kreshenko spoke for the first time. "We believe that Lester abused the Engineering Support Android in a manner that caused it to run away."

Sasha frowned. "Abused . . . how?"

The rest of the crew looked at each other. They were visibly uncomfortable. It was Wilson who answered. He had a deep, rumbling voice. "Lester tried to modify the ESA's body so that it could function as a sex surrogate. That's the theory, anyway, but none of us have gotten close enough to confirm it."

There were sexroids of course, lots of them, but they had programing appropriate to the job. The ESA didn't, and Lester's attempts to graft that function over the others had driven it insane. Which raised some interesting questions: Assuming we were able to capture the phantom, would it be able to perform the job it had been designed to do? And why had the whole thing been left so long?

I think everyone had similar thoughts, but no one wanted to say anything. To do so would be to question the way the captain did or didn't do her job and risk one's livelihood. A real no-no when there are twenty people waiting to fill your slot.

The search began in the bow. All of the *Trader*'s crew plus most of the ship's ambulatory robots had been recruited for the task. The plan was simple: Start in the bow, sweep towards the stern, and drive the phantom before us. Once it was concerned, it would be a relatively simple matter to repair the damage that Lester had done and put the android right. Or so we hoped.

I looked around. Kreshenko had armed himself with a section of cargo netting. The captain had a sandwich in one hand and a stun gun in the other. Killer had fashioned a lasso from a length of utility line and twirled it over his head. Wilson untangled his homemade bolo and Sasha looked bored. "All right," the captain said through her food, "go get him. And remember, if you hurt the little bastard, we're screwed."

Not the most inspiring speech I'd ever heard, but direct and to the point. We spread out and headed down-ship. Hand-held radios helped coordinate our movements. Each corridor, passageway, compartment, and cubicle was searched. We found all sorts of things including rats, a parrot's mummified body, a cargo module with "urgent" marked all over it and a five-year-old delivery date, the still my predecessor had maintained, plus an entire storage room packed with supplies that Kreshenko didn't have listed on his inventories and the captain ordered him to ignore. But no android.

Various members of the search party did catch glimpses of the phantom, however, always a step ahead of us, fleeing towards the stern. But large as she was, the *Red Trader* was only so big, and the outcome was inevitable. We found him huddled in a locker full of pneumatic cargo jacks, trying to blend in with the equipment around him. The things that Lester had done to his body were disgusting enough, but the artificial intelligence that stood in for his brain had been scrambled, and required three shifts of electronic therapy. The result was somewhat twitchy but functional enough to meet our needs—barring what the captain called "major catastrophes," which I was too stupid to imagine.

And so it was that I went back to petting the aniforms, finished my shift, and hit the rack. The dream grabbed my mind and pulled it down.

•　　•　　•　　•　　•　　•

"Holy mother full of grace, help me make it through this place . . ." The pilot's personal mantra was little more than a whisper now, as if the strikers might hear it, and punish us with a missile. And I couldn't really blame her, since they were damned close and had some first-class detection equipment. And why not? They had stolen it from the same place Mishimuto did. I patted her shoulder. It was slick with sweat. "You're doing good, Loot. Just a few more klicks and it'll be over."

She nodded stiffly and kept her eyes straight ahead as she slid the ship around the side of a slowly tumbling asteroid. The trick was to keep it between us and the research station for as long as possible. After all, you can't shoot what you can't see, and even the best detectors can't see through solid rock.

That was the theory, anyway, although the strikers might have surrounded themselves with a whole network of remote sensor stations that were busy screaming their heads off.

I imagined missiles leaving their racks, zigzagging away from the installations that fired them, and accelerating in our direction. The Loot might have time to detect them, might have time to say the words uttered by so many pilots before her, but would die a millisecond later along with me and the entire team.

The Loot rescued me from my own imagination. "We're twenty from the drop."

I hit my harness release. "Gotcha. I'll be with the team. Thanks for the lift."

It was macho stuff, the kind we practice in the corps, and she wasn't playing. "Your team will have sixty seconds to deploy."

I nodded, snuck one last look at her nipples, and floated free. I pulled myself down the corridor, cycled the hatch, and propelled myself into the cargo bay. The gunny yelled "Ten-hut" and the troops did their best to obey. But it's hard to look military inside a Class III battle suit, especially with all sorts of extra gear strapped to your body, and no gravity to hold things in place.

I said, "As you were," and accepted the gunny's help in donning my battle suit. It was similar to the trooper model, except for the lighter weaponry, heavier armor, and a sophisticated command and control package. It fit like a glove, smelled like the dump I had taken in it the month before, and was servo-assisted. The gunny thumped her helmet against mine. She had wide-set eyes, a pug nose, and a dusting of freckles across the top of her cheeks. "How ya doin', sir? Everything okay?"

I tried to ignore the smell. "Just fine, gunny. Couldn't be better."

She grinned knowingly. "Life sucks, don't it, sir? Well, that's why god gave us the corps. To shorten the suffering."

I laughed, knowing it was expected of me, and knowing she was scared too. And there were thirty-six men and women on our team, their helmets turned in my direction, all of whom shared the same feelings. I thought about some of the stupid gung-ho crap other officers had laid on me and tried to avoid it. "We're on final approach. You know the objective, the layout, and what you're supposed to do. Questions?"

Silence.

"Okay, then. Load the tubes."

I used handholds to pull myself towards the stern, stopped in front of the starboard ejection tube, and checked to make sure that my squad had lined up behind me. They had. I dived inside and used fingertips and toes to push myself forward. My squad did likewise. A hatch closed behind the last member in.

The gunny did much the same thing along the port side, followed by a seal check. She called thirty-eight names, got thirty-eight affirmatives, and blew the tubes.

We were in position now, ready to be fired out of both sides of the ship, falling, or in this case blasting, down towards the target below. Of course the Loot, plus the ships behind her, would cover us with cannon fire, missiles, chaff, electronic countermeasures, and everything else they had up their naval sleeves, but none of it would mean diddly if the tool heads knew we were coming. Yes, surprise was the key, that and the most fickle ally of all, luck.

"Five and counting." The Loot was tense but rational. Better than some I've flown with, but wired tight just the same. And who could blame her? Recon pilots have a life expectancy of five or six months. "One and counting."

I stared at the steel in front of my helmet and tried to ignore my surroundings. I gave thanks when the ten-second count began. "Nine . . . eight . . . seven . . . six . . . five . . . four . . . three . . . two . . . one."

The hatch, mounted up against an indentation in the spacecraft's fuselage, slid aside. I braced myself, watched the inner hatch cycle out of the way, and felt a wall of air hit the bottom of my boots. We were propelled outwards like bullets from a gun. I had little more than seconds to orient myself, to realize that it was an ambush, and feel the individually targeted micro-missile hit my chest plate.

• • • • • •

They say you can't scream if you're dead, but I proved they were wrong. It took hours to slow my pulse, to think pleasant thoughts, and drift off to sleep.

9

"Dissent is a luxury that
Mars colonists can ill afford."

*Margaret Peko-Evans, architect
of Mars Prime — the first
settlement*

The rest of the trip was fairly routine. Each shift was pretty much like the last. Get up, take a shower, drink three cups of coffee, pet the aniforms, and read for Sasha. Progress was slow, but I did my best and was reading at a second- or third-grade level in no time at all.

The whole thing might have been somewhat enjoyable if it hadn't been for the way in which the aniforms were "harvested" and passed down the ship's food chain. I had no part in the actual killing, thank god, but felt like a traitor whenever one of my charges disappeared and was replaced by a newly decanted clone, or "bud." Then, after I had spent countless hours petting it, the cow, sheep, pig, or chicken would vanish only to reappear around the captain's waistline.

Yes, the others were just as carnivorous as she was, but I held the captain personally responsible and saw her as the sole culprit. By doing so I could ignore the fact that Sasha seemed to have an insatiable appetite for steaks, pork chops, and Killer's super-crispy fried chicken.

And making a bad situation even worse was the fact that each aniform was identical to all of its predecessors. It was like killing the same pet over and over again. It got to the point where I could hardly look into their adoring eyes or touch their eager heads. So, it was with a sense of tremendous relief that I saw Mars on the main view screen. It was beautiful and looked like a sphere of reddish-orange marble set spinning on a sheet of black velvet. I was thinking about the surface and what we might encounter there when the captain burst my bubble. She moved quietly for such a large woman, and I didn't know she was present until her forklift brushed my right shoulder.

"Welcome to Mars. Ever been outside before?"

My eyebrows shot towards the top of my head. "Outside? As in outside the ship?"

"Sure," the captain replied curiously. "What? You thought we'd dump the cargo and let it drift?"

"I assumed we would dock with a habitat. Like *Staros-3*."

The captain laughed. Tidal waves of fat rippled back and forth beneath the surface of her black pajamas. "A habitat! That's a good one! As if the poor bastards had the resources to build a space station! Hell, they're lucky to meet the company's daily production quota, much less dick around with habitats. No, we unload the cargo in orbit and they take the stuff down in shuttles. So how 'bout it? You been outside before?"

I knew there was a strong possibility that I had, but I couldn't be sure, so I shook my head.

The captain clucked sympathetically. "Too bad. But don't worry, you'll catch on. And sweet buns too. When it comes time to unload, *everyone* turns to, and I mean *everyone*. Even me."

And she meant it too, which accounted for the fact that Sasha and I found ourselves adrift within the main lock four hours later. My space suit was too small, Sasha's was too large, and both smelled like an overripe armpit. The captain had taken the spin off the ship in order to provide unobstructed access to the cargo bay. The result was zero gee and nausea in the pit of my stomach. The others, Sasha included, showed no signs of discomfort.

The regular crew members had customized their suits, or purchased customized units, I wasn't sure which. The captain's was bright pink with lots of flashing red lights and a hint of chrome. Killer had co-opted Lester's suit. It had been painted to resemble a naked Hercules complete with fake sex organ. He made a production out of cutting it off and waving it over his head. Kreshenko had gone for the high-tech look, favoring a suit fitted with articulated cutters, lasers, and other accessories too numerous to mention. It made him look like a large Swiss army knife. In fact Wilson, already positioned in the cargo bay, was the only one besides ourselves who wore an unmodified suit. The outer hatch cycled open, and the captain's voice crackled in my ears.

"Okay people, listen up. Sweet buns will team with Kreshenko, and chrome-dome comes with me. Let's get it over with." So saying, the captain fired her jets and headed out into the void. She looked like a wad of pink chewing gum wrapped with Christmas tree lights.

I didn't want to go but knew I had to. I fired my jets. The suit surged upwards, bounced off the overhead, and took off again. I cut power, aligned myself with the hatch, and gave it another try. Nausea rolled over me as I passed out into the vast emptiness of space. The captain loomed ahead, dodged out of the way, and made a grab for my suit. "Maxon! Cut your jets!"

I obeyed and felt completely humiliated as she clipped a line to the eye mounted on my chest plate and towed me towards the ship's stern. So much for my secret hopes that past knowledge would surface to save the day.

The ship filled most of the view. The hull was cylindrical and covered with duct work, antenna farms, solar arrays, and other installations too arcane for me to understand. And beyond that, half hidden by the *Trader*'s hull, was Mars herself, a glowing red presence against a field of black. The sight was so awesome, so compelling, that my nausea was momentarily forgotten. No wonder the earlier me had ventured into the Big Black. There could be nothing more beautiful than the sight before me.

The cargo hatch was open, and the loading lights served to illuminate Wilson's launcher. The launcher was the equivalent of a spacegoing forklift, except that it could "launch" cargo modules, as well as move them around.

In this case that meant propelling the containers from the ship's hold towards the holding "pen" where the rest of the crew would retrieve and move them inside. No simple task when the modules were eight times bigger than you were. The launcher looked like a praying mantis with a man strapped to its stomach.

Correctly assessing my competence as nonexistent, the captain secured my safety line to the pen and issued strict instructions to stay where I was. I was happy to comply. As the rest of the crew arrayed themselves in front of the holding structure, and prepared to "catch" cargo, I examined the pen. It was anything but high-tech.

Bright orange plastic netting had been stretched over a metal framework to create a massive box or "pen" into which the cargo could be shoved and temporarily stored. Lights strobed off and on to warn ships of the pen's presence, and a system of moveable partitions had been installed to divide one load of cargo from the next.

I watched in amazement as Wilson launched the first container in our direction and the captain jetted out to intercept it. The captain was surprisingly graceful as she hurtled through space, caught the incoming module, and pushed it towards me. "Time to earn your keep, Maxon. Catch the sucker and shove it into the pen."

Mars-light winked off the top surface of the container as it tumbled in my direction. The captain had met the module with the correct amount of force, but her aim was off. To correct for that, and direct the cargo into the pen, I would have to move to the right. I gritted my teeth, fired my jets, and jerked to a halt when my safety line ran out. I felt the cable tighten under my armpit and pull me around. I was still in the process of turning back and raising my hands when the container hit. It pushed me into the net, dropped through the opening like an eight ball entering the corner pocket, and drifted towards the back wall. My jets pushed me out, the cable jerked me around, and the captain sounded cheerful. "Good going, Maxon. Keep it up."

I had barely recovered when the next module arrived, closely followed by the next, and the one after that. I felt like the goalie in a reversed hockey game, as the team fed me pucks, and I bounced them into the net. It became fun after a while as they warmed up and I gained skill. Still, the hours took their toll, and I was glad when it was over.

The captain towed me towards the ship. A pair of shuttles arrived, jockeyed for position, and disgorged a dozen space-suited figures. They headed for the pen. Their motions were so smooth, so coordinated, that our efforts looked clumsy by comparison.

A few hours later we were packed, paid, and floating around the lock as one of Marscorp's shuttles made contact. The captain had come to see us off. She extended a bejeweled hand. I took it and was surprised by her strength. "You're sure you won't stay? Kreshenko is soft on sweet buns, and your head makes a good mirror."

I shook my head. "Thanks . . . but we'll be moving on."

The captain shrugged. "Okay, have it your way, but a word to the wise . . ."

The hatch opened and we pulled ourselves through. I turned around.

"Yeah? And what would that be?"

"Be sure to duck."

The hatch closed, and I never saw her again. The stewardess had purple hair and matching day-glo nail polish. She wore a blue jumpsuit and a bored expression. She pointed towards the main passageway. "Grab any seat that's open."

We nodded and used the conveniently placed handholds to pull ourselves along. I considered what the captain had said. "What did she mean 'duck'?"

"She meant 'take care of yourself,'" Sasha replied easily. "What did you think she meant?"

I frowned. "It could have been a warning."

"You worry too much."

Sasha spotted some empty seats and pulled herself in that direction. I followed. A tiny maintenance bot, one of hundreds that roamed the ship, scuttled across the overhead. It had a screw clamped in its tiny jaws and appeared to be in a hurry. Whatever the problem was, I hoped it wasn't critical.

The rest of the passengers, an eclectic group gathered from five or six different ships, stared as we strapped ourselves in. They were what I imagined to be the usual mix of freelancers, corpies, and a zombie or two. They watched with dull, self-absorbed eyes, thinking of what lay ahead, and wishing it was over. And no wonder, since it was common knowledge that even easy Mars jobs were hard, and not everyone who came lived long enough to go back. Not a particularly friendly crowd, but not especially hostile either, so I forced myself to relax and watched Sasha out of the corner of my eye.

She looked okay, which was amazing considering what she'd been through. But appearances can be deceiving. Watching her had become a hobby of mine, and I thought I saw tension around her eyes, plus a pallor that no amount of artificial tanning could hide. And why not? The poor thing had been abducted by corpies, chased by poppers, lost an eye, and been assaulted by a sexual psychopath. All in spite of my rather questionable protection.

It made me feel like children do when their parents are troubled. Scared, vulnerable, and helpless to do anything about it. Which was strange, since *I* was the one who was supposed to protect her rather than the other way around. I wished we could talk about it and knew she'd refuse.

The deck tilted, then leveled out as the shuttle banked and dived towards the planet below. My stomach did flip-flops. There were no view ports, so I looked for something to do. A screen had been built into the back of the seat in front of me. I pulled it down and an infomercial appeared. The actor was happy, and why not? He was on Earth. He smiled and his teeth sparkled. "Hi! My name is Tom. What's yours?"

I ignored the question and he switched to the noninteractive mode. "Marscorp and its affiliates would like to welcome you to Mars. Regardless of whether you work the interface, or are passing through, our personnel will do everything in their power to make your stay as pleasant as possible. Now settle back and relax while we tell you about your next destination."

Sasha looked at my screen. "What the hell is that?"

"Some stuff about Mars. Wanta watch?"

She shook her head and yawned. "My mother pays flaks to say nice things about Europa Station too. Most of them are lies."

I shrugged and turned towards the screen. She closed her eyes and settled back for a nap. A digitally created Mars had appeared and was overlaid with text. The narration continued, but I was pleased to discover that I could read most of the words myself.

I learned that Mars has a diameter of 4,200 miles and an orbital period of 686 days, each of which is 24 hours and 37 minutes long. Mars is known as the "Red Planet" because of the pervasive orange-red color caused by the dust that blows through the atmosphere. The atmosphere is extremely thin. Ninety-five per cent is carbon dioxide, two-point-seven per cent is nitrogen, one-point-six per cent is argon, and the rest consists of miniscule amounts of oxygen, carbon monoxide, and water vapor. Not a good place to visit without a space suit. And then just to keep things interesting, there are incredible fluctuations in temperature, dust storms, and relatively light gravity. The shots of the surface faded away and the actor appeared. He smiled.

"Now, while Mars is not the wild and wooly place that the vids would have you believe, it does have an exciting history."

Smiley disappeared and was replaced by footage from the Viking lander. I pressed "scan," waited for the first landing and subsequent colonization stuff to run its course, and hit "play." The picture steadied and lost resolution as amateur video came on. I had watched the footage a hundred times back on Earth and never tired of it.

A ragtag army of men and women charged a corporate strongpoint, staggered under a hail of darts, and struggled forward. And then, just when it looked as though they might have a chance, a contingent of Mishimuto Marines, the same outfit I had belonged to, stood up from behind a barricade and gunned them down. The tool heads didn't have a chance. They danced under the impact of plastic and steel and fell in bloody heaps. Horrible though the pictures were, they provided a glimpse into the life I couldn't remember, and in spite of the fact that I had searched the faces many times before, I did so again. Maybe, just maybe, I'd been there. The narration continued.

"The brutal and completely unnecessary war started when a small group of self-styled 'freedom fighters' staged an illegal strike, and sought to impose illegal demands on the corporations and their stockholders.

"Though claiming to represent workers, and pretending to have their interests in mind, the strikers began the systematic destruction of the very facilities that gave them work. And so it was that the corporations formed the Consortium, met force with force, liberated their holdings, and returned honest citizens to their jobs."

A tidy ending to a war that had destroyed millions of lives, including mine. The rest of the program was a good deal more cheerful. It seemed that Marscorp had gambled everything on a huge city-sized vehicle dubbed Roller Three. The company was proud of the fact that while the processor traveled less than fifty feet a day, it had already consumed more than a thousand square miles of the planet's surface and crapped enough palletized ingots to turn a small profit. And, given the size of the red planet's mineral deposits, plus the fact that Roller Four was in the final stages of construction, there was little doubt that even more profits lay up ahead.

A robo-cam swooped over and around the machine while the narrator droned on. The first thing that struck me was the sheer scale of the thing. It was five miles long, three miles wide, and weighed millions of tons. Built like an enormous box, its skin covered by a landing strip, solar arrays, autocranes, and cooling fins, the processor would have resembled a mechanical dung beetle, except that it was generating waste instead of eating it.

Huge tracks, each a quarter of a mile wide, carried the monstrosity forward. Bus-sized boulders exploded as metal-bright treads fell on them. A cloud of fine red dust hung around the machine's lower parts as steel jaws gouged tons of rock out of the planet's surface and dropped it onto highway-sized conveyor belts. From there the belts fed the stuff into a nonpressurized hell where heavily armored humans supervised specially designed droids.

But that's not the sort of thing that flaks are paid to dwell on, so the scene changed and I found myself looking at a spotless cafeteria while a man in a tall white hat bragged about the quality of his food. I lost interest, touched a button, and watched while the screen was retracted into the seat back.

There was very little atmosphere to slow the shuttle down, so it fell like a high-speed elevator. My stomach went with it. It was weird to think that we'd be landing on top of a huge machine. A machine that would continue to function even as we arrived. Powerful engines and a prodigious amount of fuel kept us aloft for the appropriate length of time, but there were no windows, so the teeth-rattling thump and neck-stretching brake job came as a complete surprise. The shuttle coasted for a while and jerked to a stop.

I expected everyone to stand, grab their luggage, and head for the hatch. The newbies looked around and wondered what to do, but the Mars hands stayed where they were. The stew sounded bored. "Please remain in your seats until a pressure tube has been connected to the shuttle's main hatch and the seat belt light goes off . . ."

She had more to say, but I tuned it out. I looked at Sasha and found that she was awake. "Welcome to Mars."

She smiled. "Thanks. Now that we've arrived . . . let's see how quickly we can leave."

I nodded. The quicker we reached Europa Station, the quicker people would stop shooting at me, and the quicker I'd be able to collect the fifty thousand. Which reminded me of what I was being paid to do. "They could be waiting for us."

Her eyes narrowed. "How would they know where to look?"

I knew she was smarter than that, so I assumed it was a rhetorical question. "They would know where we are because A, there is radio communication between Earth and Mars, or B, they came on a faster ship. And what about the captain? She told us to duck. She *knew* something would happen."

"Yeah," she said reluctantly. "It makes sense."

"Yes, it does," I agreed. "So here's the plan. I get off first, trip the ambush, and you slip away."

Her eyes looked into mine. There was a softness there, mixed with determination, mixed with something else. Her voice was sarcastic.

"Great, just great. You trip the ambush, get yourself killed, and leave me all alone. What the hell kind of bodyguard is that?"

The conflicting signals made me confused. I felt defensive. "Oh, yeah? Well, what would you suggest?"

"That we wait while the others get off, leave together, and slip away."

It went against my instincts, but I nodded and touched the weapon under my left armpit. It had been loaded aboard ship, and logic dictated that it still was. I wished I could make sure. The shuttle rocked gently as the pressure tube made contact with the hull. The hatch opened, air hissed as pressures equalized, and the seat belt light went out. A newbie forgot to compensate, jumped to his feet, and hit the overhead. The resulting thud could be heard all over the ship. The Mars hands laughed, shook their heads in disgust, and stood with exaggerated slowness.

Sasha and I stayed in our seats until most of the passengers had left, stood, and eased our way forward. The last thing we wanted to do was follow the newbie's example. The stew with the purple hair and matching day-glo nails looked at my head, nodded politely, and let us pass. Was she more interested than she should be? Or was she attracted to my size, skull plate, and rugged good looks?

My heart beat faster as we walked down the pressure tube towards the terminal beyond. It might have been comical if it wasn't so frightening. There were thirty or forty people in the waiting area. The moment we stepped out of the pressure tube, three or four of them pointed in our direction and shouted, "There they are!"

The only thing that saved us was the fact that neither group had expected the other to be there. Weapons appeared, darts flew, and people screamed. Innocent bystanders, of which there were damned few, slid-scurried out of the way as the rest of us took cover behind the chrome-and-black-vinyl furniture. I placed my body in front of Sasha's, but she moved around me. A woman popped up, tried to get a bead on us, and did a slow-motion tumble as Sasha shot her in the chest. I made a note to keep my movements slow and precise.

Alarms went off as a dart whirred by my ear. It came from behind! I turned, saw the stewardess with the purple hair fire again, and felt something graze my arm. I put two darts through her throat. Blood pumped, day-glo nails clutched at her neck, and she slow-fell backwards.

The voice came over the PA system. "THROW YOUR WEAPONS ON THE FLOOR AND PLACE YOUR HANDS ON THE TOP OF YOUR HEAD!"

We never got a chance to obey, because a volley of sleep-gas canisters tumbled end over end into the waiting area and went off with a sibilant hiss. I had just started to react when the darkness rolled me under.

10

"The Class IV environment suit
is not intended for prolonged use
on planetary surfaces. Such use
constitutes an abuse of said suit
and serves to nullify all warranties
offered by the manufacturer."

*A sticker found in the right armpit
of each Jiffy Corp Class IV
environment suit*

Someone slapped my face. I felt my head rock back and forth. It hurt and, worse than that, forced me up out of the nice black hole where I'd been hiding. I made a conscious decision to hurt the person who was hurting me, gathered my energy, and reached for their throat. Or would have, if my arms had been free.

Someone laughed, a deep grunting sound, not unlike that made by primates in the zoo.

That made me *really* angry, angry enough to open my eyes and squint up into the harsh white light. It came from a ceiling-mounted fixture and served to silhouette my tormentor. I couldn't see his features, but the outline was *big*. Bigger than I am. He saw my eyes open and nodded his satisfaction. "So, sleeping beauty awakes. Time to rise and shine, sweet cakes. We're going for a little hike."

I heard a series of clicks and felt the restraints drop away. The blob withdrew and I forced myself to sit. I had what felt like a hangover and decided the knockout gas was to blame. The ambush! Sasha! Where was she? My head throbbed as I looked around. It seemed as though I was inside some sort of cylindrical vehicle, an impression that was confirmed when it hit a bump and the back of my head bounced off a heavily padded bulkhead.

A corridor ran the length of whatever it was that I was in. It was filled with half-dressed men and women. They swore when the vehicle rocked from side to side and struggled to don what looked like space suits. Almost all of them had the whipcord-thin look of people teetering on the edge of starvation. Some eyed me with open hostility. The rest seemed determined to ignore me.

My tormentor reappeared. He was big, black, and completely bald. It was supposed to look intimidating and did. He had a wedge-shaped torso, thick arms, and legs like tree trunks. I put my plans for mayhem on temporary hold. He nodded as if endorsing my decision.

"That's right, sweet cakes. Get the lay of the land before you try me on. It's nice to have a mule with a little bit of common sense for a change. Now get your big white ass down off that bunk and suit up."

Discretion seemed the better part of valor, so I slid off the bunk. My landing was feather-light and served to remind me of the planet's rather iffy gravity. I saw movement out of the corner of my eye and turned just in time to catch a loosely tied bundle. It was a suit similar to the one I had worn in orbit. I shook it out and managed to slide inside without making a complete fool of myself. I didn't know why that mattered, just that it did, especially with the black guy looking on.

The truth was that I didn't like him, but still wanted his approval, kind of like a recruit hates the DI's guts but wants his or her respect. A bit perverse perhaps, but very much in line with my need for authority figures, and the occasional bit of guidance. Which isn't to say that I wouldn't deck the bastard if I thought I could get away with it and doing so suited my purposes. Confused? Hey, join the party.

I checked the seals on my suit and tried to figure out where they had taken me and why. What had happened to the Trans-Solar goons, anyway? Not to mention the homicidal greenies. And Sasha? Was she a prisoner like me? Or lying dead in a meat locker?

Then I saw her, a reed-thin woman with stubblelike hair, piercing blue eyes, and a ruler-straight mouth. The kind that never smiles. She had sealed her suit but left the face plate open and was killing me with her eyes. Or trying to, anyway. There was something familiar about her, as though we had met before, and recently at that. On the shuttle? In the terminal? Yes, I thought I remembered a frightened face, a gun, and a dart whirring past my head.

Yeah, she'd been there, and, even more importantly, she understood what was happening. I had already taken a step in the woman's direction when a hand fell on my shoulder. It was the black guy again. "Wrong direction, sweet cakes. The lock is towards the ass end of this kidney-buster. Follow the mule in front of you."

I turned in the proper direction. The guy in front of me had "Screw you!" spray-painted across the sand-blasted surface of his oxy box. It seemed like the perfect sentiment.

The vehicle braked to a jerky halt, failed to throw any of us to the deck, and vibrated in frustration. The line shuffled forward and I followed. It soon became apparent that the lock held five people at a time, so there were a number of pauses while we cycled through. I had seen no sign of guards other than the black man, so I made plans to run. A quick check assured me that he was seven people back, well clear of the group I would share the lock with, and apparently uninterested in my activities. Good. Once clear of the lock, I would have about five minutes to disappear.

The lock cycled open, my group entered, and immediately sealed their face plates. I did the same and took the opportunity to run one last check on my suit. Unlike the one I had worn in orbit, this baby was new. So new that the chemical smell made my sinuses hurt. Because I planned to escape, the suit's six-hour air supply, four quarts of water, and two days' worth of emergency rations took on added importance. I was still in the process of wishing that I had more of everything when the lock cycled open.

The exterior landscape had a reddish tint to it and was thick with man-sized rocks and boulders: a barrier that might or might not explain why we were about to take a "little hike." Wind-driven sand peppered our suits and rattled across our helmets. I decided that I liked Mars less with each passing moment.

I followed the others away from the vehicle and turned to get the lay of the land. It was then that I gave up all hope of escape. No wonder the black guy was so relaxed. Outside of the long, tank-shaped vehicle, and the tracks left in its wake, there was not a single sign of civilization for as far as the eye could see. Six hours worth of air wouldn't begin to get me where I needed to go. I pulled a three-sixty.

A rock-strewn plain stretched off towards what my suit informed me was the south. Hundreds of dry gullies cut the west into an eye-numbing maze of channels and banks. Rocks, boulders, and ragged-looking hills marched off to the north, where they terminated at the base of the most amazing sight that I'd ever seen.

According to the video I had watched aboard the shuttle, Olympus Mons towers fifteen miles above the equivalent of sea level, making it a full-grown giant when compared to the relatively puny Mt. Everest, which stands little more than five miles high. Not to mention the fact that Olympus Mons boasts a caldera that is forty-five miles across and a base that would extend from the Montreal Urboplex all the way to what's left of the Big Apple.

But no set of statistics could possibly do justice to the out-and-out magnificence of what I saw. Olympus Mons was nothing less than a brooding presence, squatting there like an ancient monument, measuring everything against its own enormous bulk.

As for the land to the east, well, it wasn't any better, consisting as it did of a rock face fronted by a jumble of sharp-edged boulders. I noticed that while some of my companions were scoping things out, most were oblivious to their surroundings, as if they'd seen it all before or just didn't care. They stood in clusters, their helmets pressed together for private conversations, or just staring at the ground.

The lock opened and the last group shuffled out. An indicator light appeared inside my helmet, and the black man's voice filled my ears. He had a stylized "X" painted on the front of his otherwise unadorned suit. I tried to see through the polarized face plate but couldn't.

"Alright, boys and girls . . . listen up. For those of you who haven't already heard, my name is Dawkins, Larry Dawkins, Marscorp Field Supervisor extraordinaire, and one mean bastard. I ain't no lifer, and I ain't no ass-kisser, which means I got where I am by out-surviving a whole lot of dumb shits like you. So, if you work hard, and do exactly as I say, you might live long enough to get paid. Got any questions?"

Silence.

"Good . . . So here's the scoop. The company lost a shuttle about thirty miles north of here. The pilot and copilot bought the farm, but the ship's artificial intelligence thinks the cargo can be salvaged. And, since the cargo consists of ten Class IV Cargo Walkers, the first to make it dirtside, it's worth our while to go in after them. Questions?"

This time there was. The voice identified itself as Swango, and was clearly male, but I had no way of knowing which suit it belonged to. "Yeah, I've got a question. Why walk when we could ride?"

"Well, gee," Dawkins said sarcastically, "I wonder. You don't suppose it would have anything to do with those friggin' boulders, do you? Or those god-damned rocks? You know, the ones in our way?"

"Oh," Swango said self-consciously. "Sorry."

"You certainly are," Dawkins agreed. "Anyone else?"

I don't know what came over me, but the fog cleared off long enough for a thought to surface, and the words popped out of their own accord. "What about oxygen, water, and food? Will we be resupplied?"

The Field Supervisor's reply was more accurate than he knew. "Well, I'll be damned, a mule with half a brain. The answer is no, we won't. We have enough air, water, and food to reach the wreckage. Once there, we will take shelter in one of the remaining airtight compartments, resupply our suits, and recover the walkers. And here's the good news, folks: once the walkers are up and running, we *ride* out."

The supposedly good news left everyone silent. It didn't take a rocket scientist to figure out that a whole lot of things could and probably would go wrong, that the company had left us with practically no safety margin, and that Dawkins was standing in the same pile of shit we were. I thought about what he'd said earlier, about not kissing ass, and wondered if that explained why he had pulled such a rotten assignment.

"Alright," the man in question said, "enough dorking around. Line up and draw your loads."

The crawler remained where it was. Vapor outgassed into the thin atmosphere as a hatch slid open. The compartment was filled with a jumble of strange-looking equipment. Dawkins motioned us forward, grabbed what looked like a high-tech backpack from a row of similar packs, and handed it to the first person in line. I wondered why. If not supplies, what would we carry? The answer blew what was left of my mind. It quickly became apparent that our loads consisted of cyborgs! Walker Wonks, to be exact, specially engineered to pilot the huge machines, and more than a little weird.

Though human in the technical sense, the cyborgs looked like little more than gray metal suitcases to which shoulder straps and a waist belt had been attached. They had their own life support systems but were dependent on whoever was toting them for mobility and communications. Until they were united with their machines, that is, when they would take on super-human powers, and go to work on whatever task Marscorp had brought them here to do.

The line jerked to a halt, and a scuffle broke out. I missed the first part but saw the mule twist away from Dawkins. It was then that I recognized the greenie's suit. I hadn't been smart enough to wonder which side she was on, but the answer became obvious as she broadcast in the clear. "Resist the evil plan! Free the cyborgs from their devil bodies! Rise up and smite the . . ."

We didn't get to hear the rest of the woman's diatribe because Dawkins overrode her transmission. "I don't have time for this shit. Carry the load or die."

Silence ensued. Nobody moved. A woman stood next to me. I put my helmet next to hers. "What's going on?"

"Dawkins cut her air supply."

"He can do that?"

"You bet he can. Yours too. That's why we do what he says. That and the fact that there's no place to run to."

I thanked her and pulled away. No wonder a single guard was sufficient. Our suits were rigged so he could control them. The corpies think of everything. The woman surrendered about a minute later. She was gasping for breath. "I'll do what you say. Give me air!"

"A wise decision," Dawkins said, doing whatever he did to restore the woman's air supply. "Don't do that again. We've got a long ways to go, and time equates to air, water, and food. Come on . . . hurry up."

I received my cyborg two minutes later. The added weight was negligible thanks to the relatively low gravity, but the additional mass would take some getting used to. It felt as if the load was pulling me backwards and off-balance. I leaned forward to compensate.

A green indicator light appeared in my heads-up display as Dawkins shoved a jack into my external patch panel. I waited for my passenger to say something, but heard nothing beyond the hiss of an open channel. It seemed as if this particular cyborg was the antisocial type. Well, that was fine with me, since I needed what there was of my brain for other things. Like negotiating my way over the rock-strewn ground, for example.

I tongued a couple of pain tabs into my mouth and washed them down with a sip of recycled water. It tasted like what it had once been.

Once loaded, we set off in the direction of Olympus Mons, winding our way through a maze of hard-edged boulders, going where no one had gone before. Or so I assumed. It was a strange feeling after the humanity-packed cities of Earth, where you had the feeling that every corridor had been walked by thousands before you, everything you saw had been seen a million times, and "new" meant "disposable."

But the thrill of trail-blazing soon gave way to renewed anxiety over Sasha's whereabouts and the neverending task of placing one foot in front of the other. It was cold outside, minus 24 degrees F according to my helmet display, but I soon started to sweat. Turning my thermostat down helped a little, but the problem remained. Try as I might, I had a difficult time internalizing the fact that the sweat was *inside* rather than *outside* my high-tech skin. We had traveled about five miles by the time my passenger broke the silence. Her voice was synthetic, and sounded vaguely familiar, as if she'd modeled it on a holo star. "I'm sorry."

I gauged the ledge ahead, decided I could make it thanks to the lower gravity, and jumped. Slow-motion dust geysered up and away from my boots. I checked the path and started after the mule ahead. "Norgleszap? I mean, sorry? Sorry about what?"

"About you having to drag my nonexistent ass cross country."

I sidestepped a rock and laughed in spite of myself. "It isn't your fault. Or I assume it isn't, anyway."

"No," the voice said, "I've got an alibi. I was sitting in a crate aboard Roller Three when the shuttle crashed."

"Sounds airtight," I agreed politely. "Well, I sure hope you and the others know what you're doing, or this is gonna be a one-way trip."

"Oh, we know what we're doing," she said confidently. "That's not the problem."

"It isn't?" I asked stupidly. "Then what is?"

"Why, the condition of the shuttle," she answered calmly. "What if the shuttle went in hard? The walkers were in the main cargo bay. They could be spread all over the place."

I skidded down the side of a ravine and tackled the other side. "But the ship's artificial intelligence said the cargo is okay."

"The ship's artificial intelligence 'thinks' the cargo is okay," my passenger corrected me. "But doesn't really know, since it's bolted into a panel somewhere."

"Shit."

"Yeah," she agreed. "That's the prognosis, alright. My name's Loni. What's yours?"

"Max. Max Maxon."

"Glad to meet you, Max. Any chance you'd do me a favor?"

I swore as the mule in front of me came to an unexpected stop, forced me to do likewise, then started up again. "Sure, what do you need?"

"I'm tired of the darkness, Max. Tell me what you see."

Suddenly I knew something I hadn't known before. I knew that whatever I had lost, others had lost even more. Loni's brain was intact, but the eyes, ears, arms and legs designed to serve it had been taken away, either through bad luck or a conscious decision on her part. I thought of the darkness within her box, the isolation from the rest of humanity, and shivered. I turned the heat back up a notch and did my best to sound cheerful. "Okay, but I spend a lot of time looking at my feet, so I'll start there. They are size fourteen or so, large enough to qualify as battleships, and covered with reddish Mars dust."

Loni laughed, and thus encouraged, I continued. Describing what I saw to my sightless passenger forced me to realize how beautiful my surroundings were and made the time pass quickly. It seemed as if little more than a few minutes had elapsed when Dawkins announced the halfway point and declared a ten-minute break.

Mules headed in every direction as they looked for places to sit. Talking to Loni had been pleasant, but Sasha was very much on my mind, so I waited for the greenie to light on rock and ambled over. Loni was telling me about her VR-driven training, but I cut her off in mid-sentence. "Sorry, Loni, but I've got a personal matter to attend to. Hold that gafornk."

The greenie turned her helmet in my direction but made no effort to avoid me. There was plenty of room on the rock she had chosen, so I sat down beside her. My helmet thumped against hers. It's hard to be brain-damaged and subtle at the same time. I wasn't. "You shot at us."

Her reply was direct. "Yes, I did."

"Why?"

"Why what?"

"Why shoot at us?"

"Because I was ordered to do so."

"By whom?"

"Screw you."

"What about the girl? What happened to the girl?"

The woman shrugged. The suit fit fairly well and shrugged with her. "Beats me. The gas put me out."

I swore. The woman hooked her thumbs under the pack straps that held her cyborg in place. I could barely see her eyes through the sand-abraded face plate. Was it sympathy I saw?

"You really like her, don't you?"

I was confused. "Like who?"

"The girl."

"Yes, I really like her."

"Well," the woman said, "think about her before you unleash whatever technological hell you're working on."

"I'm not working on a technological rebonk."

"Really?" the woman asked. "Then what are you doing here?"

Part of me wanted to give the obvious answer, to say something about protecting my client, but the rest knew she was right. There *was* something more going on, something Sasha at least partially understood, assuming she was alive, that is.

"On your feet," Dawkins ordered. "We have about twelve miles to go and barely enough air to get there. Let's haul ass."

The next two and a half hours were difficult. Perhaps some of the others had thought to catheterize themselves prior to departure, but I hadn't and needed to pee. Add to that the fear of what we might find when we arrived at the crash site, and my concerns for Sasha, and it made for a hard, cold lump that rode my gut for the rest of the day. It was twilight by the time we hit flat ground and the mule called Swango saw the first chunk of wreckage. He sounded worried and ecstatic at the same time. "Dawkins! There it is! A piece of wreckage!"

"Good boy," Dawkins said calmly. "Now stay away from it until I get there and take a look-see. It could be dangerous."

"Or it could be loaded with goodies like oxygen," Loni said over our private intercom.

I hadn't thought about that but knew it was probably true. If the mules stumbled across some O_2, the Field Supervisor's immediate authority would be considerably lessened. And, while the mutineers wouldn't have any place to go after their rebellion, Dawkins could be more than a little dead in the meantime.

The wreckage consisted of a huge engine, one of four required to keep a shuttle aloft in the planet's thin atmosphere, and glittered with a coating of diamondlike ice crystals. I figured some sort of liquid had been liberated when the engine tore free; then it had vaporized and frozen in a matter of seconds.

We were close now, and picked up the pace without being asked to. It was relatively easy to follow the trail of debris, which, thanks to the lighter gravity, was much longer than it would have been on Earth. Judging from the wreckage, and the huge scars scored in the rocky soil, the shuttle had cartwheeled for two or three miles after it hit before finally coming to rest.

We found more and more wreckage as we followed the trail. I described it to Loni. "And there's something that looks like a piece of wing with part of an engine still attached."

The cyborg sounded concerned. "But no sign of the fuselage?"

"Nope, not yet."

"Good. The walkers can take a lot of punishment, but they'll do best cradled in the cargo hold."

The bits and pieces gradually grew thicker until someone spotted the main part of the wreckage. "There it is!" a woman exclaimed. "Straight ahead."

I arrived five minutes later and was amazed by the sheer size of the downed shuttle. The hull towered three or four stories over my head and stretched hundreds of feet in both directions. There were no signs of a fire, which wasn't too surprising, since there was very little oxygen available to feed on. All the damage was impact-related. A huge circle served to contain the Marscorp "M" and adorned the side of the hull. It was split down the middle, a fact that eliminated the need to find a hatch.

Dawkins ordered us to wait and entered through the crack. I checked my oxygen supply, saw that I was down to eighteen minutes' worth, and thought about the assumptions the corpies had used. That we would make the trip inside of six hours, that we would be able to salvage the oxygen we needed from the wreck, and that at least some of the walkers would be operable. Then I realized something that should have been obvious from the start. *It didn't matter if we got back.* As long as the borgs made it to the crash site, and Dawkins installed them in their machines, the corpies would deem the mission a success. Which explained why Mars fodder like the greenie and myself had been selected as mules. We were expendable.

Suddenly I saw Dawkins in a new light. He'd known what I'd just managed to figure out all along, and not only planned to carry out his mission, but save our asses as well. The fact was that we had been lucky, *very* lucky, and I wondered if our luck would hold.

And much to my amazement it did, as Dawkins emerged, announced that six of the walkers were operational, and started the search for an airtight compartment. We spent ten minutes on the task, but couldn't find one. So, with our air running uncomfortably low, we were forced to inflate one of two emergency shelters carried aboard the shuttle.

The second was missing. A more imaginative person than myself might have spent a significant amount of time considering what might have happened if the first tent had been destroyed, but I felt no desire to do that. No, it was much nicer to cycle through the lock with the warning buzzer sounding in my ears, strip off my suit, and seek the solace of a small but well-designed inflatable rest room.

It was only after I had taken a much delayed pee that I remembered Loni and the fact that I discarded her along with my suit. I hurried back. The shelter had been designed to accommodate twice our number, so there was plenty of room. I wound my way between people, unoccupied suits, and built-in equipment to find that a pair of mules were disconnecting Loni from my suit. I put on one of my most intimidating frowns. "Hey . . . what's going on?"

The man had his face plate open. He looked in my direction, then looked again. "Dawkins told us to collect six borgs and connect them to the walkers."

I nodded my understanding. "Great . . . but let me say good-bye."

The man looked unhappy but decided to go along. "Okay . . . but make it snappy."

Loni's umbilical was still connected to my suit. I left her on the floor, lifted the suit, and draped it across my back. The helmet felt natural after wearing it for so long. "Loni?"

"Well, if it isn't my own personal chauffeur. You disappeared."

"Sorry. I had to pee. But I hurried back."

"All is forgiven. Thanks for the ride. Try to get assigned to my walker, so I can return the favor."

"Will do. Wish we could talk some more, but they're waiting to take you away."

"No problem. If I had lips I'd kiss you."

"Traddlemop."

Then they took her away. I didn't know what the others thought about the tears that trickled down my cheeks and didn't really give a shit.

Things went relatively well after that. It took about twelve hours to grab some sleep, refill our oxygen tanks from the shuttle's supply, and bury the pilots. The sun had just started to peek over the horizon when we started the service. The walkers were equipped with a variety of attachments, and what would have taken us hours they accomplished in a matter of minutes. The graves were laser-straight and perfectly aligned.

It was a strange funeral. The sun rose higher in the sky and sent long black fingers down across the plain. Eleven space-suited mourners sang "Amazing Grace" while five four-story-tall machines stood at attention. The sixth walker, the one controlled by Loni, served as the only pallbearer, lowering the space-suited pilots into their neatly excavated graves with slow, deliberate movements of her long, spindly arms.

Dawkins called for a moment of silence, and I wondered if anyone else was struck by the fact that not a single one of us had known the pilots, or what kind of people they'd been. And what, I wondered, was the difference between the cyborgs, who lived on after the death of everything but their brain tissue, and the pilots, who were gone wherever dead people go? Was that what we were? Chunks of brain tissue? And if so, what about me? Seeing as I had lost a goodly amount of mine, did that make me less of a person? My head started to hurt, and I let the questions drift.

And so it was that a few cubic yards of rocky red soil was pushed in on top of the pilots and carefully welded metal crosses were erected at the heads of their graves. They looked kind of lonely as we turned our backs on them and boarded the walkers. And I did manage to ride in Loni's machine, not that it made much difference, since the inside of one cargo space is pretty much like another.

The good news was that it took the walkers less than two hours to traverse the ground we had covered in six. The bad news was that the ride consisted of an unending series of jolts, each one of which threatened to drop my stomach through the bottom of my feet, or lift it up through the top of my head.

But all things come to an end, even bad things, and the ride was no exception. Unfortunately, however, the end of one bad thing can signal the start of another, and such was the case.

I know that the walkers intercepted the huge machine-city

called Roller Three, and were admitted via one of the hatchways provided for that purpose, but didn't actually witness what took place. For what seemed like obvious reasons, the cargo hold was not equipped with niceties like vid screens, and Loni was far too busy to provide a blow-by-blow description. So the first thing we saw was a pressurized vehicle bay, some tool-toting technoids, and the troops sent to pick me up. It took them about ten seconds to spot me, separate me from the rest of the group, and order me out of my suit.

The guards wore red berets with Marcorps Special Forces badges on them and were very, very good. I could commit guard-assisted suicide and nothing more. The smaller of the two, a woman with corporal's stripes, handed her weapon to a steroidal sidekick and moved to pat me down. Assuming I could take her, which was a lot of assuming, Frankenstein would put a dart through my heart. Not an especially attractive option.

The corporal finished her search, took two steps back, and allowed Frankenstein to slap the gun into her outstretched hand. It had the look and feel of a well-rehearsed drill. The weapon seemed to leap into the cutaway holster and snap itself in.

"Okay, Maxon. Head for door number two."

I looked. Door number two had a big numeral "2" painted on it so idiots like me could see it. I noticed there were no threats, no promises, just "head for door number two." The woman scared the hell out of me. I shuffled towards door number two. The greenie with the piercing blue eyes yelled something, but I wasn't sure what.

I was pretty good at slip-slide walking by now and managed to stay in contact with the oil-stained deck. It vibrated as Roller Three advanced over another half-inch of Martian soil. We passed through door number two and entered a hall that was wide enough to accommodate the machinery used to build it. Airtight doors lined both sides of the corridor and were closed against the possibility of a blowout. Each bore an electro-sign. Eventually, after a trip up multiple flights of stairs, and down what seemed like miles of heavily traveled corridors, legends like "Machine Shop" and "Cybernetics" gave way to more administrative titles like "Logistics" and "Records." The corporal ordered me to stop in front of a sign that read "Executive Offices."

Frankenstein frowned, punched a code into the keypad located by the door, answered a question over the intercom, and stood aside as the door opened. The corporal gestured for me to enter, and I obeyed. I saw a receptionist backed by an entire compartment full of freelance number-crunchers. Most were wired to their computers and didn't bother to look up as we entered. The receptionist was a scrawny little guy with an artificial arm. It whirred as he jerked his bionic thumb towards the other end of the room. "Park him in the conference room."

The corporal was not one to waste words. She motioned with her head. "Move."

I moved.

A weary-looking zombie sat chained to a console. A jumper cable connected his brain to a mini-comp. He followed our progress with dull, uninterested eyes. No one else even glanced in our direction.

It made me wonder if prisoners were so common that their comings and goings were regarded as normal, or were these men and women so dedicated to the Marscorp bottom line they cared for nothing else? Both possibilities were equally depressing.

The conference room door had been decorated with fake wood grain. It had peeled along the edges and I wanted to tear it off. The door slid out of the way and we stepped inside. I saw Sasha and felt my heart leap into my throat. She was alive! Tired, edgy, but alive!

In spite of the formal nod, and the noncommittal expression, I saw relief in her eyes. It made me feel warm inside.

The corporal gestured for me to take the chair next to Sasha, and I did. The room had no decorations to speak of and didn't need any. A large picture window took care of that. A dust storm moved across the distant horizon. It drew the eye like the flames in an old-fashioned fireplace, filtering the landscape through a reddish-brown haze, and shifting with the wind.

The door swished, and I turned in that direction. A man had entered. Either Mother Nature or the biosculptors had been very good to him. He had a handsome face, ruddy complexion, and snow-white hair. His body was tall and athletically graceful. Energy crackled around him. He smiled and I smiled back. It was impossible not to.

"Mr. Maxon! Ms. Casad! Thanks for coming." The way he said it removed us from the category of prisoners and made us feel like honored guests.

The man turned to the corporal and treated her to one of his high-voltage smiles. "Thanks, corporal. I'll take it from here." The corporal, trained killer that she was, smiled bashfully, said something incoherent, and pushed Frankenstein towards the door.

The man leaned across the tabletop to shake hands. His grip was cold and limp. I let go as quickly as I could. He smiled. "Howard Norton, General Manager, at your service."

"Max Maxon. Glad to meet you."

He turned to Sasha and offered his hand. "Ms. Casad. Welcome to Mars. How's your mother?"

Sasha looked hopeful. "She was fine the last time I talked with her. You know my mother?"

Norton nodded and sat down across from us. He leaned forward. A tidal wave of cologne rolled over me. "Yes, your mother and I worked on a project prior to the war. Different disciplines, of course, but she struck me as a competent scientist, and I was impressed by the quality of her ideas."

"Mom's impressive, all right," Sasha said evenly. "We are, or were, on our way to see her."

Norton nodded sympathetically. "Yes, I'm sorry about the ambush. Marscorp had nothing to do with it. While we are aware there are differences of opinion between Trans-Solar and the Protech Corporation, we have positive relationships with both companies, and would like to keep it that way. That's why we put the surviving Trans-Solar people on a ship and sent them back to Earth."

"And the greenies?"

Norton looked my way. The smile was predatory. "We have a labor shortage. The tree-huggers were convicted of assault and assigned to a variety of functions."

I nodded. "Such as hauling cyborgs across the surface of Mars."

Sasha raised an eyebrow but I chose to ignore it. Norton cleared his throat. "Yes, Marscorp would like to apologize for the unfortunate mix-up. Someone had the crazy idea that you were connected with the greenies. By the time my office learned of your whereabouts and sought to intervene, you had arrived at the crash site and were headed back. Safely, thank god."

I started to say something, started to object, but stopped when I saw Sasha frown. The signal was clear. Go along with the program and shut the hell up. I forced a smile. "Mistakes do happen."

"Exactly," Norton said smoothly. "Thanks for your understanding. Although Marscorp does not wish to take sides, we will do everything we can to smooth the way, and remove barriers that might otherwise prove troublesome."

We must have looked relieved. Norton smiled. "You might be interested to know that no less than *three* different parties inquired about your health immediately after the ambush."

Sasha beat me to the punch. "Who were they?"

Norton's eyes were icy blue. They twinkled merrily. "A representative from Trans-Solar, a woman since identified as a greenie sympathizer, and Colonel Charles Wamba, Mishimuto Marines retired. He claimed to be a friend of Mr. Maxon's."

The name had a familiar ring, but I couldn't place it. The idea that I might have a friend seemed strange indeed. Sasha looked at me and I looked at her. We needed help, and the choice seemed obvious. Colonel Charles Wamba.

11

"If you take care of the
city, it will take care of you."

*One of countless morale holos
set free to roam Roller Three's
corridors*

Your average corpie may be a money-sucking, power-crazed jerk, but they aren't necessarily stupid, and Roller Three proved it. After all, why build cities near natural resources, only to have the resources play out? Forcing the very ground travel you sought to avoid? Especially on a planet where travel consumed time, money, and lives? No, a mobile city made a lot of sense.

But, sensible though it may have been, Roller Three took some getting used to. It was on the lowest level referred to as "Deck One" where fusion-derived power fed gigantic drive wheels and steel blades funneled ore onto high-capacity conveyor belts.

Deck two was home to the massive crushers, sorters, mixers, and furnaces, where humans and androids worked to convert ore to finished metal.

Deck Three housed the multiplicity of machine shops, electronics labs, hydroponics equipment, and computer gear required to keep the whole complex running.

Deck Four was split between living quarters, office space, recreational facilities, cafeterias, a communications center, hospital, and the ever-so-pleasant jail.

And Deck Five, the topmost level, was given over to the landing strip, cranes, and other gear I had seen in the documentary. Or so our guide said, and I believed him.

He was tall by normal standards and came all the way up to my shoulder. His name was Burns. He had carefully combed hair, expensive clothes, and the sort of eager-beaver attitude that bosses love. He was a glorified gofer but hoped to be a lifer some day and never stopped trying. That's why Burns put all doubts aside and led two rather dubious VIP's down into the bowels of the beast, where the eccentric Colonel Wamba had taken up residence.

Conditions deteriorated as we journeyed downwards. Deck Three was first. I noticed the overhead was lower, the wood-grained plastic had given way to painted steel, and the temperature had risen. Tool heads conferred, androids hurried, and an atmosphere of frantic activity held sway. The feeling was reinforced by the chatter of power wrenches, the whine of lathes, the screech of saws, and the incessant smell of ozone. Burns mouthed words, but they were inaudible over the din.

Steel shook as we descended a flight of circular stairs. We were halfway down when someone yelled "Gangway!" and a man in a pressure suit pushed past. "Move, god damn it . . . we've got a stretcher coming through!"

I looked downwards and saw three men and a droid hoist a stretcher over their heads and start up the stairs. It wasn't easy. The stretcher cradled what looked like a load of raw meat with a hole where its mouth should have been. Pieces of bone stuck out of the meat, along with rock fragments and chunks of pressure suit. Tubes ran every which way and kept the thing alive. Words popped out of my mouth. "What happened?"

"The silly bastard dropped a wrench into the rock crusher and went in after it," the man said grimly. "He won't make that mistake again."

"But why?" I asked stupidly. "Wouldn't it have been better to let it go?"

The man shrugged. "Sure, except for the five grand the corpies would deduct from his pay."

"Five grand for a wrench?"

The smile was bitter. "Wrenches are expensive on Mars."

I looked at the stretcher. It was closer now. "But why come this way? An elevator would be faster."

"It sure would," the man agreed, "*if* they worked. The mining gear is repaired first. Lift tubes are towards the bottom of the list."

The stretcher party approached. The man motioned us to the rail. Bodies rubbed as the workers shuffled by.

The man turned, spit against the wall, and looked me in the eye. "Watch your step." He took the stairs two at a time.

I turned to Burns. "He says the elevators are broken. Is that true?"

Burns shrugged. "Sure, but so what? The exercise will do them good. Come on. Time's a-wasting."

I started to reply but found myself addressing the back of his head. That was when Sasha caught my eye and frowned. The message was clear. "Don't make waves." I swallowed my anger and followed Burns downwards.

If Deck Three was bad, Two was horrible. It was a short trip from the bottom of the stairs to the unisex locker room, where a heavily dented droid gave me a bright yellow pressure suit size XXXL.

Like most locker rooms, this one contained row after row of lockers and smelled like a jockstrap. A steady stream of workers entered. Their suits dripped water from the high-pressure spray room and left trails across the deck. Most stripped to their skivvies, checked their suits for wear, and headed for the showers. Others, more modest perhaps, got into their clothes and left. No one looked at us or said anything to us. The yellow suits marked us for what we were: tourists who, if not corpies themselves, were the next worst thing.

I struggled with the final seal on my suit, traded safety checks with Sasha, and lumbered after Burns. The inside of my suit smelled better than I did. I had caught a little bit of sleep after our interview with Norton but hadn't managed a shower.

Steam drifted away from the spray room. We followed Burns through the vapor and into a parallel corridor. It was lined with safety slogans and multilayered graffiti. The passageway ended in front of a tractor-sized lock. Five humans, two androids, and a utility bot waited to enter. They looked, then turned away. Burns spoke in my ear. "Ms. Casad, Mr. Maxon, how's it going?"

The words were out before I could stop them. "If we assume normal dreeble, and gardunk aterbers, the resulting krepper would be 2678.33."

Burns was as mystified as I was. "What was that?"

Sasha hurried to cover up. "We're fine, thank you. What comes next?"

As if to answer Sasha's question, a beacon flashed and a buzzer sounded in my helmet. It took a full minute for the lock to iris open. Six filth-covered androids and two equally dirty humans stumbled out. Even the droids looked tired. They headed for a washdown while we entered the lock and watched the hatch close behind us. When it opened, it was into a hellish world of never-ending conveyor belts, huge sorters, massive crushers, gas-injected furnaces, and molten metal. All operating in what seemed like silence at the speeds made possible by computers and low-gravity refining techniques. It seemed as if the entire complex was on eternal fast forward.

Burns led us through a canyon of sealed machinery, past a river of pulverized rock, and out into a valley of man-made lava. It moved snakelike through the artificial gullies provided for its use and caused the atmosphere to shimmer with radiated heat. Burns spent a lot of time waving at workers who didn't wave back.

Then the vast bay was behind us, and the deck vibrated in sympathy to the nearest engine room. We entered an alcove. It was empty except for the layer of soil that covered everything and an empty cable spool. "This is as far as I go," Burns said happily. "The colonel owns sixty thousand shares of company stock. He can live anywhere he wants and chose this. Nobody knows why. Be careful, and watch for snakes."

"Snakes?" What the hell did that mean? I looked to see if he was kidding, but the visor obstructed his face. Sasha moved towards the stairs and I hurried to get there first. The stairs turned in on themselves and trembled under our weight. Darkness engulfed us.

Then, just as I fumbled with my helmet light, a pair of ruby-red eyes appeared. They blinked and moved closer. I reached for a weapon that wasn't there and found the switch. A cone of hard, white light located the snake and pinned it in place. The creature had a triangular head, flared hood, and long, sinuous body. It looked like a snake but was actually robotic. Its mouth opened, fangs gleamed, and a man spoke in my helmet.

"You're a sight for sore eyes, Maxon . . . welcome to Mars." Things happened in my head. Dreams flickered, voices spoke, and pain lanced the center of my brain. The voice spoke again. "Follow Kaa. He'll bring you to my quarters."

I looked at Sasha. She shrugged. We followed the snake. Light gleamed off metallic scales as the robo-serpent turned and slithered downwards. It wove in and out of the rail like a shuttle on a loom. I stayed well back, taking my time and feeling my way. A pair of luminescent eyes peered down from a ledge, blinked, and disappeared. Dirt rained down on my helmet.

The stairs ended, and a matrix of crisscrossed laser beams materialized around us. It was part of a security system, and we must have passed the test, because a blastproof door slid open. Kaa reared back, hissed through my helmet speakers, and swayed as we passed. The hatch closed and we found ourselves in a lock. It had been spacious at some point in the past but was now half filled with junk.

A robotic mouse scurried across my boots, squeaked, and scooted under a box of mother boards. The lock cycled open. I looked at Sasha, shrugged, and made my way down the tunnel. There were alcoves to the right and left. All were full.

Whatever else Wamba was, or had been, he was someone with an affinity for junk. Not just *any* junk, but robotic junk, of every conceivable shape and size. Walking through the passageway was like touring the android equivalent of a meat packing plant. Robotic cadavers were piled every which way, their arms, legs and torsos all akimbo, their long-dead sensors staring blankly from the shadows. One of them sat up, tilted its head to one side, and opened its eyes. The voice grated in my helmet. "Stop. Remove your suits. Leave them here. Have a nice day. Stop. Remove your suits. Leave them here. Have a nice day . . ."

We did as the cadaver ordered and continued on our way. The

tunnel came to an end and opened into a large chamber. It, like the
alcoves before it, was nearly filled with robo parts. Only these had
been sorted into hundreds of carefully labeled bins and were stored
in the racks that lined three of the four walls. An enormous drive
gear obscured most of the fourth wall. It moved an inch at a time.
The "Lube Here" sign was self-explanatory. Less understandable
were the things that hopped, walked, crawled, slid, and flew about
the room.

Some, like Kaa, and the mouse I'd had seen earlier, looked like
Earth animals. Others, like the foot-high pogo stick that bounced
across the deck in front of me, or the gossamer-winged flyer that
lit on my shoulder, were entirely fanciful. And there were
hundreds, maybe thousands, of them, all moving around the
compartment in concert with whatever propulsion system and
programing they'd been given.

And at the center of all this movement, on a dais that was part
control console and part throne, sat something that made me seem
normal by comparison.

It had been human once; evidence of that could be seen in the
kinky black hair, the brown, almost black skin, and the eyes that
glowed like coals in deeply shadowed sockets.

But the machinery that had been built around it came close to
obscuring the thing's human origins, and it was only through an
act of will that I was able to think of it as a "he." It was, I decided,
only right and proper that the one person in the universe who
considered himself to be my friend qualified as a freak as well.

He regarded me silently, as if aware of my emotions and waiting
for me to deal with them. His head, or what was left of it, was
surrounded by a metal cowling. A variety of lenses had been
mounted on the sides of the cowling and could be moved by means
of servo-controlled arms. His neck, shoulders, and arms were his
own, but surgical steel had replaced most of his chest. A metal
housing stood in for his hips, and tracks replaced his legs. They
whirred and threw up roostertails of reddish soil as he came down
the ramp to meet me.

Dozens of small robots hopped, scurried, and jumped out of the
way. Something the size and shape of a centipede squeaked and
was crushed under Wamba's tracks. The colonel's eyes locked
onto mine like laser beams, and his grip was strong. His voice was

identical to the one that spoke through Kaa. "Damn, you look good. I missed you."

Suddenly, and much to my surprise, I was overcome by emotion. It was as if something deep inside me recognized the cyborg and felt a kinship for him. I stepped between his tracks, put my arms around his shoulders, and gave him a hug. He hugged me back, and it felt good. Good to be valued, good to be welcome, good to be missed. Even if I couldn't remember who the hell he was. I released him and took three steps backwards.

Machinery whined as Wamba turned towards Sasha. "Hello, Ms. Casad, and welcome to my humble abode."

I had never seen the kid look shy, but she did now. "Thank you. It's nice to be here."

Wamba smiled. "I doubt that, but it's nice of you to say so. Now, tell me about the ambush, who staged it, and why."

I looked at Sasha. She managed to avoid my eyes. It was as if something kept her from talking about what we'd been through. Something she knew and I didn't. It made me angry, so I started at the beginning and spilled my guts. Wamba listened without comment. Finally, when all the words had been said, he nodded.

"You are, as my daddy liked to say, standing in deep weeds. And, while I don't know what's going on any more than you do, I might be able to offer some clues."

The cyborg paused for a moment and looked me in the eye. "You don't remember me, do you?"

I hung my head in shame. "No, I don't."

Machinery whined as his head nodded up and down. "I thought not. You were one of the craziest and most insubordinate officers I ever had the pleasure to command. And you're, well, different somehow. Changed in ways I can't quite put a finger on. What *do* you remember?"

I looked to Sasha for help, but her one good eye was focused on a spot three feet over Wamba's head. She made no attempt to help or interfere. "Nothing. Nothing prior to my discharge, anyway."

Wamba nodded as though he had expected as much. "Let me tell you a story. A story about the last time I saw you. We drew a mission, one with lots of hair on it, and were headed for a research station known as T-12. It was right in the middle of the asteroid belt and very well defended. There were three boats in all. We drew straws. You pulled the first, Captain Daw drew the second, and I came last. You led us in . . ."

My head began to throb, a door creaked open, and the dreams returned. Wamba's voice droned on, but I was somewhere in the past, living it, feeling it, *being* it.

The ejection tube worked the way it was supposed to and blasted us away from the ship. Stars whirled, then stabilized as I brought the battle suit under control and oriented myself to the target. It looked like a mountain that had been plucked from the Himalayas and set free in space. Sunlight rippled across the planetoid's surface as it tumbled end over end. I saw light glint off metal and felt something heavy fall into my stomach. Even the best suits leak heat, and I could damned near feel their missile launchers swivel in my direction. I triggered the command freq and gave the command.

"Go!"

The team arrowed in like sharks in search of fresh meat. I was vaguely aware that Daw and Wamba had cleared their ships and were headed in the same direction. It made damned little difference, though, since we were committed. The Loot would extract us if she lived long enough to do so, or we'd wait for relief. Not a pleasant thought.

A fire requires oxygen, and a battle suit contains damned little thanks to the endless vacuum around it. So the fireball that consumed Private Naglie lasted less than a second. I swore, but gave thanks too, knowing his death would give the team another surge of adrenaline. Adrenaline they needed to survive.

A buzzer buzzed, and my heads-up display (HUD) indicated the tool heads were coming out to meet us. The gunny confirmed it.

"M-dog two to M-dog one. We have four-zero, repeat, four-zero T-heads outbound our sector. Over."

Wamba had a command freq that could override the rest of us. He used it. "B-dog one to M-dog one. Team two owns twenty right. You take twenty left. Team three will cover. Over."

I switched to the team freq. "M-dog one to M-dog team. Twenty right belong to us. Three will cover. Mark 'em and take 'em. Over."

Though not supposed to take an active role, I had no desire to watch while my team fought. I picked a blip, marked it as my own, and checked to make sure that the rest were accounted for.

The tracking tone went off. A missile was headed my way. I dumped chaff, hit the electronic countermeasures (ECM) booster switch, and did a backward flip.

Bodmods Inc., a wholly owned subsidiary of General Dynamics, makes one helluva battle suit, but Krupp *"We arm business so they can do business"* Industries makes some top-of-the-line antipersonnel missiles. One of them followed me down. I spent a fraction of a second wishing I had a suit with more offensive weaponry, realized it was a waste of time, and launched a decoy.

The decoy was the size and shape of a pocket stylus and had been programed to radiate heat, radio, and radar signals identical to those emitted by my battle suit. My onboard computer dumped ninety per cent power and waited to see what would happen. The missile bought it, chased the decoy, and exploded.

Thus freed, I entered the battle sim, checked to make sure that my team had held its own, and searched for my target. He or she was busy pushing a deactivated M-dog suit up the seam between Daw's team and mine. They might have been trying to fool us, or shield themselves from attack, or who knows what. My battle sim informed me that the suit belonged to Private Kim, a tough little troop who'd been brought up in the lower levels of the London Urboplex, and played folk songs on the harmonica.

Using Kim's body as a shield pissed me off, and I fed the T-head's coordinates to one of our free-floating missile racks. They had been ejected at the same time we were, and mounted four missiles each. I knew the rack would draw fire the moment I launched, so there was no point in conserving ordnance. I put two missiles on the tool head, one on a blip I wasn't sure of, and one on T-12's antenna farm. I knew the strikers would destroy the fourth missile long before it reached the asteroid's surface, but knew the effort would cost them two or three missiles. Missiles they wouldn't be able to launch at me or my team.

I gave the order to fire. The missiles left the launcher and made dotted lines across my sim. Both the tool head and what remained of Kim's body vanished in a cartoonlike ball of flame. The enemy suit, a ridiculous-looking stick figure, disappeared a fraction of a second later. The launch rack, plus the last two missiles it had fired, were destroyed moments after that.

I switched to the big picture. The first thing that jumped out at me was that most of the strikers were dead. They were pretty good for amateurs, but we were pros, and that makes a difference. Or so the company hopes. Most of their suits, or what was left of their suits, had started the long, slow drift to nowhere. But five or six of the bastards had taken refuge behind a large chunk of free-floating rock. I saw a missile explode against the boulder's outer surface and push it towards the asteroid beyond. The tool heads answered with a crew-served laser cannon, and the battle continued.

I frowned. The team should have bypassed the rock rats and pushed for the asteroid itself. Daw's squad was damned near there. I checked, saw the gunny's light had gone out, and understood what had happened. The gunny was dead, and it was payback time. I chinned the mike.

"M-dog to M-dog team. Break, I repeat, break. You know the objective. Take it. That's an order. Over."

Sergeant Habib had filled the gap left by the gunny . . . or had tried to. He knew things were out of hand and said so.

"M-dog five to M-dog one. Sorry, sir. Breaking now. Over."

The battle sim took twenty cubic miles of space and compressed it to a single 3-D image. I saw the team break, re-form, and arrow towards the target. It looked as if they were inches apart, but at least a half-mile separated them.

I switched freq's, called the Loot, and applied full power. The team would land on T-12's surface in nine, maybe ten, minutes. I wanted to arrive at the same time they did. The Loot had survived, so far anyway, and sounded solid.

"Dodger-one to M-dog one. Shoot."

"I have five or six bad guys hiding behind a rock. Over."

"Roger that, M-dog one. Light the rock. Over."

I checked to make sure my team was clear, "lit" the rock on my sim and knew the Loot had it too. The response came right away.

She came out of the sun, fed the strikers a missile, and pulled out with a pair of surface-to-air (SAM) missiles hot on her tail. I wanted to watch, wanted to see her escape, but kept my eyes focused on the target. The Loot's ship-to-ship ordnance was a hundred times larger than the little squirts we used, and the explosion was bright enough to darken my visor. The gunny would be happy. It wasn't much as trade-offs go, but it was better than nothing.

The asteroid was closer now, close enough to fill my vision and block the star field beyond. The rock had some spin, but not a lot, so the landing would be soft.

But staying down, especially during combat, would be more difficult. Just one overenthusiastic leap and I'd be orbiting T-12 like a target balloon. Yeah, I could blast my way down, but that would take time. Time enough to track my ass and blow it clean off. Another unpleasant thought.

The strikers were out in force. Strafing runs by the Loot and a buddy softened the bastards up but antipersonnel missiles, laser beams, and bullets stuttered up to meet us nonetheless.

The major lit a sector and ordered us to converge on it. Daw's team would arrive first and have the dubious honor of securing the landing zone (LZ).

We were closer now, close enough for an honest-to-god visual, and I didn't like what I saw. Roughly half my team, about fifteen effectives, had made it through. One of them, a trooper named Raskin, took a hit and spun out of control. A vapor plume outgassed and disappeared as the suit sealed itself. A buddy called him.

"Hey, Raskin! Can you hear me? Pull out, pull out or you're going to . . ."

Raskin hit the ground, bounced, and came apart as the strikers hit him with everything they had.

I swore, added my fire to that generated by the rest of the team, and cut power. We drifted in like those puffy things that dandelions produce in the spring. Fountains of dust spurted upwards as our boots hit, paused for a moment, and drifted sideways.

Fire lanced in from three sides, and what was left of Daw's team did their best to cover us. I slo-moed my way to a crater and resisted the temptation to pull the edges in around me. I had elbowed my way to the rim and was peeking over the edge when something nudged the side of my helmet. A voice filled my ears. "Maxon?"

I damned near jumped out of my skin before I realized Wamba had arrived and placed his helmet next to mine. The sun reflected off his visor and his eyes. "Sorry, sir. You scared the shit out of me."

I felt Wamba grin. "Serves your ass right for sleeping on duty. Gather your team. We came to take T-12, and we're going to do it. Capish?"

"Yes, sir."

"Good. You lost about fifty per cent of your team, ditto for Daw, but about seventy-five per cent of my people made it through. We'll attack the dome. You hold the LZ and have the coffee ready when we get back."

I looked, saw he was serious, and shook my head. "Sorry, Major. No damned way. We're coming with you."

Wamba looked me in the eye. "Captain, am I to understand that you're refusing a direct order?"

I nodded. "Yes, sir. You sure as hell are, sir."

Wamba grinned. "That's what I thought. You're a dumb shit, Maxon, but a brave dumb shit, and what more can the share owners ask? Come on. The dome awaits."

There was a reason why the major was a major and not a captain like me. He had smarts, lots of smarts, and knew how to use them. He had analyzed the defensive fire, identified three sectors where it was relatively light, and picked the one that was *inside* the tool-head perimeter.

Yeah, that meant we had enemy troops on three sides, and T-12's main dome on the other, but it also meant that about a third of the strikers couldn't fire without hitting the dome—a dome built to withstand normal wear and tear, but not the rigors of combat.

So, while they spent time trying to readjust their lines of fire, we leapfrogged towards the dome. It was a standard tactic drilled into us from our first days in the crotch. The evolution begins with the formation of dispersed square—dispersed to lessen the casualties caused by modern weapons, and square because squared-off corners place attackers in a crossfire. During large unit actions, such a square might be spread out over five or ten square miles and would have been impossible were it not for the battle sims that allowed each trooper to monitor his or her position relative to everyone else's.

Then, while the even-numbered troopers provided covering fire, the odd-numbered troopers executed a two-mile jump. Once on the ground, it was their turn to provide covering fire, and so forth, until the entire unit had reached its objective. So that's how we leapfrogged our way to the dome. Yeah, we lost four troopers, all caught at or near the apex of their jumps, but most of them made it.

The domies did what they could, and sent volunteers out to stop us, but they were like sheep to the slaughter. We went through them like a knife through warm butter, forced the lock, and made our way inside. And that's when things went black, when the memories disappeared, when the door slammed shut. The nothingness was so sudden, so complete, that it seemed as if I had died in the dome, except that Wamba continued to talk. But what about the darkness? Then I realized that my eyes were closed. I opened them. Light flooded in. I blinked. Wamba smiled and nodded sympathetically.

"You remembered, didn't you? But the memory ended at the lock. And that makes sense, because that's where the tool heads cleaned our clocks."

Machinery whirred, and Wamba shook his head. "It was *my* fault. I assumed we had neutralized the majority of their forces. That the worst we'd encounter were some poorly trained nerds. What I didn't know was that a team of commandos had been sent to stiffen T-12's security and help the tech types evacuate. The only reason they were inside rather than outside was the shortage of battle suits. So they waited until all of us were inside, secured the lock, and let us have it. You charged them, and killed some too, before a man in an exoskeleton pulled you down."

Wamba shrugged philosophically. "I got mine about thirty seconds later. You can see what it did to me."

Thoughts burbled through my mind like coffee in an old-fashioned percolator. I felt my hand touch the top of my head and couldn't remember telling it to do so. The metal felt cold. "So, I was hit in the head?"

Wamba frowned. "No, that's the weird part. The guy in the exoskeleton peeled you like an orange. I was kinda busy at the time, but it seems to me that you eeled your way out of the battle suit, stood up, and took a slug in the chest. The skull plate doesn't make sense."

I opened my shirt and looked down at the patch of scar tissue on the right side of my chest. It was the size of an antique quarter, slightly puckered, and rougher than the surrounding skin. I had spent hours staring at it, wondering what had happened to me, but blocked by the darkness that still obliterated my memories.

I looked at Sasha and had one of those sudden flashes of intuition that come from time to time. None of this was new to her. She had known from the start. I didn't know *how* I knew it, or *why* I knew it, but I did. I could *see* it in her carefully neutral expression, *feel* it in the way she looked at me, and *hear* it in her voice. It was as if she already knew *what* had happened but wondered about the details. Her voice was filled with wonder. "But *how*? How could he survive?"

A robot scampered into Wamba's lap. He stroked it like the cat it resembled. "He survived the same way I did. The tool heads were assholes, but there were compassionate assholes, and had some damned good doctors. I spent the next three years in their hospitals and always assumed Maxon had as well."

Three years? Had I been in their hands that long? The information had been available to me all along, buried in the records I couldn't read, and obscured by the darkness that shrouded my thoughts. And what about the metal plate? Where had it come from? And who was responsible? My thoughts whirled and emptiness filled my stomach. All my assumptions, all my beliefs about who and what I was had been torn apart. I wanted answers, and Sasha was the logical place to start. But I had questioned her to no avail. No, it would take time and patience, but it was a long way to Europa Station, and my opportunity would come. I broke the growing silence. "Thanks, Major. You opened some important doors for me."

Wamba smiled and I realized what a handsome man he had been. "You're welcome, and it's 'Colonel.' A silly distinction unless you earned it the way I did." He gestured to his surroundings. "That and my kingdom are all I have left."

I nodded and glanced at Sasha. She used her one remaining eye to gesture towards the entryway. I took the hint. "Well, thanks again. We've got a long way to go, so . . ."

Wamba held up a hand in protest. "You must accept a gift.

Something to remind you of me and help along the way." He clapped his hands. "Joy! Where are you? Come to Poppa!"

A small door opened towards the front of his undercarriage. A flash of ebony caught my eye as something twirled its way into the light and struck a dancer's pose. She—for there was no doubt about her sex—was the only android in the room that had been fashioned from black metal. She was perfectly formed and stood twelve inches tall. Her face bore the slightly mischievous expression of an elf come to life. A mane of black hair cascaded down around shapely shoulders and was captured in a pink ribbon. The rest of her obviously female body was smooth and shiny, with no sign of the sensors, joints, and drive units common to less sophisticated androids.

No, this was a work of art, and it showed in the way Wamba looked at her. There was pride in his eyes, and love as well, for this was his finest creation. A surrogate daughter? Lover? It made little difference. Whatever the android was to Wamba, she seemed to know how much he admired her and drank it in.

Music came from somewhere and Joy began to move, running at first, then launching herself into a dizzying series of forward flips, twisting in mid-air, touching the ground, and going airborne again. There were cartwheels, somersaults, and dance steps, all in time with the music, all done with amazing perfection, until one last run in which she executed a series of backward flips, stumbled, and landed on her ass. Mars gravity reduced the impact, but feedback circuits fed her the robotic equivalent of pain. Her disappointment was clear to see. But she picked herself up, bowed in our direction, and scrambled onto Wamba's lap. The mechanical cat hissed its disapproval, jumped to the floor, and stalked away.

"So," Wamba inquired eagerly, "what do you think?"

"I think she's marvelous," I said honestly. "Absolutely incredible."

"She's beautiful," Sasha added sincerely. "Like a doll come to life."

The subject of all this praise beamed with obvious pleasure, and so did Wamba. "Thank you. I was an engineer prior to the war and have lots of spare time." He gestured towards the robots that continued to glide, roll, crawl and hop all over the room. "Joy is different from the rest. Do you know why?"

I took a shot. "She has feelings?"

Wamba shook his head. "No, not in the actual sense anyway, although I'll be damned if I could tell you how the simulated emotions she feels are any different from the supposedly real ones that we experience."

I was still working on that when Sasha spoke.

"The difference is that Joy can make mistakes."

Wamba pointed a finger in Sasha's direction. "Bingo. And that's one of the things that makes humans unique, isn't it? The capacity to make mistakes."

I thought about T-12, of what had happened there, and knew which mistake Wamba meant. He nodded agreeably, stroked the android's back, and looked down into her liquid brown eyes. "Go with Maxon, Joy. Make him happy and do what you can to keep him alive."

Something passed between them at that moment—something that looked a lot like love, but couldn't have been, since robots don't feel.

Joy climbed up to Wamba's shoulder, kissed his cheek, and slid back down. She jumped to the floor, dodged a mechanical dog, and ran in my direction. I felt my trousers slip half an inch downwards as she grabbed a pants leg and pulled herself upwards. Tiny hands fumbled with my jacket pocket, released the snap, and held the flap up. Long black legs flashed as she climbed inside. I looked at Wamba. "I could never accept such a gift, Colonel. Call her back."

Wamba smiled sadly and shook his head. "What's done is done, and there's no going back. Take care of yourself, Max, and let me know how things turn out."

I considered hugging him but decided on a salute instead. It felt natural, somehow, and very right. He returned it, smiled his broken smile, and turned away. Kaa met us at the lock, and Burns led us up towards Deck Four. Joy felt warm and wiggled in my pocket.

12

"Unauthorized personnel will be
prosecuted to the full extent of
the law."

*A sign posted in locks one through
twelve of the Mgundo Tug and Barge
Company's Hull 264*

Ships have names, but barges don't. Don't ask why . . . it's one
of those traditions spacers like, because it makes their profession
more romantic. It seems silly somehow, especially when the barge
is a hundred times larger than the ship that pushes it around, but
that's the way it is. Ask, and spacers will feed you some bull about
how a ship has a soul, and a barge doesn't, whereas the only *real*
difference is that ships have propulsion systems and barges don't,
or so it seems to me.

This particular barge was cylindrical in shape and at least three
miles long. Numbers, each of which was white and about three
stories tall, slipped by as our shuttle made its way towards what I
assumed was the bow. One of them, a "4," was cratered where

143

something had hit it. My stomach contracted. A meteorite? Traveling at what? Twenty miles a second? Whipping out of nowhere to hammer the barge?

No, I told myself, chances were the crater had been caused by something more prosaic. A docking accident or a collision with another barge, perhaps.

Whatever the cause, the crater gave way to an almost featureless gray hull and disappeared behind us. The barge did have some solar arrays and a small antenna farm, but nothing like the maze of sensors, duct work, and other installations that crowded the skin of the average ship. But so what? It didn't matter as long as the barge was well built and headed in the right direction. The "right direction" being defined as the asteroid belt, since passenger ships bound for Europa Station were way out of our price range.

Sasha resourceful as always, had rummaged through some of the habitat's seedier dives until she found a half-stoned shipping agent willing to accept half fare in return for a ride on the barge. A ride that, while illegal, and minus the comforts of a liner, would be quiet and peaceful.

Sasha painted a glowing picture. Rather than work as we had aboard the *Red Trader,* and kowtow to the likes of Killer, we would eat and sleep our way to the belt, grab some new transportation, and arrive on Europa Station in tip-top shape. I should have known better.

We sat three abreast with Sasha occupying the jump seat in the middle. Our pilot was a sallow little man with a pitted face. The green, yellow, and red half-light filled the craters with darkness and made the condition seem even worse. His eyes pecked at the readouts while his hands jumped from one control to the next. "You be ready now . . . I can stop for two, maybe three minutes. Any more and the tug crew will get suspicious."

I knew problems could result from the fact that the tug crew wasn't aware of us but wasn't smart enough to know what they were. Which just goes to prove that ignorance isn't necessarily bliss.

The pilot touched a series of keys. The shuttle slowed relative to the barge, tractor beams made contact, pulled the smaller vessel into place, and held it against a lock. Metal clanged and a motor whined. The pilot swiveled towards Sasha and rubbed thumb against fingers. Sasha nodded, pulled a roll of currency out of an inside pocket, and dropped it into his hand. The pilot slipped the rubber band off, counted out loud, and nodded his satisfaction. ". . . One thousand eight, one thousand nine, two K right on the nose. Grab your gear and haul ass."

We hurried to comply. Sasha went first and I followed. I had released my harness, floated free, and was pulling myself towards the stern when the pilot grabbed my ankle. "Hey, chrome-dome."

I looked back over my shoulder. "Yeah?"

"The barge is loaded with all sorts of stuff, including crystal generators."

"So?"

"So, the generators don't work worth shit during zero gee. Makes the crystals come out all weird or something. That means the tug crew's gonna put some spin on the moment they break orbit. The results could bust your butt."

"Thanks for the tip."

The pilot grinned. "Hitched a ride once myself. Nobody told me. Now get the hell off my shuttle."

I nodded and propelled myself down the short passageway. There were equipment racks, padded corners, and lockers from which most but not all of the uniformly olive drab paint had been worn away, leaving patches of shiny metal.

Sasha had transferred most of our supplies to the shuttle's lock, and I was surprised at how bulky they were. Our food was concentrated but still took up a lot of space, as did the first aid kit, a cube reader, and our clothes. I was worried about water but Sasha had assured me there was plenty on board.

And so it was that we sealed ourselves into the lock, waited for pressures to equalize, and watched the hatch iris open. It took about fifteen seconds for the airtight door to open all the way. The adjoining lock was larger and padded to protect it from damage. We pushed our duffel bags through and followed with our bodies. My boots had barely cleared the hatch when motors whined and the opening closed. A few moments later we heard a thud and felt the hull vibrate as the shuttle pushed itself away. We were alone. Or supposed to be, anyway.

A duffel bag hit me in the nose. I pushed it away. The suction pulled a piece of paper in front of my nose. I knew what it was before I grabbed it. A Mars Bar wrapper. I held it out for Sasha to examine. "What's this?"

She looked defensive. "The tug crew ran a check on this tub yesterday. One of them left it."

Spacers are a tidy bunch—they have to be—so I had doubts about her theory but knew better than to pursue it. Sasha would stick to her point of view until forced to change. That reminded me of someone else I'd known, but I couldn't remember who.

Joy had agreed to maintain a low profile aboard the shuttle, but the promise had expired. She floated free of my pocket and peppered us with questions.

"Where are we? What's going on? Why is Sasha holding that wrapper?" It was like dealing with an articulate six-year-old.

I did my best to answer Joy's questions while trying to capture a duffel bag under each arm and maintain my equilibrium all at the same time. I handled the zero-gee stuff better than I had at the beginning of the trip but was clumsy compared to Sasha. She took pity on me and grabbed the second bag in addition to her own. That left the emergency pressure suits we had liberated from Marscorp. They had been duct taped together and were floating just below the overhead. I was about to reach for them when Joy launched herself off my shoulder. "Don't worry about the suits! I can handle them."

And handle them she did, using a combination of zero-gee savvy and some highly skilled gymnastics.

Air hissed as the inner hatch irised open. Joy pushed herself away from a storage locker and drifted through the aperture. I formed words but didn't get them out in time to do any good. My stomach muscles tightened. She would draw fire if someone was waiting on the other side. Nothing happened. I heaved a sigh of relief and made a note to speak with her later. Yes, she was an android, but with a difference. Maybe it was the fact that she'd been a present, or maybe it was her pseudo-personality, but the result was the same. I liked Joy and would be sorry if she were hurt.

I passed through the hatch next, towing the duffel bag with one hand and holding my weapon with the other. I noticed that Sasha made a point of leaving her gun in its holster. I tried a flip, hoped to land feet first, and hit the bulkhead with my back. Sasha laughed, did what I had tried to do, and hung there with a smirk on her face.

I looked both ways, made sure the corridor was clear, and holstered my weapon. It wouldn't hurt to have a free hand.

Joy was disgustingly cheerful. "Hey, this is fun! Where do we go? This way or that way?"

Our head swiveled as Sasha and I considered the alternatives. There wasn't much difference. The passageway was sufficiently wide to accommodate a standard autoloader or a train of power pallets. And, judging from the longitudinal marks that scored the walls, a good deal of cargo had been hauled through this corridor. Though pretty much interchangeable during zero-gee conditions, the distinctions between overhead, bulkheads, and deck were more meaningful when gravity was present.

The deck, or what would be a deck during a normal gravity situation, was covered with heavy-duty mesh. Conduit and cable snaked along below.

The overhead was comparatively smooth, interrupted by little more than rectangular glow panels and a recessed track. Hundreds on hundreds of vertical ridges gave the bulkheads an organic look, as if we were inside a worm, or a giant serpent. The intent was obvious. By grabbing the ridges with our hands, or pushing on them with our feet, zero-gee pedestrians like ourselves could make pretty good time.

The bulkheads had other features as well, including emergency com sets, surveillance cameras, fire-fighting equipment, and slots where one could escape an oncoming cargo train. Arrows pointed in both directions and words announced possible destinations. I tried to read them and was thrilled to find that I could. The first set said, "Holds 1-12," and the second set said, "Holds 13-24."

It went without saying that someone who had legitimate business aboard the barge would know where they were headed. I didn't, but Sasha did, or pretended to. "The shipping agent said that holds one through twelve would be crammed with cargo modules. Let's try thirteen through twenty-four."

I nodded, motioned for Joy to stay behind me, and was about to launch myself in the proper direction, when something whooshed over my head. It came and went so quickly that it took me a moment to realize that whatever it was had traveled via the recessed channel. A small robot, perhaps? Rushing from one end of the vessel to the other?

I looked at Sasha, she looked at me, and both of us shrugged. The channel and whatever it was that traveled within it seemed harmless enough and could be investigated later. We needed to get where we were going, and get there fast, or we would suffer what could be painful consequences.

I repositioned my feet, pushed off, and coasted for twenty feet. The ridges were spaced about six inches apart, which placed one wherever you needed it, and a sort of rhythm emerged. Push, coast, push. Push, coast, push. Over and over again as we made our way down the corridor. It became kind of hypnotic after a while, so much so that my senses were dulled, and it was Joy who gave the alarm. "Look! Something's coming!"

I looked, and what I saw scared the hell out of me. It turned from a dot to a blob to an oncoming train in a matter of seconds. The drive unit had diagonal yellow and black stripes across its front end, mounted no less than four flashing red beacons, and filled the passageway from side to side and top to bottom. Rollers kept the vehicle from scraping against the bulkheads and explained the wear marks I'd noticed earlier. The train, if that's what it should be called, was making a good fifty or sixty miles an hour. And why not? The humans were gone, as far as the barge and its computers knew, so cargo could be redistributed by the fastest and most efficient means possible. Sasha was first to get the words out of her mouth. "The next niche! Move!"

It felt crazy to launch ourselves at the oncoming train, but the distance between us and the niche ahead was less than the distance between us and the niche behind. I put all the strength I had into the push, but the air felt as thick as old-fashioned molasses. The deck and bulkheads moved with maddening slowness, and the stripes hurtled towards me with what seemed like unbelievable speed. Seconds seemed to stretch into minutes as I willed myself forward. I saw Sasha make her way into the niche, followed by Joy. Good! Someone would live, someone would . . .

The *Beep! Beep! Beep!* of the warning buzzer filled my ears and drove all the remaining thoughts out of my mind. I felt the outermost wave of displaced air touch my face, waited for the mind-numbing impact, and felt a hand grab my jacket. The beeping sound turned into a long, thin scream as the train roared by. The heel of my left boot bounced off the side of a cargo module and threw me deeper into the niche. My head hit the bulkhead with a distinct clang. Anyone who had a full load of brains would've been injured. I was momentarily dizzy but otherwise fine. The train was gone as quickly as it came. I looked at Sasha. "Thanks. You saved my life."

There it was again. The flash of compassion, of caring, quickly hidden by a shrug and a flip reply. "It was my turn."

We paid attention after that, pushing our way down the corridor, watching for oncoming trains. That's how I spotted the change in what had been dull uniformity. The difference was hard to describe, except to say that the lighting was different, and the bulkheads had been replaced by a vague haziness. But the area acquired definition as we moved closer, rolled into focus like a carefully adjusted lens, and became a vast open space.

The bulkheads fell away and the corridor became a sky bridge that spidered out over a large cargo bay. It was filled with bushes. Hundreds, maybe thousands of them. They were lushly green, almost identical in size and shape, and heavy with purple blossoms. Light glittered off tiny wings as a host of robotic insects flitted from one blossom to the next, spreading pollen, or doing whatever it was they had been designed to do. I noticed that the bushes, and the containers they sat in, were secured to the deck.

My stomach flip-flopped as I drifted out and over the abyss. Heights don't bother me, but floating does. I wouldn't fall, not till gravity had been restored, but I wouldn't be able to go anywhere either. Not unless the air-conditioned breeze blew me against something solid. I made a grab for the railing, got it, and checked to see if Sasha was watching. She wasn't, thank god, and neither was Joy. Both had ignored the view and were well on their way to reaching the other side.

I followed, careful to plan my movements, and was grateful when the corridor closed around me. We had gone about fifty feet down the passageway when the vertical access tubes appeared and the hall ended. That was interesting, but not half as interesting as the foot-high letters that spelled out the words, "Corpies Suck!" followed by some incomprehensible lines and squiggles. It didn't take an art historian to see that the artist had used some sort of marker rather than spray paint. I turned towards Sasha. "The tug crew, I suppose?"

She gave me a dirty look and pushed herself towards the access tubes. "Come on. Let's camp on the main deck. I'd rather look at bushes than metal bulkheads."

That seemed reasonable, so I tagged along. Sasha had rigged a way to tow her duffel bag one after the other. The second one bounced off the coaming as she pushed herself down through the tube. Joy shoved her cases into position, waved cheerfully, and dropped feet first into the tube.

That left me. I pushed myself into position, planned my approach descent, and "climbed" down the rungs intended for use with gravity. It worked pretty well.

I was concerned about where Sasha would lead us once we arrived on, or in this case near, the main deck. I needn't have been. In spite of the fact that she had pooh-poohed my concerns regarding security, the girl had good instincts, and headed for the point where the bulkhead intersected the vessel's hull. While not exactly a fortress, this would protect our backs, and allow space for a kill zone between our quarters and what I increasingly thought of as the forest.

Though not as tall as your average tree, the bushes *did* tower over me, or would have if I'd been standing rather than floating. That made them a forest, as did the brooding feel that surrounded them, and the rather large amount of space that they occupied.

A cloud of glittering robo-insects rose into the air, hovered for a moment, and settled back down. Light glinted off their silvery wings and made them look like branch-grown diamonds.

It was then that I noticed the fragrance that drifted up around us. It smelled good at first, like perfume on a high-priced hooker, but grew thick and cloying after a minute or so.

Once there we found the corner already occupied by four storage modules. I tried one and found it unlocked. A quick investigation revealed that the boxes contained hand tools, fertilizer concentrate, and a whole bunch of lab equipment that I didn't understand. But density is density, and if lab equipment can shield me from darts, then I don't care what it's for.

Sasha grumbled when I freed the containers from the deck, and insisted on rearranging them into a protective semicircle, but went along with the plan. Not because she *liked* it, or thought it was *necessary,* but because I'm a crotchety old bastard who has to be humored.

Once our newly formed bulwark was in place, and was mag-locked to the deck, our next requirement was furniture. Beds had first priority, since they could do double duty as acceleration couches, and would cushion us from the effects of gravity.

With that in mind, we spread out to see what we could find. I wanted to say something cautionary, like "watch out for people with Mars Bars," but knew better than to push my luck. I took the port side and headed towards the bow, while the others took the bulkhead and headed towards the access tubes.

We'd been at it for fifteen minutes when a squadron of mechanical insects took to the air and Joy came swinging through the branches. You could see bushes swaying all the way back to where she'd come from. Her last swing, followed by a split-second release, sent her flying towards my shoulder. She hit with a thump. I fell backwards and struggled to right myself. "Damn it, Joy . . . what the hell are you doing?"

"Arriving," she said brightly. "And I found what you're looking for."

"You did? Where?"

"In a storage room near the access tubes. Cargo pads . . . lots of them."

I used the bush tops to pull myself along. Blossoms came loose and floated through the air like organic confetti. The smell of them stuck to the back of my throat. Joy held onto my right shoulder tab and chattered the whole way. I didn't pay much attention to what she said, but realized how pleasant her voice was, and understood how lonely Wamba must have been. I wondered if he'd make another Joy, or if that was possible, since she was one of a kind. I hoped so.

The cargo pads were right where Joy had said they'd be, and while some of them were raggedy, and others were stained, most were reasonably clean. It was a simple matter to free the pads from the straps that held them in place, sort them in mid-air, and take the ones we wanted. Sasha arrived towards the end of the process and helped tow them to our newly created home.

It didn't take long to discover that securing the pads to the deck was going to be a problem. But through the judicious use of magnetic clamps borrowed from here and there, and the huge roll of duct tape that I had included in our luggage, we created what looked like comfortable beds. Gravity would provide the true test.

With that effort out of the way, Sasha and I discovered that we were tired. So, after eating some rather salty ration bars, and washing them down with water siphoned from the irrigation system, we strapped ourselves in for a good night's sleep. Not that "night" had any particular meaning within the realm of the eternally lit cargo bay.

I felt one of us should keep watch, but Sasha thought it was unnecessary. So, since robots don't sleep, and she would be up and around anyway, Joy was the logical compromise. I've got to admit that I felt some qualms about entrusting our safety to a twelve-inch-tall android, but my eyelids grew heavy, sleep beckoned, and I went along.

It was two or three hours later when I was awoken by the sudden and unannounced imposition of Earth-normal gravity. And, while I was growing more and more accustomed to zero-gee conditions, it felt good. And so it was that I had just rearranged my bed, snuggled under a cargo mat, and drifted off to sleep when Joy jumped up and down on my chest. The poppers attacked two minutes later.

13

"Good for one free meal."

A pass to the Lunar Gardens Cafe found in popper number two's waist pouch

The poppers were cautious, and that was a mistake. Had they rushed in and nailed us in bed, the whole thing would have ended right there. But they didn't, and we made reasonably good use of the extra seconds. I scrambled to my feet, checked to make sure Sasha was up, and pointed to the right. "You take the right, I'll take the left!"

She nodded, held her gun in the approved two-handed grip, and took aim. There were four poppers in all. Two males, a female, and an android. A limited-edition model with three eyes, vampire fangs, and a pimp-city wardrobe. He, she, or it worried me more than the others did, because robots can be damned hard to kill. They charged the cargo modules, leaped to the top, and spent half a second looking at us.

153

I wasted half that time wishing I had the .38 instead of the dart gun, took aim, and pumped the trigger. Black holes marched across the front of the android's peach-colored jumpsuit. Jets of bright blue fluid spurted out and splashed on the deck. The robot grinned. He was still grinning when his gun came up, his finger squeezed the trigger, and Joy climbed his pants leg. The first darts blew air into my ear and the rest went wide as Joy jumped for and grabbed his gun arm. Darts splattered against the deck at my feet while hot plastic peppered my ankles.

The robot frowned, tried to shake Joy off, and died as my darts found and destroyed his central processing unit (CPU). He was still in the process of falling when I picked my next target. I fired, but she had moved, and the darts tore through empty space.

Diving onto an opponent can be quite effective if you hit and knock them down. But if the other person turns sideways as I did, and the assailant hits the deck like she did, the shoe's on the other foot. Only the most charitable of souls would have ignored the opportunity to jump on her exposed spine, and given the fact that I'm not especially charitable, I didn't.

But, instead of the yielding flesh that I had expected to encounter, my boots landed on some of Pro-Tec's finest semirigid body armor. It did what it was supposed to do, and spread the impact of my attack over a wider area. I was still in the process of absorbing that information when the woman did a military push-up. I tottered and fell sideways as she rolled. I saw her gun come up, fired mine in response, and watched a hole appear between her eyes.

The air whooshed out of my lungs as I hit the deck, and I was still struggling to breathe when Sasha arrived. She placed hands on hips and grinned sardonically. "What the hell kind of bodyguard is this? Lying around while I do all the work?"

This was less than fair, and I was planning to say so, when I saw three bodies where there should have been four. I struggled to my feet.

"I see three of them . . . where did the last one go?"

Sasha shrugged and gestured towards the bushes. "I hit him once, maybe twice, but he got away."

I looked where she was pointing and saw a trail of blood. "Damn."

She frowned and looked defensive. "It's too bad he got away . . . but we narrowed the odds."

I looked to see if she was serious. "Yeah? By how much?" I watched her think it through. If four poppers had made it aboard the barge, then why not five? Or six? Or ten? Assumptions could kill you. The voice confirmed my fears. It came from the bushes somewhere.

"Not bad for an over-the-hill head-case and a teenaged bimbo, but it ain't over yet. Not by a long shot. I'll be back! Wait for it. I'll come when you least expect me."

I jumped to the top of a storage module, saw a cloud of robo-insects take to the air fifty yards out, and considered going after him. It didn't seem wise, though, not with the cover the bushes provided, and no certainty that he was alone.

I made one helluva target standing on the storage module, and jumped down. Joy grabbed my pants and scampered up to my shoulder. She put her feet at the base of my neck, grabbed an ear, and leaned way out. She looked happy. "Hiya, boss. How's it hanging?"

I looked into her face, saw the merriment that danced in her eyes, and understood something that would have been obvious to anyone but me. Wamba had equipped Joy with the single emotion he wanted her to have, the one he hardly ever felt himself, and hoped to experience by having her around. Had the plan failed? Was that why he had given her to me?

I forced a smile of my own. "Pretty well, all things considered. Thanks for the help. You saved my life."

Joy beamed with pleasure and rubbed herself against the side of my face. The feel of her miniature breasts brushing back and forth against my ear stimulated strange thoughts. I plucked her off my shoulder, smiled reassuringly, and placed her on the deck. She giggled happily. Long, slender legs flashed and she cartwheeled away. There was no doubt about it. Joy needed some clothes.

But first there were other more pressing problems to deal with. Like collecting the arsenal of weapons our attackers had unintentionally delivered and going through their pockets. Not a pleasant task, but a productive one. We found money, about four thousand in all, lots of spare ammo, some gas grenades, enough knives to open a cutlery store, two varieties of illicit drugs, and, last but certainly not least, temporary I.D. cards of the sort that corpies provide to freelancers. They can be set for anything from a day to a year and erase themselves after that. But these were good and came with 3-D photos, thumbprints, and a scanner strip. None of which would have meant diddly except for the fact that *all* the cards had been issued by Trans-Solar. Shasha knelt beside me. I showed her the card. "So much for getting rid of them on Mars."

She was silent for a moment. "Damn."

"Yeah. I don't suppose you'd like to tell me what's going on?"

The stubborn look reappeared. She shook her head. "I already have."

I shook my head sadly and got to my feet. "Right. And corpies give to charity. Well, let's dispose of the bodies before they start to smell. I think I saw an ejection port near the storage compartment."

What would have been easy in zero gee was hard work in ship-normal gravity. People weigh more after they die, or seem to, and it doesn't make sense. Life should have weight, and leave a body feeling lighter, like a canteen emptied of water. But that's not the way it works, as the guys on the local meat wagon will be glad to tell you.

But, by rolling the bodies onto a cargo pad, and dragging them to the ejection port, we got the job done. Of course, lifting the stiffs and stuffing them down the tube was not an especially pleasant task, but better them than us. Once that was accomplished, the rest was easy. It was a simple matter to close the hatch, seal it shut, and hit the green button.

I felt a slight vibration as air was pumped out of the chamber and heard a thump as the bodies were ejected from the tube. I tried to feel something, tried to think religious thoughts, but nothing came. It's hard to empathize with poppers, dead or alive, and my religious training, if any, had disappeared along with my other memories.

The adrenaline drained out of my bloodstream and took my energy with it. I was afraid. And who wouldn't be? We were trapped on a spacegoing barge with one or more hired killers. Fear was normal, and anything else would be stupid. But fear is an uncomfortable emotion. It saps your strength and demands full attention until you respond. But what should we do? Our arrival at what had been our fortress served to underline the problem.

The android was where we'd left him. His sky-blue body fluids had oozed out, mingled with human blood, and formed a brownish crust. What had seemed snug and secure prior to the attack felt open and vulnerable now. I had just started to think about that when Sasha assumed command again. She stood hands on hips, her gun in easy reach, with a newly acquired backup stuck in her waistband. "Collect the gear, Max. We're pulling out."

I would look back later, remember how she'd taken control, and wonder how I could have been so stupid. But I *was* stupid, and still am for that matter, and it felt good at the time. I nodded slowly. "Yeah, you're probably right. No sense in staying here. We'll build a fort somewhere else."

Sasha looked grim. "No, we won't. You were right, Max. I should've listened, should've take your advice, but didn't and paid the price." Her face softened momentarily, and I saw something that might have been affection in her eyes. "You're good at what you do, and don't ever let people say you aren't. I'd be dead if it weren't for you."

Something rose to fill my throat, tears brimmed in my eyes, and a feeling of warmth suffused my body. I fought for control and got it. "Thanks . . . a letter of recommendation would be vastly appreciated. But why not? Build a fort, I mean."

"'Cause we're going to hunt the bastard down," Sasha said coldly. "And his friends too . . . if he has any left."

The idea hit my brain like the dawning of a new day. Bodyguards are reactive by nature, always looking to defend rather than attack, so the concept seemed radical at first. But the more I thought about the idea, the more I liked it. Why wait for the bastard to attack when you could find the creep, put him away, and spend the rest of the trip relaxing? The plan made excellent sense.

So we lifted the android to a standing position, checked to make sure he'd stay that way, and made an adjustment to his right hand. I thought the upraised finger said it all, and hoped the popper would see it.

It didn't take long to gather our gear, stuff it into the duffel bags, and clear out. However, things that weighed nothing in zero gee were suddenly heavy and slowed us down. Sasha carried a bag plus the pressure suits, and I toted the rest. Joy wasn't large enough to carry anything and scouted ahead. We were headed to starboard and on high alert. A second attack seemed unlikely but not impossible.

"We can't carry this stuff all the time," Sasha said thoughtfully. "We'll be dead meat if a popper comes along. No, what we need is a stash, or a number of stashes in case some are discovered."

I may be mentally challenged, but I know a good idea when I hear one, and the stash thing sounded good. My head swiveled back and forth looking for a good location. And, much to my own amazement, I found one.

The air vent was obvious really, especially to someone who lived on Sub-Level 38 of the Sea-Tac Residential-Industrial Urboplex, where good hiding places are few and far between. Four stainless-steel screws held the screen in place, but one of the recently deceased poppers had been the proud owner of a stainless-steel all-purpose pocket knife, the kind that comes with enough tools to perform brain surgery, and weighs a pound and a half. I pulled the monster out of my pocket, selected the Phillips head screwdriver, and went to work. Sasha supervised. "Don't leave any scratches. They could give us away."

I didn't think there was much chance that my scratches would show among all those left by the maintenance bots and tool heads over the years, but I kept my mouth shut. Some things are worth fighting over and some aren't.

The screen came free with relative ease. We made an arbitrary decision to divide our supplies into three equal portions, making sure there was a weapon in each—this against the possibility that one or both of us lost our weapons but remained at liberty. And, since the heavily armed poppers had contributed a total of five guns to our arsenal, that left each of us with a backup plus enough ammo to fight a small war—something I hoped we wouldn't have to do.

So, having placed a duffel bag and the pressure suits inside the air vent, and having reinstalled the screen, we followed the bulkhead towards the starboard side of the ship. Since we were located near the barge's stern, and knowing there was a great deal of space between us and the bow, it seemed logical to suppose that the popper or poppers were camped towards the entry lock or beyond. I had assumed that we'd climb up through one of the access tubes, recross the sky bridge, and retrace our steps from there. I even said as much. Sasha put me straight.

"Sure, Max, it could work, but tell me this: A popper escaped, right? Well, where did he go? If he crossed the bridge, we'd have seen him."

I frowned. She was right. The bridge was completely exposed, so we would have seen him. "How 'bout the forest? Maybe he's hiding in the bushes."

"Anything's possible," Sasha said patiently, "but he's wounded, and that makes it likely that he'll head home. Wherever that is."

Thoughts piled into each other as they tried to find a way through my head. The popper had headed home, the popper lived up towards the bow, the popper didn't use the sky bridge, ergo, the popper knew of another way to get there. Brilliant, huh? But Sasha was way ahead of me. "The way I figure it, we should make another stash, work our way around the forest, and find his escape route. The rest will be simple."

The rest would be simple? Tracking a professional killer to his lair would be simple? Was Sasha out of her mind? I looked her way, half expecting a sardonic smile, a hint of irony, but no, she was completely serious. I felt confused, very confused, and my head started to hurt. I *wanted* Sasha to be smart, *wanted* her to assume control, but couldn't quite let go. In spite of the fact that Sasha thought circles around me, and was more competent than any girl her age had a right to be, she lacked experience. A sometimes fatal flaw. I fought the headache and prepared to assert myself when and if we found the popper's escape route. We had just dropped a duffel bag containing a gun, ammo, and a third of our food into a large junction box when Joy pointed towards the other side of the bay, and gave the alarm. "Look!"

We looked, and saw what appeared to be a black dot quartering the area where the battle had occurred. Sasha kept her voice flat and unemotional. "The bastard has a spy cam."

"Yeah," I said grimly. "Or took control of a maintenance cam."

She gave me a look, the kind reserved for occasions when I'm a pain in the ass, and gestured towards the grating. "Come on, let's get the cover on." I hurried to help. The grating clanged as it dropped into place.

"Look!" Joy said for the second time. "It heard! And it's coming our way!"

We looked. The spy cam *had* heard and *was* coming our way. My reaction was to hide and hope for the best. Sasha had other plans. She pointed towards the deck. "Lie down! Pretend you're dead!"

The order went against all my instincts, all my desires, but she gave it with such certainty that I obeyed. The deck was cold and the lights were bright. I closed my eyes. Black blotches floated on an ocean of red. I heard a whirring noise, air caressed my face, and the scene grew darker.

I *felt* the spy cam hover over me, or thought I did, and wondered what Sasha would do. The answer came as the darts thumped into the spy eye's metal housing, servos whined as it tried to get away, and the whole thing landed on my unprotected stomach. Air whooshed out of my lungs, my eyes flew open, and my arms wrapped themselves around the still-struggling machine.

I was eyeball to lens with the blasted thing when Sasha drove a twelve-inch commando knife into the camera's cylindrical torso. The weapon had been liberated from one of the poppers, and the combination of the saw-toothed back edge and the high-tensile stainless-steel blade proved more than equal to the task. It passed through the housing, punctured a vital part, and ended the machine's life. The robo-cam jerked a couple of times and lay dead in my arms.

Or so I thought until a voice came out of it. A voice identical to the one that had addressed us before. "Thank you. There is nothing so boring as an easy hunt. I shall relish the days ahead."

And with that the machine discharged whatever electrical power it had left directly into my body. I awoke to the smell of burned chest hair. Two faces were looking down at me. One large and one small. Both looked concerned. Sasha was worried. "Max? Are you okay?"

I lied. "Never better. How long was I out?"

"Twenty or thirty seconds."

"Good. Let's get the hell out of here before the sonofabitch sends reinforcements."

An unspoken consensus carried us out into the forest. If the popper could send one maintenance cam, he could probably send more, and the canopy would provide at least a modicum of protection. I waited until we were a good fifty yards out before I allowed Sasha to break out the first aid kit and rub goo on my chest. It continued to hurt after she was done, but not quite as much. I sealed my shirt and we moved on. I was dizzy, sick to my stomach, and determined to hide it.

I wished there was something we could do about the clouds of metallic insects that rose in front of us, circled like windblown foil, and resettled when we had passed. They were like miniature spies, checking on our movements, and reporting them to anyone with the patience to watch. Our only hope lay in the fact that it would take the popper some time to treat his wounds and locate another surveillance cam. Or so we hoped.

The bushes were laid out in rows to facilitate the movement of various robots, and it wasn't long before we started to encounter them. They came in all sorts of shapes and sizes, ranging from box-shaped contraptions that we called "leaf suckers," to snake-like machines that slithered through the canopy and trimmed unwanted foilage.

I watched them carefully at first, afraid the popper would use them to spy on us, but, outside of sluggish attempts to move out of our way, the robots continued their work. But that could change, so I continued to keep an eye on them. The whole thing became monotonous after a while. Trees, robots, trees, and more robots, with no sign of the popper or his trail. Then it rained, a fine, penetrating mist that seemed part of the air around us. It coated the leaves, soaked our clothes, and slicked the deck. Joy loved the water the same way she loved everything else. Oblivious to our discomfort, she giggled and did cartwheels up the path.

The mist turned into a steady rain, and I found the blood shortly thereafter. Little brown dots of it, fuzzy around the edges, and dry prior to the rain. The drops came slantwise out of the forest, and a broken branch marked the point where the popper's path had intersected our own.

I motioned for Sasha to stop, took a careful look around, and considered the risks. Softened by the mist and battered by the rain, the dots were coming apart. In twenty minutes, thirty at most, the trail would disappear. The answer was to pick up the pace, in spite of the fact that doing so would make us less vigilant, and vulnerable to an ambush. The part of me that remembers and takes over at unpredictable times made the necessary decision. I waved Sasha forward and she obeyed.

It was warm, and the humidity increased as we jogged through the bushes, preceded by wave after wave of robotic insects. It felt good to run, good to push my luck, and I found myself grinning like what? An idiot? A wolf on the trail of wounded prey? The second seemed more suitable, and I hoped it was true. But too much time had passed, the trail was cold, and we reached the other side of the forest without spotting the popper. The little brown dots came less and less frequently now, then stopped in front of a stainless-steel airtight door. Had he brought the bleeding under control? Or stepped through and continued to hemorrhage on the other side? There was only one way to find out.

I positioned myself on one side of the portal and Sasha took the other. Joy jumped upwards, hit the large green button, and dropped to a crouch. Our weapons were drawn and aimed as the door swished open. I waited for defensive fire that didn't come. I started to move but the kid beat me to it. She went through the opening fast, but a hair too high, making herself a better than average target.

I followed, eyes searching for things suspicious, but found nothing more than some unimaginative graffiti. Though a good deal smaller, the corridor was similar to the first one we'd been in, complete with vertical ridges, emergency com sets, fire-fighting gear, and surveillance cameras. I saw no escape slots, however—an omission which could mean that the automated trains didn't travel this particular passageway, or they did and pedestrians were S.O.L.

Satisfied that the popper had cleared the area, we looked around. There were ten to fifteen drops of blood, all clustered together, and smeared by a bootprint. Some partial prints marched into the distance and disappeared: a clear indication that our quarry had rigged a bandage. I looked at Sasha and she nodded. We hugged the sides as we made our way down the hall, hoping the popper had better things to do than watch the security cameras, fearing that he didn't. Motors whirred as they tracked our progress.

It was a weird feeling, knowing something was watching, but unsure of whether it mattered. The situation must have spooked

Sasha too, because she opted for the vertical ladder the moment we encountered it, and I followed. For reasons I couldn't quite articulate, I assumed the popper had continued down-corridor, but cameras made me nervous, so I kept my feelings to myself. The cameras tilted to follow us and stopped when they could tilt no more.

The ladder led to a narrow maintenance tunnel. If cameras were present, I couldn't identify them. Though equipped with rudimentary hand- and footholds, the passageway had been intended for robots, one of which blocked our path. It was shaped like a large turtle, and judging from the noises it made, was engaged in cleaning the gratings beneath our feet. The strong smell of disinfectant reinforced that impression.

Sasha solved the problem by stepping onto the robot's gently rounded back and off the other side. Joy jumped, caught hold of my pants leg, and held on as I followed suit. If the turtle-shaped machine objected to this treatment, it gave no sign of its displeasure.

We followed the corridor for a hundred feet or so, stopped in front of still another airtight door, and took the usual positions. Me to the left, Sasha to the right, and Joy wherever she wanted to be.

The hatch slid open and I saw darkness beyond. Darkness and the flicker of what looked like flames. The kid made eye contact, nodded, and stepped onto a narrow balcony. I joined her. Below us, three-quarters filled with thousands upon thousands of crates and boxes, was a space similar in size and shape to the one occupied by the forest.

And there, at the hold's epicenter, burned a large bonfire. The barge's automatic fire-fighting systems had been defeated somehow. The flames leaped higher as they consumed an especially choice piece of fuel, then fell back, as if tired by their exertions. And, moving around in the foreground, their forms silhouetted against the flames, were people. Lots of people, fifty or sixty at least, all talking, laughing, and swigging from a variety of containers. There was something primitive about the scene, and ominous as well.

I had just turned towards Sasha, and was about to say something stupid, when a beam of white light shot across the hold and pinned us against the bulkhead. The voice came from everywhere and nowhere at all. It belonged to the man who had addressed us through the maintenance cam. "Well! Look what we have here! I hoped you would follow. Welcome to hell."

Sasha turned, hit the door release, and nothing happened.

Another light popped on. This one roamed the crates below, paused each time it touched someone, and moved on. They were a motley lot. I saw men, women, and yes, children. And, judging from the way they avoided the light, as well as the generally ragged condition of their clothing, it was obvious that they had no more right to be aboard the barge than we did. The voice spoke to them. "Look! Look at the catwalk! They are worth ten thousand dollars each! Do as you will to the girl, but keep the man alive."

There was silence for a moment while the stowaways considered what the man had said, followed by a howl of approval, and the sounds of movement.

Sasha tried the door, found it still wouldn't budge, and set out along the balcony. I stuffed Joy into a pocket, checked my weapon, and followed. It's funny how life works. Just when you think things couldn't possibly get worse, they sure as hell do.

14

"Surgeon flees after botched operation."

The headline on a press clipping wadded up in the bottom of Doc's duffel bag

Our fellow stowaways had been on board at least as long as we had and knew their way around. They swarmed up ladders, dashed through passageways, and burst onto the catwalk. The hatch that refused to work for Sasha opened smoothly for them.

We ran for the other end of the platform. Our boots pounded the metal gratings and our breath came in gasps. I put a dart into every surveillance cam that I saw, but knew that a long sequence of disabled cameras would be like an arrow pointing towards our destination. It felt good, though, and might provide an edge later on.

The catwalk ended where it met the port bulkhead. Sasha pounded on the green button and swore when nothing happened.

We turned to face our pursuers. Knowing we were trapped, and eager to collect the reward money, the stowaways charged. A couple of scroungy-looking men led the attack with some equally ragged women close behind. A collection of scraggly-assed kids brought up the rear. One of the men brandished what looked like a homemade dart gun. The rest were armed with a wild variety of clubs and knives. The balcony was narrow, so they had little choice but to come at us two at a time — a factor that didn't exactly even the odds but didn't hurt either.

I turned sideways in an effort to reduce the target profile and felt Joy scramble down my leg. I had no idea where she was headed and couldn't take time to look. A dart whispered by my shoulder and clanged off metal. I raised my pistol, took aim, and fired. The lead man, the one with the gun, stumbled and fell. The rest jumped over his still-twitching body and kept on coming.

Sasha fired. A woman clutched her throat, staggered, and fell. A little girl cried, "Mommy!" and stopped to help.

I heard someone yell, "Stop! Stop, damn you!" and realized it was me. But they didn't stop. They screamed their hatred and kept on coming. My stomach felt queasy, and bile filled my throat as I continued to fire. It was a one-sided battle in which their weapons were completely ineffectual and ours were deadly. The imperative "kill or be killed" is written in our genetic code somewhere, and that's what we did.

Finally, when the last adult had fallen, and the children were sobbing at their sides, it ended. Some were wounded. I wanted to stay and help, but a series of inarticulate yells followed by the clang of distant footsteps forced a retreat. I was about to grab Sasha and drag her the length of the balcony when Joy tugged at my pants leg. "Come on! I opened the door."

I looked, saw wires dangling from the now-open control box, and realized that Wamba had given his creation something more than a pleasing personality. Joy had initiative, technical expertise, and who knows what else. I made a note to kiss Wamba when and if I saw him again.

The next set of pursuers moved out onto the balcony, saw us, and charged. Their shouts became muffled as the door closed behind me. That's when I realized that a stranger had joined us: a boy who was crying, knuckling his eyes, and looking to escape.

Sasha held the kid with one hand and a pistol with the other. Her eyes flashed with anger. "We need to find that bastard and find him now!"

I shrugged. "Great. But how? He could be anywhere."

She gave me one of those looks, the kind that reminds me of how stupid I am, and knelt beside the boy. Her voice was level and tight. "Security cameras imply a control room of some sort, and that's where the popper will be. Isn't that right, boy? Where's the control room?"

The boy looked resentful and tried to pull free. "You shot my sister!"

I expected Sasha to say something nice, to comfort the boy, so imagine my surprise when she put the gun to his head. "Now listen, you little shit! I shot your sister because she tried to kill me. Now, tell me where the control room is or I'll splatter your brains all over the wall! Take your pick."

Voices yelled and fists pounded on the door. I looked at Joy. She shook her head and smiled. Whatever she'd done to the lock mechanism would hold for a while. I turned to the boy. You could see the wheels turn. He hated our guts but wanted to live. It didn't take long to arrive at the proper decision. The tears stopped and his eyes drifted towards my skull plate. "I won't tell you where it is . . . but I'll show you."

The kid was no dummy. The longer he held onto the information, the longer he'd live. That's what he assumed, and Sasha nodded agreeably. "Good, very good. Lead away. And remember, one false move, and I'll blow your brains out."

The kid knew his way around or was leading us on a wild-goose chase. One or the other. We followed him down the corridor, up a ladder, through an accessway, and out into a large passageway. It was littered with scraps of half-eaten food, empty booze bags, and pools of dried vomit. There was no doubt about it, the poppers liked to party. A box-shaped maintenance bot beeped and ate an empty food pak.

The boy held a finger to his lips; we nodded, and followed him down the hall. I went first, followed by Sasha and Joy. Though nearly obliterated by orange spray paint, the words "Control Center" could still be seen on the hatch at the far end of the corridor. I was proud of my ability to read them. There was no way to know if the popper was inside or not. A security cam stared unblinkingly back at me. Was the popper monitoring that particular shot? Waiting for us to walk into his trap? There was no way to know. He paused ten feet short of the hatch. I checked my weapon. "I'll go first. Cover me."

The kid nodded. Her face was pale, and her lips made a long thin line. She was scared, one of the more sensible things I'd seen her do, and a sign of inevitable adulthood.

I turned, planning to lecture the boy, and discovered he was gone. My heart beat a little bit faster, since I knew the little shit had every reason to run for the nearest com set and scream his head off. Time was critical.

I touched the button, and the hatch opened. I dived, rolled, and came up feeling foolish. Control panels lined the bulkheads. Vid monitors displayed miles of empty corridors. Air whispered through the vent over my head. The compartment was empty, or seemed to be, and my pulse started to slow.

The kid stepped through the door, swept the room with her weapon, and looked in my direction. I was halfway through a shrug when the popper dropped out of an overhead crawl space, landed on his feet, and shot Sasha in the back. She looked surprised, took a step in my direction, and fell flat on her face.

My weapon was light-years out of position. I fought to bring it around, cursed the gravity that slowed my hand, and prayed I would beat him.

There was time, plenty of time, time enough to notice that his eyes were cesspool black, that his teeth were very, very white, that he wore a gold crucifix around his neck, that his left shoulder had been bandaged by someone who knew what they were doing, that the weapon in his hand was a Ruger Dartmaster, that his finger was squeezing the trigger, that the pistol was jerking in my hand, that darts were walking their way up the middle of his body and punching holes through his throat.

The popper grabbed his neck, hoping to staunch the sudden flood, but blood oozed out between his fingers and dripped down the front of his shirt. I think he fainted then, and bled to death a minute later, but didn't really care. The kid was, well, I didn't know what she was, not a friend exactly, because friends don't keep secrets from each other, but not a client either, because clients are about money, and I hadn't thought about the fifty K in a long time.

No, the girl fell into some weird category I couldn't quite put a name to, but felt as a confused mishmash of anger, fear, and sorrow. I knelt by Sasha's side, searched for a pulse, and found one. I felt relieved, and scared because she needed help and I didn't know what to do. The back of her shirt was wet with blood and her skin was whiter that it should've been. I saw a lump where her head had hit the deck.

"Excuse me . . ."

The voice came from behind me. I whirled, saw a middle-aged man standing in the doorway, and was in the process of squeezing the trigger when Joy ran towards me. "Don't shoot! He's a doctor!"

The man smiled and held his hands palms out. "Not a doctor, but a physician's assistant."

I must have looked doubtful because he gestured towards the dead popper. His voice had a sardonic quality. "I bandaged his wound . . . though the effort seems wasted."

"He offered to help," Joy added brightly.

I remembered the popper's bandage, the expertise with which it had been applied, and got to my feet. The physician's assistant watched me. He had thinning gray hair, a nose that looked larger than it should have, and about two days' worth of stubble. I noticed that while his clothes were old, they were fastidiously clean, and had been fashionable once. His eyes were blue, as clear as a tropical sea, and free of fear. I got the feeling that everything that *could* happen to him already had. The choice was no choice at all.

"He shot her in the back, Doc. Do everything you can."

The man nodded, knelt by Sasha's side, and went to work. Metal flashed as he cut through blood-soaked fabric. Gauze appeared from the case by his side. Blood welled up and was wiped away. The entry wounds were high and to the right. Doc checked for exit wounds, found them, and slapped self-sealing premedicated pressure bandages over the holes. The bleeding stopped. He nodded his satisfaction, slipped a needle into her arm, and handed me a bag full of liquid. "Here, make yourself useful."

There were words on the bag, but they defied my ability to read them. Whatever it was trickled down a tube and into Sasha's body. Doc slipped his arms under the upper part of her body. "She's stabilized, but who knows what's happening on the inside. Could've nicked a lung. Help me move her."

Joy had scrambled to my shoulder. I gave her the I.V. bag and slid my arms under Sasha's legs. We carried her to a counter and laid her out. I took the I.V. bag and sent Joy for some water. I used it to wipe away the worst of the blood while Doc attached self-adhesive disks to various parts of her body and used a hand-held monitor to check her vital signs. Then, having nodded a couple of times, and mumbled to himself, he tended the bump on her forehead. The eyepatch was askew, and he fixed it. "What happened to her eye?"

"She sold it."

He gave me the same look most people reserve for corpies. "Asshole."

I gestured, and the I.V. bag swung back and forth. "You've got it all wrong, Doc! I didn't have a thing to do with it!"

He started to reply but was interrupted by a third voice. "Freeze."

I turned and found myself looking into the bore of a Colt Space Master. I was zero for two. My primary weapon was in its holster and the backup was stuck down the back of my pants. It might as well have been on Mars for all the good it would do me. The man with the gun was short, paunchy, and better dressed than the twelve or fifteen people gathered behind him. Something about the way he held the Colt told me he knew how to use it. His voice was calm. "Move it, Doc . . . you're in the way."

Doc shook his head and looked stubborn. "There's been enough killing."

The man was unmoved. "Tell it to Kirtz, Nichols, Chin, and a couple more. They're dead."

Doc shook his head slowly and turned into the line of fire. Training, or maybe it was instinct, told me to use that moment to pull a weapon, fire through Doc's body, and drop the guy in his tracks. I listened to Doc instead. His voice was calm. "Kirtz, Nichols, and Chin took their chances and lost. It was self-defense, and you know it. You want the money? Well, there it is, lying over there. Help yourself."

The man glanced towards the popper's body, gave a slight inclination of his head, and backed in that direction. The crowd tripped over each other getting out of the way. I watched for guns and wondered if I could get to Sasha's backup. It was sticking out of her waistband. All I needed was two, maybe three seconds to pull it and fire.

The man was good, and kept his eyes on me the whole time. The Colt never wavered as he knelt by the body, patted it down, and found the wallet. He thumbed it open, glanced at the contents, and nodded. "Okay . . . fair enough. How 'bout it, chrome-dome? You willin' to let it drift?"

I get tired of the "chrome-dome" thing at times but didn't want to kill anyone over it. I nodded. "Fine with me."

The crowd mumbled a little, angry at the loss of their friends, and resentful about the money. But the man knew what made them tick and pointed towards the boxes piled on the far side of the room. "Those boxes have food and god knows what else in 'em. I got a feelin' the poppers ain't comin' back. Help yourselves."

There was something akin to a stampede as the crowd headed for the boxes and tore them apart. The man smiled, made the gun disappear, and strolled our way. He held out his hand. It was hard as steel. "The name's Dan. Dan Riler."

"Max Maxon."

"Glad to meet you, Max. Welcome to our little community. Sorry about your friend. Hope she'll be okay."

Doc took the I.V. bag. "She'd be a lot better if you took this conversation somewhere else."

We stepped aside. I didn't want to leave her, but couldn't afford to ignore Riler either. "Yeah, I hope so too."

Riler gestured towards the popper's body. "Was I right? His friends won't be back?"

I shook my head. "Nope. They jumped us at the other end of the barge. We stuffed their bodies into an ejection tube."

Riler nodded agreeably. "Nice of you to clean up. They were a mean bunch. Boarded as a group. Checked us right away. Said they were looking for a man with a chromed head and a girl with an eyepatch." Riler lifted an eyebrow. "Call me crazy, but it seems as if someone wants you dead."

I ignored the invitation and shrugged. "Maybe it's my deodorant or something."

Riler laughed and gestured towards the scavenging crowd. They were like crows on a road kill. "Well, your troubles are over. For a while, anyway. There were some bad apples in the crowd, but you thinned 'em out, and the rest are too scared to attack head-on. Course you gotta sleep . . . and so do I. Tell you what . . . you watch my back, and I'll watch yours."

I looked at Sasha. The Doc had located an emergency stretcher and convinced two members of the crowd to carry it. The kid looked pale, real pale, and it scared me. Partly because I liked her, but partly because I needed her, and didn't want to be alone. Yes, she had lied to me, yes, she had hidden things from me, but I hadn't been lonely in a long time, and the thought of losing her made my gut feel empty. So I'd stay with her, do what I could to nurse her back to health, and hope for the best. But I had to sleep, and Riler's offer made sense. I stuck out my hand. "You've got a deal."

It took the better part of two hours to get Sasha down to the main deck, make a home for her among the crates, and settle in. She remained unconscious, which worried me, but didn't seem to bother Doc. Or maybe it did, and he hid the fact. In any case, I felt as if I should stay awake but found it hard to do. So when Riler offered to stand watch, and suggested a nap, I took him at his word.

I was gone within seconds of putting my head down. I don't think I dreamed right away, but who the hell knows? I know this, though: Like some of my previous dreams, this one was real, or had been real, however you want to look at it. As with the previous dreams, this one picked up where the last left off.

The initial sensation was that of fighting my way up from a deep sleep, coming almost to the surface, but not breaking through. I heard voices, two of them, one male and one female. They were arguing. The man was against something and the woman was for it. "It isn't right, I tell you . . . and that's all there is to it."

"Right?" the woman demanded. "Is war right? Is theft right? Because that's what's going on. He killed some of our friends, would've killed us, if the commandos hadn't been here."

"Two, three, or any number of wrongs don't add up to a right," the man responded stubbornly. "He's a human being, and what you propose goes beyond all standards of decency."

"And what would *you* know about decency?" the woman asked scathingly. "A man who lied, cheated, and stole his way out of the gutter? How dare you lecture *me* on right and wrong!"

"It's true that I've done all these things and more," the man replied calmly, "but none of my transgressions even come close to what you propose. I refuse to be part of it. More than that, I plan to tell the union."

There was silence for a moment, as if the woman was thinking things over, followed by the muffled thud of a gas-propelled dart. I heard glass shatter, metal clang, and something go thump. I strained to open my eyes, struggled to see what had happened, but found that I couldn't quite break through. I heard the woman say, "Asshole," and felt darkness drag me down.

But I floated to the surface now and again, snatched whatever sensation was handy, and carried it with me. I felt movement, heard laughter, smelled feces, felt cold, tasted water, and experienced pain. Lots of pain. Pain from the chest wound, pain from the needles in my arms, and pain I couldn't quite identify. It hurt to be me, to exist where I was, so I fought my way upwards, determined to break into the light, to tell them how I felt, to make the pain go away. And suddenly I was there, looking around, seeing Sasha, Riler, and the crates. It was disappointing somehow, and less than I had hoped for. Riler saw my movement and gestured with a fork. A meal pak sat balanced on his knee, and the smell made me salivate. "Welcome back. You've been out for nine hours."

I rolled over and came to my knees. Sasha looked the same as she had before.

"No need to worry," Riler said evenly. "She came to about three hours ago. Doc gave her something and she went to sleep."

I nodded and felt a tremendous sense of relief. We were down but not necessarily out. Riler tossed a food pak in my direction. I caught it, pulled the tab, and felt the container warm my hands.

Suddenly I wanted to be in the asteroids, on Europa Station, or back on Earth. But they were a long way off and no more friendly than where I was. I opened the meal pak, tried the stew, and liked it. Riler nodded, and we ate in silence.

15

". . . So, given the workers' already
ambivalent feelings about the company,
it's our opinion that the existence of
a toxic waste dump deep in the heart
of asteroid DXA-1411 should be
kept secret until such time
as morale improves or the planetoid
can be abandoned."

*An excerpt from a "Board Eyes Only"
memo on file at Trans-Solar HQ*

The next couple of weeks passed with agonizing slowness. Although Sasha seemed to rally at first, an infection set in, and her condition worsened. What had been a clean wound produced a gray-green pus that looked horrible and smelled even worse. And as her health nose-dived, so did her spirits, leaving her in a passive, almost vegetablelike state.

Doc gave it everything he had, but the medical bag was little more than a glorified first aid kit and offered few drugs to choose from. He did manage to slow the rate of deterioration, however, for which I was extremely thankful.

The artificial days dragged by. Each brought with it an endless round of sponge baths, wound cleanings, and when the kid was conscious, hand feedings.

In the meantime Sasha came and went, said weird things, and held my hand in a grip of steel. There were times when her mother seemed to be present and times when she wasn't. Whenever she was, the two of them had long, rambling conversations that almost always left Sasha in tears. Of course, what I heard was rather one-sided, and might have been totally inaccurate, but I got the impression of a mother who wasn't around much and had high expectations. So high that her daughter would rather give up an eye than fail to please.

But there were other times too, like when Sasha opened her remaining eye, smiled and said, "I love you," before slipping off to the dreamy-strange world she spent so much time in. I didn't know who she saw at that particular moment, whether it was me or someone else, but I hoped it was me, and felt warmed by the possibility that it was.

The partnership with Riler went well and prevented the others from slitting our throats while we were asleep. Our supplies ran low after a while, and he watched Sasha while Joy and I journeyed to the other end of the barge for supplies. Supplies we shared with him.

And so it went until Riler's calculations put us only a day or two out from the asteroids: a time when the tug crew might be expected to board. I was worried about the possibility of discovery, but Riler shook his head. "Come on, Max . . . think it through. The tug crew knows the score and are paid to ignore our presence. They have every reason to want us off the barge *before* they board."

"Maybe," I said doubtfully, "but the guy who put us aboard was worried."

Riler shrugged. "Maybe he cut them out, put on an act, or who knows? Main thing is they aren't gonna bother us."

Riler's words made sense, but so does brotherly love, and god knows there's damned little of *that* floating around the solar system. Still, Riler was proved correct when a pair of space-armored heavies appeared and offered us the only deal we were likely to get. I noticed that while their pressure suits were relatively new, they *looked* old and worn. Both rigs were highly personalized and bore the painted-on equivalent of tattoos, bumper stickers, and graffiti.

The bigger of the two, a guy armed with twin blasters, and with the words "Miners do it deeper" emblazoned across his chest, spoke via his external suit speaker. His partner stood back a ways, her scatter gun covering the crowd, her jaw working a wad of gum. "My name's Quint. Welcome to the 'roids. Anyone that wants off this bucket should gather round. Anyone that wants to stay and enroll in a two-year, all-tuition paid course in 'roid mining can take a nap."

With the exception of Sasha, and some of the kids, we gathered round.

Quint had brown eyes, a fist-flattened nose, and a three-day beard. The unlit cigar roamed from one side of his mouth to the other, as if searching for the perfect spot to land. He nodded, as if to say that we'd made the right decision. "Good. Okay, here's the deal . . . For two thousand dollars, or the equivalent in drugs, metals, or gems, we will haul you, plus twenty-five pounds of personal gear, to a Zebra-free landing in Deep Port. Kids under twelve travel half-price. Pets, robots, or personal gear over twenty-five pounds are subject to negotiation. We'll take 'em if weight allows. If you don't have the money, don't waste my time. I've heard every hard-luck, I-got-screwed-life-sucks sob story in the solar system and simply don't give a shit."

As Quint spoke, his hands drifted towards the blasters at his sides. "Now, last but not least, don't even think about trying to grease us. You may be armed with some nasty-assed hardware, and you may be the meanest sonofabitches that ever lifted off Mother Earth, but we've got a ship and you ain't going nowhere without us. Got it?"

We had it, or I did anyway, and I assumed the others did too. A line formed as people hurried to pay. Most, if not all, of our fellow stowaways had anticipated the moment and set aside money or other valuables to pay for it. Neither Sasha nor I had been quite so provident, but our work aboard the *Red Trader,* plus the four thousand appropriated from the poppers, had given us a modest stash. I checked to make sure there was enough and got in line. There were pauses when the people in front of me offered trade goods rather than money, but the line jerked forward with reasonable regularity, and I found myself eyeball to eyeball with Quint. He squinted. "What the hell happened to your head?"

I shrugged. "What the hell happened to your nose?"

He grinned. "I stuck it into somebody else's business. I do that from time to time. How many bods you planning to move?"

I gave thanks that Joy was hidden in my pocket, and said, "Two, but the second one is ill, and needs some help."

Quint nodded agreeably. "No problem, long as you can pay the five-hundred-dollar surcharge."

Five hundred seemed like a lot of extra money. I looked for signs of weakness. There weren't any. I could pay the freight or work in the mines. The choice was mine. I peeled the bills off my quickly dwindling roll and handed them over. Quint nodded, and his cigar bobbed up and down when he spoke. "Where's your friend?"

I pointed towards the spot where Sasha lay. "Over there."

Quint murmured into his throat mike, and a pair of space-suited figures came on the double. They'd been out of sight until now, and wore riot guns slung across their chests. A ready reserve in case of trouble. They were identical twins, or had been until one of them ran face first into a piece of mining equipment and forever settled the question of which one was which.

Scarface was very gentle, as if she knew what pain was all about, and treated Sasha like fragile china. The kid's dressings were due for a change, and smelled horrible, but the twins gave no sign of it. They loaded Sasha into her stretcher and did their best to make her comfortable. That's the funny thing about goodness: it can bubble up when you least expect it, and disappear just as quickly.

The kid was only half conscious and regarded me through bleary eyes. I patted her hand, promised everything would be all right, and hoped it was true.

Everything went fairly smoothly after that. The twins carried Sasha aboard the shuttle, and I followed. The gravity created by the barge extended to Quint's ship. Like most of the craft used out among the 'roids, it was heavily armored, highly maneuverable, and equipped for everything under the sun. The stretcher slid into one of four recesses provided for that purpose and was clamped in place. I took a nearby seat. My duffel went underneath. Others plopped down all around me. It was then that I remembered our pressure suits and realized that I'd left them behind. I spent five seconds wondering if I should go back and decided to let it slide. It would take forever to get Sasha into a suit, so to hell with it.

The lock closed, the children were strapped in place, and the shuttle broke contact with the barge. The transition to weightlessness was almost instantaneous. I checked to make sure that Sasha was secure, saw that she was, and tightened my harness. The pilot increased power and we were on our way.

The ensuing trip lasted about eight hours, which was at least seven more than I was psychologically prepared for, and eight more than was good for the kid. Doc fought to keep her temperature down, but she continued to run a fever and her wound smelled worse than ever. Every minute was like torture, knowing her condition was deteriorating, and unable to do anything about it.

Joy escaped from my pocket and, much to the children's delight, put on a demonstration of zero-gee gymnastics. But when Quint threatened to charge me five hundred bucks for bringing an "unauthorized passenger" aboard, I ordered the little robot into my pocket. She complained but did as she was told.

After what seemed like an eternity, Quint announced that we were closing with asteroid DXA-1411, better known as "Deep Port." There were no windows, but I imagined a rocky planetoid, covered with impact craters, tumbling along the path it had followed for millions of years.

Most of the living quarters would be deep underground, as on Earth's moon, so there wouldn't be much to see except for docking facilities, zero-gee cargo storage, antenna farms, and the half-salvaged skeleton of the linear accelerator that Riler had told me about. He said it looked like a ramp and had once been used to shoot ore at waiting ships.

Minutes passed, the shuttle bumped something solid, and gravity reasserted itself. Not Earth gravity, or Mars gravity, but something in between.

I figured everyone would take off and leave me to move the kid by myself, but such was not the case. Doc stayed, as did the twins, and I had plenty of help taking Sasha in through the habitat's lock: a lock that was labeled "For Emergency Use Only," and clearly off the beaten track. And that was a good thing, considering the reception we got on Mars. A motorized cart and driver were waiting. I watched as the twins strapped the stretcher into place.

"Climb aboard. The driver will take you to the hospital."

I turned to find Quint standing next to my shoulder. The ever-present cigar rolled from one side of his mouth to the other. "Thanks for the transportation."

He shrugged. "It's all part of the service. She looks like a nice kid. I hope she makes it."

I looked around, hoping to enlist Doc's help, or at least thank him, but he had disappeared. I threw my duffel in the back, took the seat next to the driver, gave Quint an optimistic thumbs-up, and held on as the cart jerked into motion. Beacons had been mounted front and back. They flashed on and off as we whirred down the corridor. The walls were made of machine-cut rock and were plugged where core samples had been taken.

We came to an intersection, paused, and took a right-hand turn. This corridor was five lanes wide. The centermost space was reserved for a monorail. The train approached from the opposite direction, roared by, and blasted us with displaced air. I had the impression of windows and hundreds of helmeted heads.

Our driver waited for a break in traffic, pulled into the fast lane, and activated his siren. It made a bleating sound, and he grinned as vehicles pulled out of the way. The driver didn't get many opportunities to drive full out and put his boot to the floor. Rubber screeched, and I felt G forces push me against the back of my seat. Convinced that we were in at least semicompetent hands, I studied my surroundings in the hopes of learning more about our temporary home.

The first thing I noticed was the orderliness of our surroundings. There were signs of it in the lighting, the well-maintained pavement, and the graffiti-free walls. And it wasn't that people didn't have spray paint, because you could see where they'd used it—only to have their efforts masked by neatly applied squares of rock-gray paint.

No, the unrelenting neatness gave the impression of centralized control, of rules that couldn't be broken, of punishments waiting to be imposed. Which, though not especially surprising in what amounted to a company town, gave the place a repressive feel, and went against my somewhat rebellious grain.

But if I missed the free-for-all atmosphere of home, I didn't miss the trash-filled corridors, neon-lit dives, and the two-legged scum that frequented them. And speaking of scum, what about our poppers? Had they killed us, rather than the other way around, they'd be reporting in about now, and clamoring for their pay. So what would happen when the call didn't come? When the corpies discovered that their goons had disappeared? People would come looking for us, that's what. People with guns.

A person with a full set of brain cells might have come up with a plan, might have hatched some sort of scheme, but not me. All I could do was feel frustrated, get medical help, and hope for the best.

The cart negotiated a corner, wove between a scattering of parked vehicles, and screeched to a halt. A pair of almost identical androids hurried over. Both wore red crosses painted across their otherwise bare chests and had names stenciled on their foreheads. Fric had blood splattered on one shoulder and Frac had a faulty wrist seal. A steady stream of green fluid dribbled down his plastiflesh fingers and dripped to the pavement. He smiled reassuringly. "May we help?"

I gestured towards the stretcher. "Yes, you can. The lady is ill. Would you take her inside?"

The robots could and would. I thanked the kid, grabbed my duffel, and gave him a tip. He nodded and got some rubber as he left. Joy tried to escape from my pocket and I shoved her back in. The last thing I needed right then was a naked robot running around.

The emergency room looked like they all do. Bright lights, stainless steel, and lots of signs. The place was packed with miners. All wore loose-fitting pressure suits under filthy orange overalls. Most had bandages wrapped around their heads, splints on their legs, or other signs of injury. A few had other less obvious problems. They had a tendency to stare through the walls, their eyes slightly out of focus, as if their minds had gone someplace else. I knew how they felt.

A nurse with bushy eyebrows and hairy arms ran a scanner over Sasha's body, peeked at her wound, and wrinkled her nose in disgust. "Hey, Doc! We've got a ripe one over here!"

The doc broke away from a miner and came our way. She was

middle-aged, slightly plump, and more than a little crotchety. She fired questions like grenades from a launcher.

"Who are you? Who is she? What happened?" The questions came one after another, and I answered them as honestly as I could without confessing to larceny, assault, or various degrees of homicide. But the doctor didn't care about anything unconnected with her job and downloaded me to a desk droid. He was one of those stationary models that are hard-wired to the desks they sit on. It took about twenty minutes to pump him full of phony information, hand over most of our remaining money, and work my way free of his bureaucratic grasp.

It didn't take long for the doctor to remove the dressing, draw blood, and snap orders at the nurse. She started an I.V., injected something into the tubing, and ordered Frac to take her away. The doctor was following along behind when I tapped her on the shoulder. She turned and looked annoyed. "Yes?"

"Where are they taking her? When can I see her?"

The doctor looked me up and down. Her opinion could be seen in her watery blue eyes. "Your friend is one sick puppy. We need to open her wound, drain it, and close it again. Then, assuming things go well, she'll be released in five or six days. You can see her during visitor's hours tomorrow. Have you got a place for her to stay after that?"

I shook my head.

"Well, get one. And not some piece-of-shit dive, either. She'll need time to recuperate."

I tried to thank her but found myself talking to her back instead. Ah, well, as long as she took good care of Sasha, it hardly mattered. I watched until the gurney had disappeared from sight, hoisted my duffel, and headed for the sliding glass doors. As has been established by now, planning is not my strong suit, but the doctor had pointed me in what I hoped was the right direction. I would find a place to stay, get a job to pay for it, and wait for Sasha to get better. But, as with most things that seem simple, it wasn't.

I passed through the sliding glass doors, followed some pedestrians towards an automated sidewalk, and climbed aboard. There were two lanes to choose from: the "arterial" lane, favored by retired mine workers, androids in need of repair, and newbies like myself; and the "express" lane, which catered to the likes of hyperactive children, robo-couriers, and amphetamine addicts, all of whom whizzed by at lightning speed. Thick, almost junglelike foliage passed to the right or left, interspersed with slower than normal waterfalls, and piped in bird sounds. It had the feel of a third-rate amusement park. Joy had made her way up to my shoulder and talked in my ear.

"Hey, boss . . . where we headed?"

I felt the usual sense of shame, considered a cover story, and decided to level with her instead. "I don't have the foggiest idea."

Joy grabbed my ear and swung out next to my face. She was naked as hell and still needed some clothes. Her voice was matter-of-fact. "Maybe I can help."

"Yeah? How's that?"

"Take me to a public terminal and I'll show you."

An elderly woman was staring at us so I stashed Joy in a pocket, waited for the next exit, and hopped off. There were some unisex rest rooms, fast-food stands, and yes, a public terminal. The only problem was the fact that a Zebra was using it. I turned my back, bought a soydog, and smothered it with chili. It tasted surprisingly good and filled the time while the Zeeb did whatever it was he was doing.

People came and went, a small maintenance bot ran over my foot, and the Zeeb stayed where he was. I bought an Americano, and was halfway through it when the Zeeb sauntered away. I hurried to replace him.

Like most kiosks, this one had a grubby, overused feel. Doodles, limericks and com numbers covered all three walls. The word "Greetings" was white against the inevitable blue background. It blinked off and on.

Joy scrambled out of my pocket and made her way to the stainless-steel shelf. The terminal was voice or keypad activated. Joy chose neither one. She winked in my direction, wet her right index finger, and shoved it into a small recess located under the screen. Most high-function androids could do the same thing, but I was impressed nonetheless. Hundreds of screens' worth of information scrolled by during the two minutes that we stood there. I used the time to puzzle out the words printed over the terminal. "Property of Minestar, a wholly owned subsidiary of Trans-Solar Inc."

The knowledge seeped through my body as if someone had poured ice water into my veins. I wanted to run, pull my jacket over my head, and scream all at the same time. I remained motionless instead, but cursed myself for being seven kinds of idiot, and not asking the right questions to start with.

When Joy had everything she thought she'd need, she removed her finger from the machine, blew on it, and returned the imaginary weapon to its imaginary holster. I laughed in spite of myself. Joy received the visual and auditory cues that she'd been programmed to elicit, felt whatever robots feel when they're pleased with themselves, and cycled to the "ready" mode. It was a strange interaction, but better than none at all.

"So," I said, moving aside to allow an impatient miner access to the terminal, "what did you learn?"

Joy sat on the palm of my hand and let her legs dangle. She smiled coyly. "What would you like to know?"

I considered what I'd learned. "I need a disguise, a job, and a place to live."

Joy nodded as if disguises were the most natural thing in the world and squinted as if the reflection from my head might blind her. "You could wear a bandana tied around your head the way the miners do, one of those black ball caps, and let your beard grow for a couple of days."

I nodded. "Sounds good. Where can we get that stuff?"

Joy spent part of a second canvassing her newly acquired data. "Tom's Gear Shop is closest. Follow that autocart."

We followed the autocart for a while, took a left down a corridor packed with side-by-side stalls, and hung a right shortly after that. I kept a sharp eye out for Zeebs, poppers, and other homicidal maniacs but didn't see any. Tom's was two stalls down on the right. Tom was middle-aged and decked out in some of his own finery: a dirty T-shirt, some orange overalls, and a pair of work boots. He treated us to the same suspicious stare that most people reserve for chrome-headed giants. "Welcome to Tom's. What can I do for you?"

"I'm looking for a bandana and a ball cap."

"Big spender, huh? Well, take a look over there."

We left five minutes later. I had to admit that between the bandana and the hat, you couldn't see any of my telltale white hair or highly reflective scalp. Not exactly foolproof, mind you, but better than nothing. And, safely wrapped in her new saronglike bandana, Joy was a lot less noticeable as well.

We paused by a rock garden. I said, "So, how 'bout a job?"

Joy twirled and admired her reflection in the water. "There's an opening for a metallurgist on sub-level six."

"Funny. Very funny. I need a *real* job. One I'm qualified for."

The ensuing thirty seconds of silence signaled how many jobs I was qualified for. Finally, when I was about to give up, she spoke. "There's *one* job that you're qualified for . . . and the pay's pretty good."

I picked her up. "Really? What is it?"

She looked me in the eye. "They need a bouncer at a nightclub called Betty's."

It took the better part of half an hour to find Betty's. Like most establishments of its kind, the nightclub was located in a seemingly run-down section of the asteroid known as "Old Port." I say "seemingly," because the seediness was somewhat calculated and about as genuine as the bird calls emanating from the surrounding jungle. And, since drinking, gambling and fornicating are often associated with night, even the street lights were kept artificially low.

There were lots of joints, lots of miners, and lots of Zeebs to keep an eye on them. I checked to make sure my bandana was in place, stepped over a drunk, and made my way down the main drag. Dealers offered me dope out of the sides of their mouths, whores signaled me with sign language as old as their profession, and everybody else got out of my way. It pays to be big sometimes.

Like its neighbors, Betty's was housed in what had been a processing plant of some kind. Noise, light, and the smell of booze leaked out through a variety of holes and beckoned us in. We accepted. I sidestepped a pair of whacked-out miners, stepped through the swinging doors, and took a moment to check the place out.

Betty, or an interior designer from hell, had taken full advantage of what was already there. The floor consisted of not-so-smooth native rock. Huge, rusty-looking I-beams held the ceiling up. A stage consisting of odd-sized cargo modules occupied the far end of the room. A fifty-foot bar took up most of the right-hand wall. It was made of hull metal and rested on a string of clapped-out mining carts. The floor was packed with miners, spacers, dealers, pimps, whores and scam artists of every description. I noticed that the furniture was made out of metal and looked damned near indestructible. I strolled over to the bar. A human was in charge and had two robotic assistants. I waved him over. He wore a brightly flowered shirt, black suspenders, and red pants. He plucked an empty off the bar and tossed it towards a recycle bin. "Yeah? What'll it be?"

"I'm looking for the owner or manager."

The bartender was in his early thirties, had slightly dissipated features and a somewhat arrogant manner. "What for?"

"You need a bouncer, and I'm interested in the job."

The bartender looked me up and down like a butcher appraising a side of beef. "You're big . . . but size ain't everything."

"No, it isn't," I agreed patiently. "Can I see the owner?"

"That would be me," a soft, rather melodious voice said. I turned to find an absolutely beautiful woman standing before me. She had black hair, black skin, and a bod that wouldn't quit. Kind of like a full-sized, flesh-and-blood Joy, clad in a long black evening gown rather than a bandana. Her dress was covered with black sequins. They shimmered with reflected light.

I took the ball cap off and held it in my hands. "My name's Max. I'm looking for a job."

The woman smiled. "Good. My name's Betty and I'm looking for a bouncer." She held out her hand. I took it, got lost in her eyes, and barely remembered to let go. Joy climbed up on my shoulder, and Betty smiled as if seeing herself in the miniature robot.

A ruckus started on the other side of the room. A pair of men stood, exchanged words, and started to square off. Betty gestured with her head. "Fights are expensive, Max. Break it up."

I nodded soberly, placed Joy in a pair of well-manicured hands, and made my way across the room. My goal was to get there in a short period of time but do it in a low-key, almost casual way. The usual pre-fight war of words was well under way by the time I arrived. I interrupted. "Good evening, gentlemen. Having a good time?"

The bigger of the two, a mean-looking dude with the words "Eat shit and die!" tattooed across his forehead and fists the size of miniature hams, looked me up and down. The sweet-sour stench of alcohol rolled over me as he spoke. "I'm going to rip this asshole's head off and shove it up his ass. You got a problem with that?"

It's always been my opinion that actions truly speak louder than words. That's why I turned towards number two, smiled, and side-kicked number one's left knee. Something crunched, and he went down gushing swear words.

Number two's eyes got wide, like he couldn't quite believe what he'd just seen, and his right fist went back in preparation for a roundhouse swing. I jerked my head to the side, let it pass, and sunk my fist into his gut. He bent over, barfed on his boots, and fell to his knees.

Pain lanced up through my right leg. I turned to find that bozo number one had sunk his teeth into my right calf. I shifted my weight to that foot, back-kicked with my left, and felt his teeth tear loose. The rest was relatively easy. I bounced number one's head off a nearby pillar, towed him over to number two, got a grip on both their collars, and dragged them towards the door. An obliging patron helped me roll them out into the street, where the Zeebs would eventually cart them away. I thanked him and followed the path of blood and vomit back into the night club. Betty was waiting for me. Joy had taken up residence on her shoulder. The nightclub owner smiled. "Your methods are rather messy, Max. I prefer bouncers who use as little violence as possible."

I felt my heart sink. The brain-cell shortage had surfaced again. A normal person would have used psychology, would have bullshitted the drunks out onto the street, then sent them packing. But not me, oh no, I had to kick the shit out of them, and blow off the only job I was likely to get. I looked down toward her elegantly clad feet. "Sorry."

"On the other hand," Betty said levelly, "talk's cheap and doesn't work all that often."

I felt my spirits rise and dared to look up. She smiled encouragingly. "Tell me something, Max, is your little friend for sale? She looks like a miniature version of me."

Joy seemed oblivious to Betty's words and toyed with one of her diamond earrings. The thoughts plodded through my mind. I needed money, that was true, and Joy would bring a pretty price. But you don't sell friends, even if they don't qualify as human. I shook my head. "Sorry, but Joy was given to me by a friend, and she's not for sale."

Betty nodded understandingly. "Good. I like people with principles. You're hired."

16

"Once entrenched, new technology grows like an evil weed. Given sufficient time, it will overwhelm the garden of man and destroy that which sustains us. Our task is to identify the first twisted tendrils as they appear above the ground and destroy them before they can spread."

From an "Ecological Manifesto," by Hans Schmidt, father of the Radical Action Committee of the group known as Green Earth

Visiting hours started at 1000 standard and we were there when the doors opened. The women's surgical ward was just that, a big open room with two rows of bio beds, each adjusted to meet that particular patient's needs. Depending on what sort of surgery they had undergone or were about to have, the women lay on their backs, sides, or stomachs. Tubing and multi-colored wires snaked all around them. Most were miners, clearly identifiable by their short, easy-to-wash hair, but there was a scattering of spacers, tool heads, and freelancers as well. No corpies, though, since they had private rooms with hot and cold running robots to keep them comfy. My calf hurt where the drunk had chewed on it. I limped slightly as I made my way down the corridor.

The kid was located about halfway down the ward. Pull-out curtains screened her bed from the rest. Someone had combed her hair and given the bed permission to prop her up. Sasha was pale, and somewhat emaciated, but far better than when I'd seen her last. She managed a smile and held out her hand. It felt cold and weak. "Hi, Max. Hi, Joy. I like your dress."

The little android squealed with pleasure, did cartwheels up the bed, and snuggled into Sasha's lap. I perched on the edge. "Hi yourself. Howya feeling?"

"Like warmed-over vat slime. How do I look?"

"Never better," I lied cheerfully.

"Liar," she said equably. "They say I can bust out of here in three or four days."

"Glad to hear it," I replied. "We'll have the apartment ready by then."

She looked to see if I was serious. "Apartment? What apartment?"

"The one I rented this morning," I said importantly. "Gotta have a place to stay, you know."

Sasha frowned, and I saw the wheels start to turn. "That was thoughtful, Max, very thoughtful. Can we afford it?"

This was fun. I grinned. "Yup . . . my job pays pretty well."

She looked genuinely surprised. "You've got a job?"

"Sure do. I'm the bouncer at a nightclub called Betty's."

I watched her absorb and process that piece of information. She looked up to where the bandana and hat covered the top of my head. "I like the fashion statement."

I almost said, "That isn't a fashion statement, it's a disguise," and realized my mistake. I nodded wisely. "Thanks, it seemed like a good idea at the time."

"A *very* good idea," Sasha said seriously. "I hope you'll continue to think along those lines."

I winked broadly. "Don't worry, Mary. I will."

Sasha rolled her eyes at the sound of the phony name. "Good. See that you do."

I was about to respond with something witty when the bed interrupted. "The patient is tired. The patient is tired. Please leave now. Please leave now." I felt a buzzing sensation under my butt. I stood. Joy ran to join me.

"Okay, okay. I'm leaving, already. Take care of yourself, Sash, I mean Mary, and I'll see you tomorrow."

The kid smiled, held up a hand, and let her head fall back against the pillow. She managed to look pretty in spite of the eyepatch, pasty skin, and nonexistent makeup. Sasha was tough, you had to give her that, and I felt a sense of almost fatherly pride. I forced myself to leave.

The next couple of days developed into an almost pleasurable routine. Get up, shower, dump the fast-food containers left from the night before, drink two cups of Americano at the local expresso stand, visit Sasha in the hospital, and walk to work. Something I took seriously.

After some rather arduous thought, I discovered it *is* possible to handle most troublemakers without resorting to violence. The first step is to *look* intimidating. That'll control about seventy or eighty per cent of your typical barroom yahoos right off the top. That's why I took to wearing black leathers, chrome-plated chains, and a semipermanent sneer.

Of course, some drunks are talkers rather than fighters. Nine times out of ten you can bullshit them out the door, and as Betty likes to say, "Why fight if you don't have to?"

Still, real honest-to-god barroom brawlers *like* to fight, and build their reps on how many bouncers they wax. The best way to deal with them is to launch a preemptive strike that is *so* unexpected, *so* violent, that they never have a chance. The trick is to sort them out from the rest of the crowd, and that's what I was working on when trouble arrived.

The whole thing started about four hours into my shift. A few thousand miners had just come off duty, and two or three hundred of them had decided to spend some of their hard-earned pay at Betty's. It wasn't long before we had the usual number of arguments, squabbles, and scuffles. I sorted them out and took a break by the bar. Then something unusual happened. A set of honest-to-god, dyed-in-the-wool corpies walked through the doors, looked around, and headed for a recently vacated table.

I was clear across the room when they entered, but it was easy to tell who and what they were from the way they moved, and the greyhound-thin zombie that tagged along behind them. It didn't take a genius to know they'd attract trouble. After all, miners have a tendency to blame corpies for everything from pressure leaks to the quality of their sex lives. I moved in and tried to see their faces, but the combination of smoke and heavy shadow made it difficult.

Nothing happened at first. The corpies ordered drinks, argued amongst themselves, and laughed at private jokes. Their zombie sat on the floor, rested her head against someone's thigh, and stared into space. I wondered what she was thinking, *if* she was thinking, and how she'd wound up the way she was. I was still thinking about that when Betty came along.

"The rounds," as Betty called them, were something she was known for. They were her personal touch, the way she made her club different from the rest, and built a loyal clientele at the same time. Such was her beauty, and the personality that went with it, that everyone wanted to know and be known by her.

Betty started by the autotellers, worked her way down along the bar, and drifted out onto the main floor. A robo-spot tracked her progress. Smoke eddied as it drifted through the light. Canned music thumped in the background. Betty knew the regulars, hundreds of them, and called them by name. All the rest were addressed as "honey, sweetie, or darling."

"Murphy, nice to see you tonight . . . Rawlings, nice earrings. Where'd you get them? Hello, sweetie, welcome to Betty's. Lopez, behave yourself tonight, Max is getting tired of throwing you out . . ."

And so it went until she approached the corpies. I tensed, hoping things would go well and sensing that they wouldn't. She addressed their leader. He had his back turned in my direction. Her voice was husky sweet and carried over the noise. "Hi, honey, how are you tonight?"

"Horny as hell," came the answer. "Why don't you sit on my lap?"

I saw Betty frown and was already in motion when she replied. "Thanks, sweetie, but not right now. Some other time, maybe."

I was halfway there when a hand grabbed Betty's arm and pulled her down. She struggled but he held her down. "What's the problem, bitch? You hard of hearing or something? I said sit on my lap."

I approached from behind, looped the garrote around his neck, and pulled the handles in opposite directions. He let go of Betty and reached for the wire. She stood and I released the handles. The garrote fell away as the man turned in my direction. That's when I realized that we'd met before.

It was Curt, the same Curt I'd called "pretty boy" back on Earth, though his looks had deteriorated since I'd blown half his nose away. The docs had done a good job on him, but it would take time and more operations before anyone called him "pretty" again.

I waited for him to recognize me, but the disguise worked. You could see it in his eyes. He didn't know who the hell I was outside of some jerk that he wanted to hurt. Yeah, Curt was pissed, seriously pissed, and he started to rise. I hit his already damaged nose, felt it break, and grinned.

"Max! Max! Over here!" I turned to find that one of Curt's bodyguards was on his feet. He was struggling to peel Joy off his face with one hand while reaching for his gun with the other. I measured the distance, kicked him in the balls, and watched him go down. That was a mistake.

The third corpie, a woman this time, executed a textbook-perfect spin-kick and hit me in the side of the head. I stumbled backwards, felt the zombie hit the back of my knees, and fell over backwards. The floor hit hard. The corpie was still celebrating when the bartender sapped her from behind. She slumped to the floor. I got up. The room tilted, swayed from side to side, and stabilized. I turned to the bartender. "Thanks."

He shrugged and slipped the sap into a pocket. "I did it for Betty." I nodded my understanding.

Some of the regulars grabbed the corpies, roughed them up, and carried them towards the doors. Curt, supported by a miner on each side, held his nose with one hand and pointed towards me with the other. Blood dripped off his chin. "Mgmpf!"

It didn't make sense, but I understood. He planned to kill me, or have me killed, whichever was most convenient. I shrugged. So what else was new? The bastard had tried to grease me for months now.

The miners split into teams, vied to see which group could throw their corpie the furthest, and cheered their scores. It would have been fun to watch, except that a group of drunks had corralled the zombie and were pushing her around. She offered no resistance and bounced from one person to the next. She had a nice figure, and at least two members of the crowd were taking unfair advantage of that fact.

I walked over, thanked the miners for their help, and sent them to the bar for a free drink. The miners grumbled but obeyed. They were afraid not to. The zombie gazed at me through vacant eyes. I took her leash, led her outside, and gave control to a Zeeb. He frowned, started to say something, thought better of it, and led the zombie towards her master.

In spite of the fact that Zeebs aren't exactly known for their humanitarian efforts, four of them had gathered around Curt and were loading him onto a stretcher. After all, corpies outrank everyone, Trans-Solar owned the company they worked for, and if it hadn't been for the money that Betty paid them to stay off her back, the Zeebs would have hammered me right then and there. But they'd remember, yes they would, and the bill would eventually come due.

I turned and went back inside. My head hurt, and one eye had started to close. It was too bad, really, because if my vision had been unimpaired I might have seen the greenies and been prepared for what happened later. But I didn't and wasn't.

Two days passed. Days in which Curt could have sought revenge but didn't. Sasha was released from the hospital. I took her home to the apartment. It was a one-room affair, similar to my pad on Earth, though a good deal cleaner. I was proud of the artificial roses on the fold-down table and hoped she'd like them. "So," I said, gesturing to the room, the blanket that divided her sleeping space from mine and the miniscule kitchen, "what do you think?"

"I think it's wonderful," Sasha said sincerely. "And I love the roses. Thank you."

My heart swelled with pride. "She liked it! Not only that, but I found and paid for it all by myself! Well, almost by myself, since Joy had helped.

Life was good, truly good, or so I thought as I left for work. Sasha was better, the worst was behind us, and the end of the assignment was in sight. Yeah, right.

The club was half empty when I got there, with only a scattering of customers left over from the first shift. I grabbed a cup of really bad coffee from the bar, sauntered over to my favorite stainless-steel table, and took a seat. I hadn't been there for more than a moment before a man sidled up, pulled over a chair, and sat down. I was just about to snarl at him when I saw who it was. An ugly orange jumpsuit had replaced the green coat, but the man was the same. Still combed, still serious, and still Nigel Trask, greenie extraordinaire. He smiled, and the frown lines vanished. "Hello, Mr. Maxon. We meet again."

I lifted my coffee cup in a mock salute. "We certainly do. Take a hike."

Trask spread his hands on the tabletop. "Now, is that any way to speak to someone who traveled halfway across the solar system to see you?"

I got to my feet. "You people are nuts. First you try to kill me, then you want to talk. Get out before I throw you out."

Trask stood. "All right, take it easy. The Mars thing was a mistake. I opposed it, but the locals disobeyed my orders."

"They sure as hell did. Now get out. I won't say it again."

Trask backed away. "Okay, okay. But Trans-Solar knows you're here, and would've nailed you too, if Curt was smarter. One of us will get you, Maxon, mark my words, and we're nicer than they are."

I stepped forward. He turned and walked away. I watched him go. Things were getting complicated, real complicated, and Sasha would want to know. I resolved to tell her the moment that I went off duty.

Time passed. The second shift got off and flooded in through the doors. I kept a sharp eye out for Curt, his friends, and anyone who looked like a popper. I saw some, but they were regulars. I watched them anyway.

A fight broke out. I cleared it. A spacer threatened to commit suicide. Betty and I talked her out of it. A miner slapped his girlfriend. I decked him. Then, just as I was helping him up off the floor, all hell broke loose.

A chair flew through the air. Insults were exchanged. Fists started to fly. I pushed and shoved my way through the quickly gathering crowd. When I reached the center of the disturbance, I found that four men were pushing each other around. Not fighting, mind you, just shoving the way kids do, and calling each other names. I was just about to break it up when they turned on me.

What ensued was quick, professional, and well coordinated. A man wrapped his arms around my chest, smiled, and blew mint-fresh breath in my face. I tried to move and found that I couldn't. My feet were lifted clear of the ground. Something bit my left thigh. My thoughts slid apart, reassembled themselves in strange ways, and swirled as the chemicals pulled me downwards. Complete and total darkness followed.

I awoke to the smell of freshly brewed coffee. Not all at once, mind you, but gradually, until I wanted a steaming hot cup of Americano in the worst possible way.

It seemed as though my eyes were glued shut. It took a conscious effort to force them open. First the right, then the left. The picture was bleary. I blinked it clear. A room full of empty desks, computer consoles, and office equipment surrounded me. The clutter gave the impression of employees who might return at any moment. Curt sat two feet in front of me. A bandage covered the bridge of his nose. A thin red line signaled where the garrote had been buried in his neck. I sensed people behind me but couldn't see them. My arms and legs were bound to a chair. The lifer nodded pleasantly and took a sip of coffee. "Well, look who decided to join us. Welcome back."

I tried to muster a smart-assed reply but couldn't seem to come up with one. Curt nodded understandingly. "A little short on repartee? That's too bad, but nothing to be ashamed of, considering your low IQ."

Curt took another sip of coffee and gestured with his cup. "Tell me something, Max, how smart are you, anyway? Nothing to say? Well, the experts say you have an IQ of about eighty, realizing that most people score between ninety and a hundred. Not too good, is it? Nothing like the 124 you scored prior to joining the Mishimuto Marines. They say you were one smart hombre back then, until you checked into a research station called T-12 that is, and had your ass kicked. Do you remember T-12?"

I mustered some saliva and used it to moisten my mouth. "Yeah, sort of."

Curt nodded agreeably. "I thought so. And after your capture? Do you remember what happened then?"

I tried to shrug. The ropes made it difficult. "Bits and pieces. Nothing much."

"And the girl? What did she tell you?"

I thought of Sasha and whatever it was that she'd been hiding. "I asked but she didn't tell me anything."

Curt placed his coffee cup on a table and leaned back in his chair. "Not too surprising, because if she told you the truth you'd run *to* us instead of away from us."

I felt an almost overwhelming need to know what he knew, to be in on the secret, to understand my past. "I would?"

"Yes," Curt replied quietly, "you would. Here's what Sasha Casad doesn't want you to know . . . Her mother, a more than competent physicist named Marsha Casad, worked for a company called Protech. She and a group of other scientists came up with a breakthrough, something worth a lot of money, and were just about to cash in on it when the war started. We know, because one of her closest associates was employed by us. Unfortunately for Dr. Casad and her fellow entrepreneurs, Protech was taken over by rank-and-file employees, and the scientists had little choice but to go along for the ride. A ride that started guess where?"

"On an asteroid called T-12?"

Curt pointed a finger in my direction. "Bingo! Not bad for an idiot. So, along comes Captain Maxon and his gung-ho Marines. They attack, get waxed, and the survivors wind up as prisoners."

Curt leaned forward so the front legs of his chair hit the floor with a thump. "Now pay attention, Maxon, because this is the interesting part. It seems that Marsha Casad and her scientist friends had no desire to share their newfound discovery with the great unwashed horde. But where to hide it? In the computers that any tool head worth his or her salt could hack? On cubes the unionists could check? No, they needed something better, a hiding place where no one would ever think to look."

I waited for Curt to continue, but he shook his head and smiled. He wanted *me* to think of it, to solve the puzzle with what was left of my brain, to . . . My god! That was it! The bastards had stored their data in my brain! Had used me as a zombie, or a *near* zombie, leaving just enough mental capacity to survive.

Curt saw the understanding fill my eyes and laughed. "That's right, stupid. Sasha Casad was guarding *you* rather than the other way around. She may not *look* very imposing, but Sasha Casad has been in training for this mission since she was born."

It all came back. The countless times when Sasha had been more competent than she should've been, when people came after *me* instead of her, when I should've smelled a rat. But not me, oh no, I was too stupid for that.

I fought the bonds, tried to pull free, but hands gripped my shoulders. Curt waggled a finger in my direction. "Naughty, naughty! We wouldn't want to damage that shiny little head, now would we? Not after all we've been through. There were others, you know. Backups. A man and a woman. The man committed suicide shortly after discharge. I found the woman in a mental institution. Our shrinks siphoned a lot of crap out of her head, but very little of it made sense. That's the trouble with schizos. They make piss-poor storage modules. The R & D types are working on that. We have high hopes for you, though."

I remembered the greenie called Philip Bey, how he'd told me about the others, and how Sasha had refused to comment. The rotten little bitch. I struggled but the ropes held me in place.

"So," Curt said, getting to his feet, and cracking his knuckles. "Enough of this bullshit. First, I'm going to break your nose. Then we're going to drain your brain, dump the data to my pet zombie, and beat Protech to the punch. Adios, asshole."

Curt planted his feet, pulled his fist back, and swung. I tipped my head forward, felt the impact on the top of my skull, and heard him scream. He was still dancing around holding his broken hand when a tox dart took him in the neck. He looked surprised, tried to say something, and collapsed.

I heard a commotion, tried to turn, and felt the hands leave my shoulders. Someone yelled, "Shoot her!" and swore as he took a dart. Feet scuffled, dart guns hissed, and bodies thumped as they hit the floor. That was when Joy appeared next to my knee, scrambled onto my lap, and went to work on my bonds. She was her usual exuberant self.

"Damn boss . . . you get yourself into the most amazing situations! I followed you here, called Sasha, and hung around until she arrived. Sorry it took so long. Are you okay?"

The last of the ropes fell away. I stood. My wrists hurt. I rubbed them to restore the circulation. "Yeah, I'm fine, thanks to you."

Joy giggled happily, made her way up to my shoulder, and grabbed my ear. I turned to find three bodies sprawled on the floor, the zombie huddled in a corner, and Sasha going through some-one's wallet. "What the hell are you doing?"

She didn't even glance in my direction. "Borrowing some money so we can get the hell out of here."

I shook my head. "The farce is over, Sasha. Curt told me all about it. How your mother used me, how you lied, the whole thing."

Sasha looked up. I couldn't place her expression. Was it concern I saw? Relief? Or another part of the performance she'd been trained to give? There was no way to know. "I'm sorry, Max, I really am. I wanted to tell but promised I wouldn't."

I searched for the words that would tell her how much it hurt, how much I hated her guts, but couldn't find them. So I walked to the door, stepped through, and heard it close behind me.

I walked for a long time. Through the residential areas good and bad, past the heavily guarded scientific section, and out into the cathedral-sized atrium. It was one of those things that the corpies hated to pay for, but did because the shrinks said the workers would go bonkers if they didn't.

The park consisted of carefully maintained flower gardens, patches of green grass, and gravel-covered paths. The gravel had been coated with white paint, but most of it had worn off. Genetically engineered trees grew around the edges and softened the hard gray rock behind them.

It occurred to me that the vegetation served to supply supple-mental oxygen as well, and I wondered where the thought had come from. How did I know that? Was I as stupid as Curt said? What part was me and what part wasn't? My thoughts whirled, and my head started to hurt.

People strolled around me, clustering around the trees as if seeking strength from them, or shelter from the duraplast sky.

A pair of Zeebs, both women, looked my way, invented a "chrome-headed weirdo with a robot on his shoulder" category, and dropped me inside it. They subvocalized to each other and watched me from the corners of their eyes as they passed.

I sat on a park bench, tried to look normal, and let my chin rest on a fist. The knowledge of what had been done to my head, what had been hidden in my brain, weighed heavily and increased the pain. I forced myself to think, to wonder what it was that Sasha's mother had sacrificed my life to, and if I would approve of it. What had she hidden there, at the center of my being? A medical miracle? A doomsday weapon? And what should I do about it? Blow my brains out? Make my way back to Earth? What?

A bright red ball rolled towards me and came to rest against my foot. A little boy ran up, wiped his nose with the back of his hand, and said, "Ball. My ball."

I forced a smile and toed the ball in his direction. He picked it up, said, "My ball" again, and ran away.

"My ball." The words seemed to echo through my mind, transformed themselves into "my head," and refused to go away.

Suddenly I had it, one of those wonderful moments of clarity that had rescued me in the past, and knew what I wanted to do. *Must* do. My head belonged to *me,* damn it, regardless of what Marsha Casad had stashed there, and *I* would decide whether it would be released or not. So, given the fact that the greenies didn't seem to know much more than I did, and Curt wasn't about to tell, I had little choice but to obtain the information from Sasha's mother. And do so without getting caught, brain-drained, or killed. All of which reminded me of Sasha, my little bodyguard, liar, and corpie-in-training. I would use her just as she had used me.

The decision felt good. I grinned, scared the hell out of a little girl, and headed for our apartment. Dr. Casad had sent for me, and I was on the way.

17

"The captain and crew request your
attendance at the Jupiter Ball.
Please RSVP."

*From the invitation sent to passengers
aboard the* **Solar Queen**

A lot of people would like to take the grand tour, but few can
afford it. Those who can choose between two great ships, the *Solar
Queen* and the *Solar Princess,* both owned and operated by the
Regis Line, one of the few companies to go head-to-head with
Trans-Solar and emerge at least even, if not slightly ahead. And
that's why Sasha and I felt reasonably safe boarding the *Queen.*
Trans-Solar might have agents aboard, but we could count on
Regis security to keep them in check. Or so we hoped.

Once we were aboard, the ship would become part of a journey
that had started on Earth, paused off Mars, and stopped in the belt
on the way to Jupiter and Europa Station. The very place we
wanted to go.

Like the *Princess,* the *Queen* had been designed to meet the rigorous demands of the extremely wealthy, none of whom were anywhere near the C Deck lock, through which lowlies like ourselves passed. The line was fairly long and consisted of robots, zombies, and freelancers.

One of them, a woman with blonde hair, blue eyes, and bright red lips, caught my attention. She was one person ahead of me in line and stood out from the rest. Maybe it was the way she held herself, the carefully coordinated clothes, or the expensive perfume that floated back to tease my nostrils.

Whatever it was caught and held my attention. She seemed to sense my interest, turned, and smiled. I felt a sudden sense of warmth and smiled back. But months of running had made me wary. Yes, she could be attracted to my obvious charm and rugged good looks, but there were other possibilities as well. What if she was a killer in nice-lady drag? An assassin android? Or a carefully disguised bomb? Still, she *looked* innocent enough, and my libido said she was the greatest thing since sliced bread. I was getting ready to say or do something stupid when the line jerked forward and took her with it.

I turned and saw Sasha frown. She had monitored the interchange and didn't approve. Well, too bad. Gone were the days when she gave orders and I obeyed. I had my own reasons for going to Europa Station now, reasons that went beyond the fifty K they had used for bait, and it didn't matter if Sasha came along or not. I appreciated the fact that she had stolen enough money to pay her fare, and would cover my back if it came to a firefight, but could get along without her too. And she knew it. So the silence was complete as we stepped through the hatch, waited for the lock to cycle open, and entered the *Queen*'s opulent interior.

Everything was spotless, even on C Deck, which was a far cry from the glory found on A and B. In space there is nothing so rare and frivolous as genuine wood, and that's what the ship's architects had used to cover the standard durasteel bulkheads. Everywhere I looked I saw highly polished wood, brass fittings, and deep pile carpets. It made quite a contrast to life on the barge.

Sasha had suggested that we share a stateroom in order to reduce expenses and enhance security, but I said no. The less I saw of the traitorous little minx the better, and besides, some privacy would be nice for a change.

Though smaller than the cabin I had occupied aboard the *Red Trader,* my stateroom managed to be a good deal more luxurious. The plumbing worked, for one thing, never a surety aboard the *Trader,* and there were lots of extras too, like a high-quality virtual reality entertainment console, a fully stocked minibar, a toaster-sized automaid that nearly went crazy trying to pick up after me, plus rotating storage lockers that could accommodate a large, but in my case nonexistent, wardrobe.

So, doing my best to get into the spirit of the thing and enjoy the many amenities, I took a long, wasteful shower, left the thick terrycloth towel for the automaid to tow away, donned my most presentable set of clothes, and set out to explore the rest of my temporary home. Joy wasn't too happy about being left behind, but I figured I was noticeable enough without a miniature android perched on my shoulder. The hatch closed on her protests.

I set out for the far reaches of C Deck, knowing that while A and B Decks might have been more interesting, the denizens of C Deck weren't allowed to visit their betters without a specific invitation to do so.

The corridor curved gently to the right. Almost everyone I encountered, children excepted, managed to ignore my chrome-plated scalp and smile at me. It was as if my head had been magically transformed from the grotesque to the merely eccentric.

The change puzzled me at first. What the heck was going on? Were these people especially nice? Or was there a more believable explanation? After giving the matter some thought, I decided that I was the accidental beneficiary of "situational niceness."

The logic went like this: Special people rode the ship, Max rode the ship, ergo, Max was a special person and would be treated as such. If, on the other hand, the same people encountered me in a dimly lit alley, they would perceive me as a seven-foot-two-inch-tall chrome-headed homicidal maniac, and run like hell. Ah, well, it was pleasant to be accepted by other human beings even if the pleasure was only transitory.

An airtight door slid out of the way and I entered a large multi-purpose lounge. There was a bar against the far bulkhead, an open area where people stood about in conversational clumps, and semicircular tiers of acceleration couches that dropped away to a vast expanse of transparent duraplast. Sunlight glazed Deep Port's rocky surface, and stars twinkled as light generated millions and even billions of years before hit my retinas and was recorded by what was left of my brain.

I had no more than entered the area when an artificially sweet voice said, "Welcome to the *Solar Queen*. The ship will depart in fifteen, I repeat, fifteen minutes. The captain requests that those passengers still in their cabins lie down and strap themselves in.

"Those passengers presently located in the public areas may proceed to their cabins or make use of the acceleration couches available in each of our lounges. Please check to ensure that your restraint system has been activated. Children must be accompanied by an adult or a Class IV android. Autostewards are available to answer your questions. Welcome to the *Solar Queen* . . ."

The voice droned on in the background as I wandered down the center aisle, descended five or six tiers, and turned towards the center seats. Some were occupied but many were still available. I selected one, lay back, and activated the restraint system. Servos whined as heavily padded arms wrapped themselves around me. The couch came equipped with a variety of accessories. I was still in the process of investigating them when a voice came from my left. "Hi, it seems we're neighbors."

I turned and was pleased to find that the voice belonged to the same woman I had salivated over in line. She wore a bright red pants outfit that most women would have avoided like the plague. It looked great on her. I gave her what I hoped was my most charming smile.

"So it seems. My name's Max. Max Smith. What's yours?"

She smiled. Her teeth were wonderfully white. "Linda Gibson. Please to meet you, Max."

Her outstretched hand bridged half the distance between us. It felt small and warm. I was in the process of shaking it when Sasha appeared in the distance. Her eyepatch seemed out of place, or was it me? Our fellow passengers seemed as oblivious to the patch as they had been to my chrome-plated head. Same deal, probably. She treated me to one of her characteristic frowns and sat where she could watch. Alerted by the loss of eye contact, Linda turned and looked over her shoulder. "Am I missing something?"

I shook my head. "No, an old acquaintance, that's all." I plastered a phony smile on my face and waved. Sasha glowered in response.

I turned my attention to the lovely Linda. She had pale blue eyes, and they fastened on me as though I was the only man in the world. Her voice was soft and confidential. "Can I tell you a secret?"

I nodded earnestly. "Please do."

"I sat here on purpose."

Blood roared in my ears. She liked me! The only woman who had liked me prior to this time had been paid to do so. Had I been equipped with a tail, I would've wagged it. Now to say something clever. "Really? Well, I'm glad you did."

"Me too," she said sweetly. "Have you chosen a costume yet?"

"Costume?" I asked stupidly. "For what?"

"Why, the ball, silly," Linda said lightly. "It will be held on A Deck, and everyone's invited. I hoped you'd be my escort."

A storm of conflicting thoughts and emotions whirled through my head. Pleasure at being asked, fear of having to dance, and a sense of confusion. "Why no, I mean yes, I'd love to go. When is it?"

"2000 hours day after tomorrow," Linda answered smoothly. "I'm coming as an eighteenth-century noblewoman. You'd make a marvelous pirate."

"And so I would," I replied in my best pirate cackle. "Hoist the mainsail and belay the hatches!"

Linda giggled, I felt a rush of pleasure, and the ship broke contact with the asteroid known as Deep Port.

•   •   •   •   •   •

If the Jupiter Ball had been invented to keep the passengers busy, it did an excellent job. The next twenty-four hours were a whirl of preliminary fittings, intermediate fittings, and final fittings, all under the rather autocratic supervision of an android named Perkins.

It was Perkins who adjusted the plume on my hat just so, dictated that Joy would be dressed in an outfit identical to that worn by Linda, and helped rehearse our entrance. An entrance that would be judged against all others for one of three prizes. Prizes that meant nothing to me, but seemed important to Linda.

And we were typical. All the people around us were caught up in an absolute fever of preparation. And, just to make sure that everyone got involved, the ship's staff did everything they could to hype the occasion by running stories on the internal news system, holding pre-party parties, and peppering us with invitations, gifts, and special meals.

Though somewhat stiff at first, I found myself becoming more and more involved in the pre-party activities, until I actually worried about the color of my waist sash, the fit of my vest, and the edge of my aluminum cutlass.

Which is why I was exhausted by the time that Linda and I parted company and welcomed the opportunity to sleep. It came quickly, floating upwards to wrap me in its arms, then holding me in its dark embrace. What followed was similar to the dreams I had experienced in the past and was clearly related.

●　　●　　●　　●　　●　　●

My first impression was of lying on my back watching ceiling tiles pass overhead. My thoughts were slow, ponderous things, weighed down by the drugs the medicos had given me, and wholly unfocused. The ceiling tiles were interspersed with glow panels. I felt sure that someone wanted me to count them, to make an exact record of how many glow panels I had seen, but the numbers had a slippery, eellike quality and eluded my grasp. People walked to either side of my gurney. One, a woman with swept-back hair, a long straight nose, and a white lab coat, glanced at me but addressed her comments to the balding man on my left. "You're sure this will work."

"No, I'm not," the man replied calmly. "Bio-storage is a fledgling science. I *believe* it will work but make no guarantees."

It was as if the woman hadn't even heard him. "A zombie would be too obvious. The trick is to stash the research in his head, yet leave him functional. The unionists are almost sure to discover it otherwise."

"I'm aware of that threat," the man said dryly. "I'll do the best I can."

The woman wanted to say more but gave a short, jerky nod instead.

The autogurney turned a corner, I lost count of the glow panels, and felt a desperate need for water. My mouth felt dry, terribly dry, and I croaked pitifully. The woman glanced in my direction but made no effort to learn what the problem was.

An airtight hatch came and went. The ceiling panels disappeared and were replaced by a seamless surface. It was translucent, and light seeped through.

The gurney stopped under a vent. Cool air caressed my face. The smell of disinfectants stabbed my nostrils. I caught a glimpse of OR greens. An operating room! They were taking me into an operating room! But I wasn't sick . . . was I? I struggled against my restraints, and feeble though the movements were, the woman noticed them. She frowned and turned towards the person behind me. "The pre-meds are wearing off . . . take him down."

"But not too far," the bald man cautioned. "I need access to his reactions."

I fought to free myself, gave up, and floated on an ocean of light. I heard voices, felt the gurney move, and knew we had entered the operating room when the large circular lights came into view. Metal clanked as the side rails were released. Hands felt along my sides, took hold of the sheet beneath me, and a voice said, "On three. One . . . two . . . three."

I felt myself lifted into the air and lowered to the surface of the operating table. A distant part of my mind told me to do something, but I was unable to respond.

Time passed. There was talk of "local anesthetics," "head preps," and "neural interfaces." None of which meant anything to me. Then it started, the general sense of inflow, of words and numbers that tumbled around me to build vast informational structures so large and complex that they could be compared with cities, except that try as I might I was unable to comprehend them in their entirety, to back away far enough to see and understand their function and purpose.

But I did notice that as the city grew larger and larger, I became smaller and smaller, until it towered over and around me. The air grew thick with words and numbers until I choked and couldn't breathe. It was then that I decided to escape, to leave the whole affair behind, and exist somewhere else.

And no sooner had the thought occurred to me than I was gone, drifting up to hover under the ceiling, while the bald man and his staff shouted to each other and struggled to bring me back. I saw my body jump as they passed electricity through my heart and watched as drugs were injected into my veins. The light grew even brighter, and seemed to beckon me onwards, but I hung there unsure of what to do. And then, like fishermen pulling in their catch, the medics reeled me in. My head was full. So full I thought it would explode. I screamed . . .

•   •   •   •   •   •

. . . and was still screaming when I awoke to find myself in bed, the sheets soaked with sweat.

It was a terrible dream, made all the more horrible by the certain knowledge that it or something like it had actually happened, leaving me forever crippled. I was afraid to sleep and spent the rest of the cycle staring at the ruby-red light over my head. It belonged to the smoke detector, and blinked on and off with machinelike patience.

•   •   •   •   •   •

The first day of my relationship with Linda Gibson had passed without much in the way of serious conversation. By the afternoon of the second day, I wanted to know more about her. Perkins had approved our costumes, the ball was hours away, and Linda had agreed to a drink.

The Constellation Room consisted of a clear duraplast bubble accessed through a pipelike structure that connected it to the hull. The place was half full. Glasses clinked and conversation hummed. Linda was beautiful. Stars decorated her hair, diamonds twinkled at her ears, and her perfume made my head spin. I raised my glass. "To us."

Linda smiled and did likewise. "To us."

We took a sip and placed our glasses on the table. "So, tell me about Linda Gibson. Where she's from, and where she's going. Besides Europa Station, that is."

Linda laughed. "There isn't much to tell. Mom and Dad were

high-priced freelancers, the kind who get lots of work, but aren't willing to make the sacrifices required of lifers."

"*Were* freelancers?"

A cloud passed over Linda's eyes. "They were killed when the Mundo-Tech fusion plant went critical and destroyed Caracas."

"I'm sorry."

She shrugged. "Don't be. It was one of those crappy this-is-the-real-world kind of things, that's all."

I nodded. "Then what?"

Her eyes went out of focus. She seemed to see through me and into another time. "I was in college. There was some money, enough to finish my degree, and I did. Then the war started and I graduated just in time to get drafted by General Electric. I did fairly well and wound up as a captain."

I nodded respectfully. "GE has some tough troops . . . what outfit were you in?"

Linda smiled. "Logistics . . . I spent the whole war using a computer to shuffle supplies from one place to another. How 'bout you? How did you spend the war?"

I used my drink to buy time. The wine felt cool as it trickled down my throat. How honest should I be? Semi-honest seemed best. "I was a Mishimuto Marine, or so they tell me. I don't remember much after being hit in the head."

She smiled and gestured with her glass. "Which explains the rather unusual hairstyle."

"Exactly."

Linda leaned forward. Her cleavage made a wonderful canyon. A hand touched the side of my head. I fancied I could feel it there, warm through an eighth-inch of polished steel, accepting the thing that kept me apart. Nothing could have meant more to me, and I was sorry when the hand was withdrawn. She nodded as if satisfied. "I like the skull plate. It makes you look dangerous."

"You like dangerous men?"

"No," Linda answered thoughtfully, "I like men who *look* dangerous. There's a difference."

Word games are not my strongest suit. Not with a gazillion megabytes of god knows what occupying a significant portion of my brain. I let it drop.

"So, what did the logistics expert do after the war?"

One carefully plucked eyebrow rose higher than the other. She smiled. "Logistics . . . what else? GE liked my work and hired me as a freelancer."

"This is a business trip, then?"

Linda laughed. "Of course. I could never afford this. My boss is up on A Deck, where she can hobnob with her peers. You'll meet her at the ball. How 'bout you? What's an ex-Mishimuto Marine doing on his way to Jupiter?"

I delivered what I hoped was a nonchalant shrug. "I won the northwest regional lotto. Haven't had a vacation in years. Thought it would be fun."

If Linda thought the story was far-fetched, she gave no sign of it. She hoisted her glass. "To fun!"

Crystal clinked as our glasses touched and the conversation turned toward less dangerous ground. Time passed, and the ball neared. We stood. I bent slightly, felt her lips brush mine, and wallowed in her perfume. Bright blue eyes searched my face. "I'll expect you at 1945 hours. You won't be late?"

"Pirates are punctual."

"Well, noblewomen aren't, but I'll do my best. Our entrance is scheduled for 2017. Perkins would be most annoyed if we missed it."

"God forbid."

I escorted Linda through the access tube and watched her walk away. And what a walk it was. I turned, and was headed for my stateroom, when Sasha appeared at my side. She had lain in wait. Her voice was determined. "We need to talk."

"I doubt that very much."

"Your friend, if that's what she is, lied to you."

I stopped and turned to face her. The other pedestrians looked annoyed and walked around us. "Oh, really? And how do you know that?"

Sasha looked serious, and something else as well. Sympathetic? Sad? No, those were human emotions of the sort that her mother would never countenance. "I know because she's a greenie."

I frowned. "Says who?"

"Says all the propaganda lying around her stateroom."

My jaw dropped. "You searched her quarters?"

"No," Sasha said evenly, "Joy did. The air-conditioning ducts are like a highway for someone her size. The woman is not only a greenie, she's Trask's boss, and here to take you out." ·

Part of it was true, anyway. With no orders to the contrary, Joy would do whatever Sasha asked. And, given her rather unusual programing, surveillance work was well within her abilities. I felt resentment, fear, and rage all at the same time. "You're lying!"

Sasha spoke as if to a child. "No, I'm not. Believe what you will about my motivations, but I'm telling the truth."

I didn't know what to think, what to believe, so I turned and walked away. I was still confused by the time I ordered my door to open and stepped inside. Joy was dressed as a miniature noblewoman, and Perkins had left my costume on the bed. It was time to dress, and I allowed inertia to carry me along.

Before I knew it I was dressed in a wide-brimmed hat with plume, a snow-white shirt, a black vest, scarlet waist sash, black breeches, knee-high boots, a brace of flintlock pistols, and my aluminum sword. Even I, something of a cynic when it comes to my own appearance, was impressed when I looked in the mirror.

And Joy, cheerful as always, looked wonderful on my shoulder, her hair done up in a beehive, her petticoats arranged just so, and a tiny parasol tilted over one shoulder. She giggled happily. "We look great, boss . . . A prize is in the bag."

But if *we* looked good, Linda looked even better. She was nearly ready when we arrived. She wore her hair piled high, like Joy's, and a dress so daring it barely covered her nipples. I must have stared because she laughed and pointed over a shoulder. "Would you be so kind as to zip me up?"

I moved behind her and found in place of the buttons or hooks that would've been part of a *real* noblewoman's gown, this one had been equipped with a most sensible zipper. A wonderful invention that reduces the amount of time it takes women to dress and undress. The second being more important than the first.

But as I zipped Linda's dress, and looked over her shoulder I scanned the compartment looking for the evidence that Joy had allegedly uncovered, but saw no sign of it. That being the case, I decided to wait and see what happened.

We stepped out of Linda's stateroom and into something verging on a traffic jam. Everyone but everyone was going to the ball, and the corridor was jammed with people wearing a fantastic assortment of costumes, all in a festive mood. Cheers welcomed us into the crowd, and every man within ten feet maneuvered for a chance to look down Linda's dress. Being closest, I had the best view.

The line jerked forward by fits and starts, passed through a lounge where we were sorted and rearranged according to our entrance times, and sent into the lift tubes in proper order. The ride to A Deck took about fifteen seconds. The doors slid open, a uniformed crew member gestured to the left, and we obeyed.

The flow steadied as guests were funneled into the ballroom. The drill was to listen for your name, take three steps forward, strike a pose, and proceed across the open floor to the other side. That gave the residents of A and B Decks time to look at the costumes, compare them to the others they'd seen, and record their votes via small hand-held boxes. Each had thirty votes and could assign them in any way they chose. Winning meant absolutely nothing, but the knowledge did nothing to lessen the empty feeling in my gut, or slow the beating of my heart. Linda's hand felt damp through my sleeve, and I knew the tension had affected her as well.

A voice called, "Frank Stanton and Mary Tomari," in loud stentorian tones, and the couple in front of us, a somewhat portly sultan accompanied by a willowy dancing girl, stepped out into the ballroom. The music segued, and the sultan stood with arms crossed while his more athletic companion treated the crowd to a passable belly dance. The applause was light but sustained. Then, long before I was ready, it was our turn. The voice announced our names: "Max Smith and Linda Gibson."

Linda, her fingertips resting on my arm, looked up and smiled. I took three steps forward, pulled the sword, and used it like a cane. Joy, already on her feet, curtseyed at the same exact moment that Linda did. No small trick while standing on someone's shoulder. The two of them, dressed exactly alike, earned a roar of approval. We were already in motion when the next names were called.

I heaved a giant sigh of relief when we reached the other side of the ballroom, checked to make sure no one was looking, and wiped my forehead with a sleeve. "Thank god it's over."

Linda fluttered her eyelashes and looked over the top of her fan.

"Over, my lord? Whatever do you mean? The dancing has yet to begin!"

A rock fell into the bottom of my stomach. Assuming that I'd known how to dance once, the knowledge had been obliterated along with the rest of my memories. Sweat trickled down my temples.

The next two hours were pure torture. I stepped on Linda's toes at least five times, tripped on my sword, and dumped Joy on the floor. Nor did the humiliation end there. I danced Linda into a collision with another couple, spilled wine on her boss's dress, and delivered five seconds' worth of mathematical gibberish to the ship's captain.

But, just when I was about to declare the evening a total loss, a miracle occurred. The winners were announced, and we copped third place, right behind the juggling Rinaldo sisters, and the barbershop androids. Linda was thrilled, and hurried to collect our prize, a rather handsome chunk of plastic. It seemed that all my sins were forgiven. So, borne along on high spirits, and fueled by alcohol, we dropped Joy at my stateroom and headed for Linda's.

Even a pirate wouldn't go into the details of what happened next, but suffice it to say that it took Linda less time to get *out* of the gown than it took to get *into* it, and I did what I could to assist. And while I would have been happy to join her in the buff, she liked the pirate costume, and insisted that I continue to wear most of it, minus the hat and the unwieldy sword.

I enjoyed the next hour or so, and got the distinct impression that Linda did too. She had wonderful breasts, and I liked the way they moved when she handed me a drink. "I had a wonderful time, Max. Thank you."

I took a sip and smiled. "No, it is *I* who should thank *you*. Especially your feet . . . which paid a high price indeed."

She laughed, but it was a halfhearted laugh, as if her mind was on something else. Something that made her sad. I took another sip and felt my head swim. I tried to move and found that I couldn't. Something, a drug of some kind, held me in a paralytic grip. I could see, hear, and to some extent think, though the process was slow and somewhat ponderous. I tried to speak but croaked instead. Linda nodded understandingly.

"I'm sorry, Max, I really am, but we lack the means to erase whatever Dr. Casad stored in your brain without destroying the rest of you as well. Yes, our operatives had a long and somewhat unpleasant conversation with Curt. We learned all sorts of things, including the fact that while Trans-Solar doesn't know *what* the good doctor stashed in your gray matter, they know it's worth billions, and would sacrifice anything to get their hands on it. But there's enough techno-evil in the world already without creating more. Think about it, Max; think about the things they did to your brain, the Urboplex where you used to live, the condition of our home planet. It has to stop."

I struggled against the chemical bonds. My limbs twitched ineffectually. I felt drool slide down my chin.

Linda shook her head sadly. A tear rolled down her cheek. "I wish there was some way to help you, some way to restore what they took, but there isn't. And by the way, no one *told* me to make love to you. I wanted to."

It was a nice compliment, the nicest I'd had in some time, but didn't make up for the plan to murder me. Linda left me to drool, donned a robe, made a com call, and went about restoring the few items of clothing that I'd been allowed to remove. She had foresight, you had to grant her that. The skin-tight breeches offered the most difficult challenge, but by dint of such tugging, swearing, and lifting Linda got them on.

The door announced visitors, and she ordered it open. My old friend Nigel Trask entered and stood over the bed. Philip Bey, the guy I had met aboard *Staros-3,* was right behind him. Both wore nondescript costumes. No wonder Linda wanted to party with someone more colorful. I ordered my limbs to move, and they twitched spasmodically. Trask shook his head sympathetically.

"Sorry, Mr. Maxon . . . nothing personal. If only you had agreed to work *with* instead of against us. But it's too late for that, I'm afraid. Philip, give me a hand."

Philip pitched in, and between them they managed to get me into a slump-shouldered standing position. I'm heavy, so it was no small task to drag me across the cabin to the hatch. Linda spoke, and it disappeared. I wanted to see her face, to see if she cared, but my head refused to turn.

I thought they were crazy at first, dragging me out in the hall like that, but I was wrong. Passengers, most of whom were still in costume, and about three sheets to the wind, roamed the corridors in groups, and found the sight of a drunken pirate most amusing. Which is why the greenies were able to drag me through a lounge while the rabble laughed, and yelled things like "Yo, ho, ho, and a bottle of rum."

The crowd thinned as we made our way down a series of little-used passageways. I hoped for a crew person. Someone who would question our presence and demand an explanation. The corridors were empty. Or so I assumed, since my view was restricted to beige carpet, followed by high-gloss decking, followed by unadorned steel.

Coping as they do with zero-gee conditions, spacers have a tendency to print directional signs on every available surface, including the deck. The Regis company was no exception. The words "EMERGENCY LOCK," and an arrow pointed toward the right, disappeared under my toes as they dragged me around the corner. A lock! They planned to eject me from a lock! I could imagine the investigation and perfunctory report. ". . . And so, with no evidence to suggest foul play, and no history of mental instability, we conclude that passenger Smith was inebriated, wandered into the lock, and cycled himself into the void . . ." A tragic but understandable mistake.

Both men were panting by now, tired from lugging my dead weight a quarter-mile or so, and eager to be rid of their burden. "There is it," Trask said, "at the end of the corridor. Come on."

Philip renewed his grip around my waist and helped drag me towards my death. I imagined what it would be like to hear the hatch close, to feel the vibration as the pumps started, to gulp air in a desperate attempt to prolong life, to know it was hopeless, to feel my lungs start to burst, to see the outer hatch start to open, and to catch a glimpse of the stars before the vacuum sucked me out. I screamed, but nothing came.

That's when three sets of boots appeared in front of me and I heard Sasha say, "I think you took a wrong turn, gentlemen. The lounge is thataway."

18

"By protecting the proprietary nature of Project Freedom, and regulating access to it, Protech will earn excellent returns for its share owners while changing the course of human history."

From Draft 16.2 of an unpublished Protech press release

The kid saved my life, there's no doubt about that, even if her motivations were a bit clouded. The moment they were confronted by Sasha and two members of the *Solar Queen*'s security force, Trask and Bey pretended they were drunk and requested directions for the bar. No one believed them, least of all me, but it offered the security people a way to avoid conflict with the greenies, assuming they knew who the players were, and I was betting that they did. The security types made a big production out of escorting us to our respective staterooms and admonishing us to stay sober.

Yeah, like it or not, Sasha and her stubborn ways had saved me from a one-way trip through the lock. And that being the case, I knew it was simply a matter of time before the greenies or someone else tried it again. So, given the fact that the security people remained carefully neutral, I reversed my earlier decision and moved in with Sasha. It was a tight fit but a good deal safer than living alone.

Though afraid to launch a frontal assault, Linda tried to tease me out of the cabin with seductive voice-mail messages, Trask made futile attempts to bug our quarters, and the Regis folks monitored everything we did.

We, on the other hand, sent Joy on reconnaissance missions through the air ducts, watched entertainment videos, and ate elaborate meals obtained from room service. And, since it was difficult to eat without talking to each other, I allowed myself to be friendly.

Sasha seemed to welcome that, and, with the big secret out of the bag, let her guard down. She wore her eyepatch, a Regis Line T-shirt, and a pair of shorts. The food sat on the bed between us. She told me about her childhood, and it sounded depressing as hell.

". . . So, even though I received training in the martial arts, I didn't know why until Marsha called me into her office, and told me about the mission."

I raised an eyebrow. "You call her Marsha?"

Sasha smiled. "Everyone else calls her Dr. Casad."

I shook my head in amazement. "Go on."

"Well, she told me how a man had been captured during the war and used as a storage module for valuable research. Research it would take years to duplicate, and she needed to complete an important project. The mission was to find and bring the man back, but to do so in a manner that left him unaware of his significance, and fooled the competition." She smiled wryly. "I'm zero for three."

I ignored the joke. "So, what did you say?"

Sasha allowed her eye to drift down towards the bed and brought it up again. "I didn't say what I should have said. I didn't say that it was wrong, I didn't say that I was horrified, I didn't say no. I said 'yes, ma'am,' and did as I was told."

There was a moment of silence. Tears trickled down Sasha's cheeks. Something broke inside me, and tears trickled down my cheeks too. I wiped them away. "So what will you do? When we reach Europa Station?"

Her eye wandered away. "I honestly don't know. What Marsha did was wrong, but she's my mother, and this project means a lot to her."

I nodded. It was an honest answer, and a step in the right direction.

•　•　•　•　•　•

Thanks to Joy, and the time she spent camped in the air ducts over Linda Gibson's stateroom, we knew about the plan to abduct me well before the ship docked at Europa Station.

Europa, the smallest of Jupiter's four largest moons, was little more than an ice ball, its light-colored surface crosshatched with reddish fracture lines where water had erupted from the ocean below and frozen in place. Not especially hospitable until compared with Jupiter herself, playground for anticyclones large enough to swallow planets, and an atmosphere composed of ninety-five per cent hydrogen and helium.

It was no wonder, then, that Protech had established its base on a satellite rather than on the planet itself, and selected the one that not only had an abundance of water, but, thanks to Jupiter's tidal action, a partially molten mantle that provided the scientists with a ready-made source of geothermal energy.

Since the station had been founded, financial necessity had forced Protech to lease some of the ever-growing habitat to other corporations, but they were still in charge, and kept the rest of the corpies on a short leash.

Which made it all the more amazing that the greenies had hatched a plan to grab me right out from under Protech's nose. A plan that involved snatching me as the passengers disembarked, and either killing or holding me prisoner, they couldn't decide which. Bey, bless his ecological heart, was for letting me live, while Linda favored the death penalty and Trask vacillated back and forth.

I opposed both plans, needless to say, and Sasha's too, since it amounted to giving myself over to her mother. So, unbeknownst to my teenaged companion, I had a plan of my own, flawed as always, but better than nothing.

Everyone watched the approach on the ship's entertainment system, and we were no exception. The bed doubled as an acceleration couch, and we strapped ourselves in place.

The moon was little more than a cue ball at first but quickly grew larger. It didn't take long for the ship to fire powerful repulsors and come to terms with the satellite's rather anemic gravity.

Viewed from space, Europa Station was an intricate maze of solar arrays, antenna farms, observatories, storage tanks, catwalks, and other installations too arcane to identify with a single glance. But the single most noticeable feature was the fact that the entire complex rested on platforms like those that dot the California coast. Only larger.

I was struck by the look of anticipation on Sasha's face. What seemed strange and alien to me was the place where she'd been born, spent her childhood, and been trained . . . as what? An extension of her mother's will?

One of the ship's officers provided a rather nasal explanation of what we were seeing. Sasha replaced his narration with one of her own. There was genuine enthusiasm in her voice as she told me about the columns that held Europa Station aloft, how they extended down through ice and semiliquid slush to the top of a seamount hundreds of feet below, and functioned as gigantic shock absorbers in case of a moonquake or other geological disturbance.

I found myself watching her face rather than the screen, entranced by the energy I saw there, and impressed by the amount of scientific knowledge she had accumulated. Knowledge natural to someone of her background, yet hidden until now. From me? Or from a mother so strong, so domineering, that any sign of talent similar to her own was interpreted as a threat? My head started to hurt, and I let it go.

The ship swung out and away from the station, melted ice with the heat from its repellors, and vectored through a cloud of its own making. A sign appeared and disappeared as vapor drifted past the external vid cams. "WELCOME TO EUROPA STATION—HOME TO THE PROTECH CORPORATION."

I felt a hand grab my stomach and squeeze. Here it was, the

place where I would learn what they had stored in my head or die trying. I was scared, but eager too, wanting the whole thing to end.

The ship lost altitude, hovered for a moment, and dropped towards frost-covered metal. Other ships shared the deck, including freighters, couriers, and some strangely configured research vessels, but the *Queen* dwarfed them all, and cast her shadow across most of the landing platform and a substantial amount of sulphur-stained ice. Our landing jacks touched steel, and the hull creaked as it accepted the unaccustomed weight. We had arrived. A tone sounded, and the captain came on the PA system.

"On behalf of Regis Lines, and the Protech Corporation, it's my pleasure to welcome you to Europa Station. I would like to thank those departing our vessel, and wish them a productive visit or happy homecoming, whichever the case may be. As for the rest of our passengers, this is but the halfway point in what I hope is the best vacation you've ever had. The ground crew is hard at work connecting pressurized tubeways to our locks, and the moment they're done, you'll be free to leave the ship. Please consult a host or hostess for more information regarding . . ."

I ordered the screen to black, touched my harness release, and swung my feet over the side of the bed. Sasha hit her release a second time. "Hey, Max, this thing's jammed."

I stepped over to the storage locker, ordered it open, and grabbed the bag I had packed six hours earlier. "Really? That's too bad. I'll tell maintenance to take a look."

Sasha swore, tried to free herself, and gave up. Her first reaction was anger. *"You* did this!"

I looked in the mirror, polished my skull plate with a hand towel, and straightened my collar. "No, I asked Joy to do it."

Always happy to hear the sound of her name, Joy climbed my pants leg and claimed her place on my shoulder. She was cheerful as always. "Sorry Sasha, but he's the boss. I had to obey."

Sasha strained against the harness, hit the release five or six times, and fell back against the pillow. Her expression changed to one of concern. "What will you do?"

"Find your mother, ask her what she stored in my head, and decide what to do with it."

The kid shook her head in amazement. "You're nuts. Absolutely nuts. You know that?"

I nodded agreeably. "So I've been told, although most people are less charitable and say I'm stupid."

She gave me one of those looks, the kind that turn me gooey inside, and said, "Take care of yourself."

I said I would and let myself out. There was lots of traffic, most of which was headed towards the C Deck lock. It was tempting to join the flow and let it carry me along, but I wasn't that stupid. Assuming the greenies still planned to grab me, and I had no reason to doubt it, the lock was the logical place to do it. No, the crew's lock, which was located one level down on D Deck, would be a safer bet.

I fought the current like a long-extinct salmon fighting its way upstream and made my way to one of the more utilitarian lift tubes frequented by the crew. And, given the fact that beyond the occasional tryst, passengers had no reason to visit crew quarters, there was nothing to prevent me from doing so. I wound up on a platform with a couple of stewards. They pretended I wasn't there. No small task where I'm concerned.

The doors opened as the platform stopped on D Deck. The stewards got off and I followed. Europa's gravity was a good deal lighter than the Earth-normal conditions maintained while the ship was in space. I moved carefully and used the slide step I'd learned on Mars.

The wood paneling had disappeared. Steel bulkheads, liberally sprinkled with safety slogans, morale boosters, and other corporate propaganda passed to either side. I noticed that androids and crew people alike had the ability to look right through me. I found the lock, joined a load of palletized cargo, and cycled through.

The corpies grabbed me as I stepped off the ship. There were four of them, all heavily armed and clearly expecting me. I considered giving them a tussle but it seemed pointless. They located my weapon within a matter of seconds. Joy bailed out of my pocket and was halfway to the deck when a man grabbed her. She struggled, but it was useless. Their leader, a skinny woman with a pink crewcut, glanced at her hand term and nodded. "Yup, he's the one. And right on time too. Put the zappers on him and get a move on. The doc's extra pissy today."

Even *I* could figure out who "the doc" was. I should have been afraid but was ashamed instead. The fact that they had taken me so easily was worse than whatever lay ahead. It struck at the little bit of pride I had left.

The zappers were shaped like fat bracelets and felt slimy as they wrapped themselves around my wrists. The woman with the crewcut held a control unit in front of my face. I nodded my understanding. The yellow button would "zap" my nervous system, the amber button would induce temporary paralysis, and the red button would stop my heart. I wondered if the woman had orders to stop short of that. I figured she did. Casad would have a hard time getting any information out of a refried brain. That gave me an edge, but a damned thin one.

Crewcut gestured for me to move, and I obeyed. My escorts walked two ahead and two behind. I didn't see much of the habitat at first. Just a bunch of maintenance ways, freight tubes, and high-gloss corridors. After all, why march a prisoner through the station's public areas if they didn't have to? Still, they were forced to lead me across an enormous observation deck about halfway through the trip. It was packed with people just off the *Queen*. Most stared open-mouthed at the enormous Jupiter that hung overhead. It was beautiful, and there were lots of "oohs" and "aahs" as people struggled to look up through the triple-thick duraplast.

I scanned the crowd for people I knew, came eyeball to eyeball with Bey, and was about to say something when crewcut jammed something hard into the middle of my back. Bey looked surprised, alarmed, and agitated all at once. He pushed an elderly woman out of the way and burrowed into the crowd. A pair of doors marked "AUTHORIZED PERSONNEL ONLY" swung open to admit us, and the open area disappeared behind.

The first hint of our destination was a passing glimpse of a laboratory packed with esoteric equipment and staffed by a crew of lab-coated techies. That signaled me that we had moved from the outer world into Doctor Casad's private domain, a place populated by facts and figures.

We passed a room filled with light so intense that some of it leaked through the plastifiber walls, heard a rhythmic thumping sound, and smelled something so foul it made crewcut swear out loud. Then we passed through an emergency lock and entered an area that screamed "executive offices" with every inch of its deeply carpeted floor, art-covered walls, and wood-accented, fiber-formed furniture. The reception area was large and rectangular. Everything was spotless and arranged with the same precision that a staff sergeant admires in a footlocker. The reception desk was circular, stood about chest-high, and had been designed to accommodate the four-armed android mounted at the center of it. He, she, or it had paisley-covered skin, four arms, and a no-nonsense attitude. "Dr. Casad is waiting. Take him in."

I felt my heart beat faster as I was led through double doors and into the presence of the person who had stolen my life. Marsha Casad was smaller that I had expected, and the similarities between her appearance and Sasha's were made all the more obvious by the fact that they were standing next to each other. I should have been surprised, but wasn't. Nothing else had gone properly . . . why would this?

The elder Casad was prettier than the woman who haunted my dreams and had the same brown eyes, pretty face, and shapely body that her daughter did. A fact that the primitive male part of me noticed and reacted to in spite of the fact that to do so was stupid—proof positive that I'm at least three rounds short of a full magazine. But the mother was harder than the daughter, her flesh closer to the bone, her eyes like lasers. Power surrounded her like a cloak and was so much a part of her that it was taken for granted.

Both women stood with their backs to a steel-framed Jupiter. Its storm-lashed surface moved with dreamlike slowness. Sasha spoke first. She was apologetic. "I'm sorry, Max, I really am, but you forgot to disable the com set."

I swore softly. Of course! The com set had been voice-activated. It had been a simple matter to call a steward, have herself released, and contact her mother. Damn. All that energy, all that effort, only to have it end like this. I shrugged. "Don't worry, kid. You did what you had to do."

Sasha nodded, but her chin trembled, and I saw a tear trickle down her cheek. Not so her mother. She was brisk and rather cheerful. Her eyes glittered like those of the robo-snake outside Wamba's quarters. There was no understanding or mercy in them, just her unrelenting will. The voice was cold and distant. "You are no longer equipped to appreciate the importance of this, Maxon, but thanks to the information stored in your head, a new era is about to begin."

I saw the ego in her eyes, the pride in what she had accomplished, and took advantage of it. "A new era? What does that mean?"

The elder Casad smiled. "It means freedom! Freedom to travel beyond the limits of our solar system!"

Sasha got it first, confirming that she hadn't known the reason behind her mission, and cementing my affection for her. "Beyond our solar system? A star drive?"

Her mother nodded. "Yes. It will be known as the Casad Drive, and it will carry millions, even billions of human beings to distant stars. "Imagine," she said, momentarily caught up in a glory of her own making, "a new beginning! A breakthrough so important, so liberating, that it will change the course of history. And *I* made it happen!"

The way Dr. Casad said it called for applause, and judging from her expression, I think she actually heard it thunder across a thousand years of immortality.

But the rest of us were silent. Shasha looked uncomfortable. The guards shuffled their feet. Metal pinged in response to a temperature fluctuation. Finally, after what seemed like minutes, but was actually seconds, the scientist's eyes rolled into focus and she returned from fantasy land. Her words were precise and to the point. "Take him to Lab 16. Tell Sanchez to wire him up. I'll be along in fifteen minutes or so."

Sasha tried to move in my direction, but her mother grabbed an arm. Crewcut nudged me towards the door, and there seemed to be little point in resisting. What with zappers on my wrists and four able-bodied guards, there was no chance of escape.

That being the case, I tried to come up with a suitably nonchalant response and failed. The four-armed android didn't even bother to look up as they marched me down the hall. I heard the same thumping I'd heard before, saw light leak through plastifiber walls, and was ordered down a side corridor. The air smelled of ozone. An equipment-laden autocart whirred by. I assumed these were among the last sounds, sights, and smells that I would experience. Everything seemed hyper-real, the way it always does when adrenaline pours into the bloodstream and death looms near.

A door marked "Lab 16" appeared in front of me, sensed my presence, and slid open. A worried-looking lab tech hurried forward. She wore a severe pageboy, no jewelry, and an immaculate lab coat. An I.D. badge hung from her breast pocket and identified her as Carla Sanchez. She gave me the same sort of look a butcher gives a side of beef and pointed over her shoulder. "Place him on the table and strap him down."

The table looked like the kind you find in well-equipped operating rooms. It was backed by a wall full of vid screens and banks of computer equipment. The autosurgeon stood crouched over the table. Its arms whirred as servos were tested and found to be in working order.

I remembered the dreams that weren't dreams and tried to escape. The zappers clamped down on my wrists and pain lanced through my nervous system. I screamed and kept on screaming as the guards lifted me onto the table, applied the straps, and removed the zappers. The pain disappeared and left me sobbing for breath.

Sanchez appeared between me and the ceiling, waved a scanner in front of my eyes, and squinted at the reading. She smelled of soap, and the fragrance remained even after she had disappeared. I liked the smell, even though I knew it was stupid, and marveled at how the male part of me never quit. I whimpered pitifully and nobody came.

Things got complicated after that. More people entered the room. Needles entered my veins, wires were hooked to various parts of my anatomy, and people talked as though I wasn't there. Their voices seemed to float on an ocean of drug-induced happiness.

"Is this the one?"

"Yup, that's him."

"Holy shit."

"Yeah."

"What happens next?"

"The doc comes, we pump him dry, and break for lunch."

"Just like that."

"You got a better idea?"

"No."

"Then shut the hell up and align this equipment. One glitch, one error, and everyone pays."

There was more of the same, but I lost interest and drifted away. That's where I was when I heard someone shout, heard the steady *thump, thump, thump* of an automatic flechette gun, and felt something heavy land on my chest. It smelled of soap.

Then I heard someone call my name, struggled to respond, and discovered that I couldn't. I heard more thumping as someone fired back. A man yelled, "Hit the switch! Start the transfer!" and data rose around me like a suffocating tide. Words, images, and numbers filled my throat, mouth, nose, and ears. And then, just when I seemed certain to drown in a flood of information, something powerful started to suck the data away, pulling me along with it. I fought the sensation for a while, determined to save what remained of my personhood, but the effort was pointless. The suction was too powerful for me to resist. I let go and was removed from my body.

19

"Unauthorized use of this
equipment can result in
permanent brain damage."

*A warning sticker posted on
the control panel in Lab 16*

Someone flicked a switch, and I came into existence. I opened my eyes. Nothing. I moved an arm. Nothing. I attempted to speak. Nothing. Words arrived from somewhere and echoed slowly through my brain. "Hi-i-i-i-i boss-s-s-s-s! Order-r-r-r-r the-e-e-e-e computer-r-r-r-r to-o-o-o-o provide-d-d-d-d an-n-n-n-n interface-s-s-s-s."

The voice was gender-neutral and could have belonged to anyone, except for one thing: Joy was the only person in the solar system that called me "boss." I had formed the words in my mind and was about to speak them through a nonexistent mouth when the computer obeyed. A fuzzy-looking picture appeared. It was shaped like a rectangle. I thought the word "focus," and the view became crystal clear. I was looking down from the corner of a large room. I saw an autosurgeon, an operating table, and a body. *My* body, or what *had* been my body, until the techies sucked it dry. Wires ran into and around it like worms feeding on a corpse.

I screamed. The computer took the thought and turned it into a high-pitched squeal. There were ten or fifteen people in the room. They winced and covered their ears.

A feeling of warmth and happiness flooded around me. A giggle came out of nowhere and rippled through my mind. "Joy?"

Her voice seemed closer now, and the echo had disappeared. "Hi, boss. Sorry about that . . . it took a moment to find you. This computer has an incredible amount of memory. They stashed you in a file called " 'Project Freedom.' "

I was happy, confused, and worried all at the same time. "I'm in a computer file? Then where are you?"

Joy giggled. "Pan right and you can see my body. I left my operating system out there . . . but most of my personality program is here with you."

I thought the words "pan right," and the picture moved accordingly. A camera! I was looking through one of the many security cameras placed throughout the habitat. Joy appeared. It seemed as if she was too far away. The camera zoomed in. I ordered it to stop and saw that she was naked again. Pieces of duct tape still clung to her arms and legs. Always dramatic, the diminutive android had struck a pose prior to sticking her finger into an interface socket. "There you are . . . showing off as usual. Thanks for riding to the rescue. But why would a Protech computer obey *my* commands?"

Joy laughed. The sound had a wonderful bubbly quality that made me want to smile. "Because I *told it to* . . . that's why."

I was still marveling at the gift Wamba had given me when a voice came from what seemed like a thousand miles away. "Max-x-x-x-x? Can-n-n-n-n you-u-u-u-u hear-r-r-r-r me-e-e-e-e?"

I wished the echo away and wondered if there were other cameras besides the one I was looking through. The thought was still in the process of being born when my vision was routed through three additional lenses in the lab, out into the hall, and into spaces I hadn't seen before. I ordered the computer to return my vision to the lab. It took conscious effort to ignore my own circumstances and focus on the outside world.

Crewcut and two of her subordinates lay sprawled on the deck. Sanchez lay draped over my body, and Linda, impeccable as always, stood with a gun in her hand. It was gold-chromed and matched her earrings.

Trask was there, as was Bey, and a woman I had never seen before. She was dressed in Protech overalls, which suggested a spy of some sort. All three had their weapons aimed at a group of terrified technicians. You had to give the greenies credit. Subsequent to spotting me on the observation deck, Bey had wasted little time finding reinforcements and tracking me down. I realized Linda had spoken, and thought my reply. It boomed through the PA system. "Yes, I can hear you."

Linda frowned and looked around the room. I panned a tiny bit. A motor whirred, and she looked into the proper camera. Judging from her expression, she either cared about me or was one hell of an actress. I suspected some of both. "You've seen what Dr. Casad is like. She wants to destroy you. Joy can bring you back. Order her to do so."

I laughed. The electronic translation had a maniacal quality. "Get serious. You tried to kill me. Why would I place myself in your hands?"

"Because we represent the lesser of two evils," Linda said calmly. "Because you have *my* word that we will protect you."

I had just started to consider Linda's offer when the door burst open. An assistant entered, followed by Dr. Casad and Sasha. The scientist took a quick look around, understood the situation, and shoved the technician towards Linda. He stumbled, collided with Linda, and jerked as she fired two darts into his abdomen. He fell, Linda tried to catch him, and Casad turned. She took two steps and stopped when she found herself staring down the business end of her daughter's gun.

The older woman was furious. "Sasha! What are you doing?"

Sasha's face was pale and drawn. "You can't do this. It isn't right."

I switched to another camera and watched the scientist marshal her considerable will and focus it on her daughter. Lightning flashed in Marsha Casad's eyes, and her hands were clenched at her sides. "How dare you interfere with my work! Don't you understand? Life isn't easy. Sacrifices have to be made. I worked for it. The knowledge belongs to *me*. Now put that gun away, or better yet, shoot the greenies."

The people in question didn't like that idea and aimed their weapons at Sasha. She didn't even look in their direction. Tears streamed down her cheeks. "No! The decision belongs to Max. The knowledge is stored in *his* brain, and it belongs to *him*."

Her mother's eyes bulged with emotion. "Have you lost your mind? The man's an idiot! You traveled with him . . . you know how limited his capabilities are. I worked ten long years to gather and analyze the information stored in his head. The data is mine. Think about it, Sasha . . . Project Freedom could put billions of unemployed people to work. It could launch a thousand ships to distant star systems and save the human race from slow suffocation!"

The words had a rehearsed sound, as if they had been said countless times before and long since reduced to a catechism. I watched Linda take the information in, process it, and come up with a greenie-style response. "She's lying. A star drive won't solve humanity's problems. Androids will build the ships, Earth will be stripped of the few resources she has left, and the corpies will leave us to die."

Marsha Casad walked towards her daughter with outstretched hand. Her voice was calm and soothing. "Give me the gun. Everything will be fine. Protech has wonderful doctors. They can replace your missing eye. How 'bout one of Maxon's? The tissues will match. You know why? Because Maxon is your biological father, that's why. I needed a warrior, someone who could bring him back, so I used his sperm to make you. That's why this is so symmetrical, so perfect, so right. I stored the knowledge in his head, I created you to get it back, I . . ."

I was still in the process of absorbing the part about my sperm when Sasha fired a tox dart into her mother's throat. The older woman looked surprised, removed the projectile from her flesh, and held it up to the light. She was still in the process of examining it when she slumped to the floor.

A klaxon started to beep. Joy was worried. "Uh-oh. It looks like the doctor was wearing a biomonitor. Security was notified the moment her vital signs dropped below normal. They're online now, trying to regain control of the computer."

Though not directly involved, I could feel some sort of struggle as powerful forces tried to take control of my electronic universe and Joy fought to stop them. I wanted to help, but my new existence hadn't made me any smarter than I was before. Sasha knew that and did her best to focus my thoughts.

"There isn't a lot of time, Max. Security is on the way. Make your decision."

I watched Trask move towards Sasha and saw Linda shake her head. He frowned but stayed where he was. I felt calm and strangely detached. Sasha was right. The decision was mine. And it was easier than I thought it would be. The human race wasn't ready for the stars. Not by a long shot. No, the knowledge should be destroyed, even though someone would reassemble it. Time, even a little time, might make a big difference. Maybe man- and womankind would grow up, get a little smarter, and behave a whole lot better. Maybe they would *deserve* the stars. Hey, a guy can hope, can't he?

And that meant a brain-wipe. Not a *partial* brain-wipe, as in erase the data and leave everything else alone, because no one had figured out how to do that. No, this would be a complete brain-wipe, as in the whole enchilada.

Which is why I asked Joy to store this narrative in her hard drive and download it into whatever remained of my brain moments after she deleted the file named "Project Freedom." I hoped it would give the future me some idea of what the past me had been through.

The hard part was accepting what amounted to death, having just acquired something worth living for. Suddenly I had a daughter, and more than that, a connection with the past and the future. But there was no helping it, no way to avoid what I had to do, so I ordered Joy to wipe my brain. Darkness fell, and I ceased to exist.

Epilog

More than five years have passed, but I never tire of hearing how Sasha and Joy joined forces with the greenies, how Linda ordered Trask and Bey to carry my mind-wiped body to a specially chartered freighter, and Joy forced the Protech computer to supply us with the necessary clearances.

The new me is something of a legend among the greenies, which is just as well, since Dr. Casad is very much alive, and willing to pay a cool one hundred thousand credits for my chrome-plated head. Not for what's in it, mind you, since the data is gone, but for the satisfaction of seeing me dead.

So, I give the greenies what assistance I can, including interviews like this one, and work at learning all the things a five-year-old should know. I'm way ahead of my experiential age, thanks to special therapy and fast-learn techniques, but still something akin to an over-the-hill teenager.

But, thanks to a nicely crafted blond wig, and some well-executed biosculpting, I can pass for a regular Joe. It wouldn't be healthy to tell you where Sasha, Joy, and I live, but suffice it to say that we run a little café, and look on the regulars as part of our family.

As for the future, well, who knows? We may have slowed 'em down a little, but one thing's for sure, they're working on it.

*"When it comes to military SF, William
Dietz can run with the best."*
—Steve Perry

WILLIAM C. DIETZ

__THE BODYGUARD   0-441-00105-X/$5.50

In a future where violence, corruption, and murder
grow as rapidly as technology and corporations, there
is always room for the Bodyguard. He's hired muscle
for a wired future—and he's the best money can buy.

__LEGION OF THE DAMNED
                              0-441-48040-3/$5.50
*"A tough, moving novel of future
warfare."*—David Drake

When all hope is lost—for the terminally ill, for the
condemned criminal, for the victim who can't be saved—
there is one final choice. Life...as a cyborg soldier.

__DRIFTER'S WAR   0-441-16815-9/$4.99
"Entertaining, fast-paced adventure."
                              —Locus

A million credits' worth of technology on a high-tech
drift ship could leave smuggler Pik Lando set for
life—if he can live long enough to collect.

Payable in U.S. funds. No cash orders accepted. Postage & handling: $1.75 for one book, 75¢
for each additional. Maximum postage $5.50. Prices, postage and handling charges may
change without notice. Visa, Amex, MasterCard call 1-800-788-6262, ext. 1, refer to ad #519

Or, check above books Bill my: ☐ Visa ☐ MasterCard ☐ Amex	
and send this order form to:	(expires)
The Berkley Publishing Group Card#_____	
390 Murray Hill Pkwy., Dept. B	($15 minimum)
East Rutherford, NJ 07073 Signature_____	
Please allow 6 weeks for delivery. Or enclosed is my: ☐ check ☐ money order	
Name_____	Book Total $_____
Address_____	Postage & Handling $_____
City_____	Applicable Sales Tax $_____
State/ZIP_____	(NY, NJ, PA, CA, GST Can.) Total Amount Due $_____

THE FUTURE IS NOW!
THRILLING NEW SCIENCE FICTION

■ ■

__CRASHCOURSE by Wilhelmina Baird 0-441-12163-2/$4.99
Cass, Moke, and Dosh had it all figured out. The three cyber-slackers
would get off the planet by starring in a new cyber-cinema film. But the
line between real life and *reel* life becomes blurry. And their new costar
seems intent on killing off the rest of the cast.
> *"A pungent, gleamy-dark street-future."*–William Gibson
> *"Wilhelmina Baird is wicked, wild, and kicks butt."*–Pat Cadigan

__PASSION PLAY by Sean Stewart   0-441-65241-7/$4.50
The Redemption Presidency has transformed America. Adulterers are
stoned. Executions are televised. But sin still exists. And so does
murder...
> "Passion Play *is a wonderful debut novel from a talented new voice."*
> –Charles de Lint
> *"Nastily believable...Sean Stewart (is) a talent to watch."*
> –William Gibson

__HARD DRIVE by David Pogue   1-55773-884-X/$4.99
On December 18, a computer virus destroys the files on a single
terminal. In a matter of weeks, it will infect the world...
> *"A thrilling cautionary tale... exciting and entertaining."*
> –David Bischoff, author of Wargames

__SPINDOC by Steve Perry   0-441-00008-8/$4.99
Venture Silk is a government spindoc. When a tragedy occurs—a space
crash or an alien virus—Silk reels off the "appropriate" articles. But when
Silk becomes entangled in a web of assassins, he must cut through the
"facts" to find the one thing he's never worried about before—the truth.

Payable in U.S. funds. No cash orders accepted. Postage & handling: $1.75 for one book, 75¢
for each additional. Maximum postage $5.50. Prices, postage and handling charges may
change without notice. Visa, Amex, MasterCard call 1-800-788-6262, ext. 1, refer to ad # 471

Or, check above books	Bill my:	☐ Visa	☐ MasterCard	☐ Amex	

and send this order form to: (expires)
The Berkley Publishing Group   Card#_____
390 Murray Hill Pkwy., Dept. B
East Rutherford, NJ 07073   Signature_____   ($15 minimum)

Please allow 6 weeks for delivery.   Or enclosed is my: ☐ check   ☐ money order
Name_____   Book Total $_____
Address_____   Postage & Handling $_____
City_____   Applicable Sales Tax $_____
                                          (NY, NJ, PA, CA, GST Can.)
State/ZIP_____   Total Amount Due $_____

"A genuinely gifted newcomer."—*Locus*

Wilhelmina Baird

CLIPJOINT

Two years have passed since Dosh died during the making of a cyber-drama. Cass and Moke have safely buried the horrors of the past and gone on. That is, until someone sends Cass a vidclip of the latest hit cyber-film—starring an actor who bears a striking resemblance to Dosh. Now Cassandra's coming back for answers...and revenge.

__0-441-00090-8/$4.99

CRASHCOURSE

"A pungent, gleamy-dark street-future."
— William Gibson, award-winning author of *Neuromancer*

Cass, Moke, and Dosh had it all figured out: Sign a movie contract and you had it made, right?...Not if you're starring in the new cyber-cinema and the audience plugs into your emotions. Not if you can't tell the difference between real life and *reel* life. And especially not if your costar is a mass murderess...

__0-441-12163-2/$4.99

Payable in U.S. funds. No cash orders accepted. Postage & handling: $1.75 for one book, 75¢ for each additional. Maximum postage $5.50. Prices, postage and handling charges may change without notice. Visa, Amex, MasterCard call 1-800-788-6262, ext. 1, refer to ad # 455

Or, check above books   Bill my: ☐ Visa   ☐ MasterCard   ☐ Amex _____
and send this order form to: (expires)
The Berkley Publishing Group   Card#_____
390 Murray Hill Pkwy., Dept. B   ($15 minimum)
East Rutherford, NJ 07073   Signature_____
Please allow 6 weeks for delivery.   Or enclosed is my: ☐ check   ☐ money order

Name_____   Book Total $_____

Address_____   Postage & Handling $_____

City_____   Applicable Sales Tax $_____
                                                     (NY, NJ, CA, GST Can.)
State/ZIP_____   Total Amount Due $_____